# I TOO HAD A BREAK-UP STORY

PARTEEK DHAWAN

Made with ♥ on the Notion Press Platform
www.notionpress.com

# About the Author

**IRENE SULLIVAN**, a retired Florida Circuit Judge, served twelve years as a family and juvenile judge, presiding over cases involving child abuse, domestic violence, family conflict and juvenile crimes. She is now appointed as a Guardian ad Litem to be the voice of the child and make recommendations that are in the child's best interest in divorce and paternity cases.

Irene is a graduate of Northwestern University's Medill School of Journalism and worked for a few years as a newspaper reporter and magazine editor before attending law school—Stetson University College of Law in Gulfport, Florida, near St. Petersburg. For 22 years she practiced law with a large St. Petersburg firm. In 1998, Irene was elected as a Circuit Judge and served for 12 years before retiring and becoming an adjunct professor of juvenile law at Stetson University College of Law until 2022.

Irene is the author of Raised by the Courts: One Judge's Insight into Juvenile Justice, real stories about the children in her court. She is the co-author of You Can't Raise Children by Text: Better Co-parenting in a Digital World, written with child psychologist Dr. Lisa Negrini, a guide to improve coparenting in divorce and paternity situations.

Irene is very active in her community, sitting on the boards of many nonprofit organizations and has received many awards for her judicial service and community involvement.

For everyone who has ever loved deeply and lost — may you find the strength to love again.

And to those who supported me through this journey, this is for you.

# Contents

# Preface

Writing this book has been a deeply personal journey for me. It stems from my own experiences, and in many ways, it has helped me come to terms with events that I once struggled to understand. Love and heartbreak are universal themes, and through this story, I've tried to capture the intensity of those emotions.

I hope that as you read, you find pieces of yourself in these pages—whether you've loved, lost, or are still on your own journey of healing

# Acknowledgements

A heartfelt thank to Vikas for inspiring me to write this book and for his invaluable help in editing.

I'm also grateful to Hairat for her assistance with editing and feedback, and to Sunidhi for her unwavering support throughout this journey.

To my family, for believing in me when I didn't believe in myself.

Lastly, to the readers, for taking a chance on this story. Your support means the world.

# When Love Blossomed

January 15, 2017—the day I walked into my new office, full of excitement and nerves. The air was crisp, charged with the kind of energy that only comes with starting something fresh. A new chapter. I had just joined as an Executive HR in a company in Panchkula. It felt like the beginning of a whole new adventure, one that I had been waiting for, but little did I know how much this job would become valuable to me.nikhil

The office was massive—over 700 people on that floor, all of them bustling around, heads down, focused on their tasks. As soon as I entered, I could feel the weight of hundreds of eyes glancing in my direction. It was that unmistakable "new guy" feeling, and I wasn't sure whether to feel excited or petrified. And before I even had time to settle in, I was told I'd need to introduce myself to the entire office. My heart jumped into my throat. Giving an introduction was one thing, but standing in front of a sea of unfamiliar faces? That was a whole different story.

Still, I knew this was part of the job, and I couldn't afford to stumble on my first day. I took a deep breath, walked to the front, and launched into a small introduction. I tried my best to sound confident, though inside I could feel my heart racing. My voice wavered slightly, but I pushed through. I wasn't looking for perfection—just to make it through without embarrassing myself. Somehow, I managed, and after that, things got a little easier.

Over the next few days, the awkwardness slowly started to melt away. I found my rhythm, learning the ropes of the company and understanding the dynamics of my new role. It took about a month for me to really settle in, but by then, the office had started to feel less intimidating, more like a second home.

I wasn't alone in this. The HR department was tight-knit, and the team welcomed me with open arms. There were six of us in total, each with our own quirks and personalities, but we clicked quickly. Ashish, Vinay, and Rahul became my closest confidants, and we often bonded over cups of chai during breaks.

The camaraderie helped ease the work stress. After a few weeks, my shift was rotated, and I met Dipaansh, the HR lead for the night crew. He was sharp, quick with a joke, and immediately made me feel like part of the family.

With each passing day, I felt more and more connected to the office, but as part of HR, I had to maintain a certain distance. It wasn't easy—there were a lot of girls in the office, and sometimes, it was hard not to notice them. There were moments when someone's smile or a glance would catch my eye, but I knew better. My role came with responsibility. As part of HR, I was often referred to as "Sir," a title that carried weight. It meant I had to maintain boundaries. After all, HR wasn't just about managing people—it was about setting the right example.

But even though I had to keep things professional, I made sure to be approachable. It was my mission to break the mold of the typical HR, the one who only ever seemed to scold employees. Instead, I wanted to be someone they could turn to, someone who could listen and offer real solutions.

I remember one particular day, when a young employee came up to me, looking visibly shaken. She wasn't here to talk about work. Instead, she wanted to share a personal issue that had been weighing heavily on her, and it was starting to affect her performance. As she talked, I could feel the tension she had been carrying. It was in her voice, in the way she sat on the edge of her seat, clutching the armrests as if she were holding on for dear life.

I listened carefully, nodding as she poured her heart out. It wasn't just about offering HR advice—it was about being human. When she finished, I gave her some suggestions, and her shoulders visibly relaxed. That moment stayed with me. I realized then that this job wasn't just about rules or policies—it was about empathy. It was about understanding the human side of the business.

Even though work kept me busy, my friends in the HR department often teased me about my single status. Ashish was happily married, Dipaansh was engaged, and Rahul was practically glued to his phone, constantly talking to his girlfriend, Sonia—whom we affectionately called "Sonaliya." And then there was Vinay, who always had some love story brewing on the side. I was the odd one out, the last man standing in the HR department, single and eligible—but honestly? I didn't mind. Love had always been a bit elusive for me, and I'd long accepted my role as the guy sitting at the back of the class in the school of romance.

But everything changed on February 2.

That day, I was sitting in the office cafeteria, sipping on a cup of coffee, when out of nowhere, I saw her—a tall, slim, fair girl who seemed to float into the room, as if carried by some unseen breeze. My breath caught in my throat for a moment. She was strikingly beautiful, the kind of girl who instantly commands attention without even trying. But what really caught my eye, surprisingly, was the little detail in her hair—a small, butterfly-shaped clip, the kind you usually see little girls wearing. It was so unexpected, so innocent, and it made her seem almost dreamlike.

As she moved, there was a certain grace to her, an effortless beauty that I couldn't look away from. My coffee, which had been my sole companion just moments before, was now forgotten. I was completely captivated.

With every sip of my coffee, I found myself stealing more glances at her. She had a delicate smile on her lips, and her eyes sparkled with a kind of mischief that intrigued me. I couldn't help but wonder who she was. Was she already taken? Did she have a boyfriend? My mind started arguing with itself. "Of course, she has a boyfriend," I thought. "A girl like her? There's no way she's single."

But a part of me, a hopeful part, refused to let that thought settle. Maybe, just maybe, fate had something else in store.

As much as I wanted to stay and steal more glimpses of her, my coffee cup was empty, and reality was pulling me back to the office. I reluctantly picked up my jacket, paid for the coffee, and headed for the door, casting one last glance her way before stepping out.

Even as I walked back to my desk, I couldn't shake the thought of her from my mind. Who was she? Would I ever see her again? The cafeteria, once just a place for a quick coffee break, now held a kind of magic, and I knew I'd be back there, hoping to catch another glimpse of the girl with the butterfly clip.

I had always known she was in my office, part of the designing department. Her presence was like a quiet whisper in the air, something that lingered in the back of my mind. But, being responsible and conscious of my position in HR, I knew I couldn't just approach her out of the blue. We worked in different shifts, and it had become a routine—just as I arrived at work, she would be leaving. It was like two ships passing in the night, our paths crossing for mere moments, yet never long enough for anything substantial.

Still, those brief glimpses of her stayed with me. She had this effortless beauty, the kind that you notice even when you're not looking. Every time I saw her, it felt like something inside me shifted, a pull I couldn't quite explain.

One day, I came to the office a little early, hoping—if luck was on my side—that I might catch a longer glimpse of her. I headed straight to the cafeteria, where she usually waited with the other girls from her shift for their cab. And there she was, sitting at a table with a group of her colleagues, laughing softly, her smile lighting up the room. My heart thumped in my chest like it always did when she was around, but I forced myself to keep my cool.

Vijay, a friend from the office, was sitting nearby. He waved me over, and I joined him at his table. Coincidentally, she was sitting diagonally across from me at the adjacent table, close enough that I could hear the soft rhythm of her voice mixed with the laughter of the other girls.

Vijay saw my mobile lying on the table. He looked at it and said - I love this mobile. Xperia W550i isn't it? It's amazing while playing music. He grabbed my phone and started playing a song. As the music filled the cafeteria, I noticed something—a small moment that felt like magic. She seemed to be enjoying the song, nodding her head lightly to the beat. Every now and then, her eyes would flicker in my direction. It was only a brief moment, but it felt like the world stopped for a second, as if she had silently acknowledged something that had been unspoken between us for a long time.

She looked at me, held the glance for a heartbeat longer than usual, and then, with a small smile, she stood up and left with the rest of her group, disappearing into the hustle of the office.

Then, as if fate had decided to give me a hand, everything seemed to change. A few days later, we were both assigned to the same shift. It was my chance, but I wasn't sure how or when I could even approach her. Being in HR, I had to maintain professionalism, but there was this small, burning hope inside me that our paths would finally cross in a more meaningful way.

And then, as if the universe was listening to my silent plea, she came to me. I was in the middle of taking attendance when she approached, her presence lighting up the space around her. "Mandira won't be coming today," she said softly, her voice gentle and polite, like music in the air. "She's not feeling well."

Her words were simple, routine, but the way she said them—there was something in her tone that made my heart skip a beat. She was wearing a yellow Patiala suit that day, and it suited her perfectly, as if that shade of yellow had been made just for her. It was impossible not to notice how stunning she looked, but I had to keep my emotions in check. I nodded, trying to act casual. "Thank you for the information," I replied, hiding the fact that just hearing her voice had already made my day.

Before she turned to leave, I gathered the courage to ask, "What's your name, by the way?"

"Jolene," she said, her voice carrying a warmth that matched her name perfectly.

Jolene. Somehow, her name was even more beautiful than I'd imagined. I couldn't think of anything else to say, so I simply thanked her again. My heart, however, was racing like I'd just ran a marathon. The entire day passed in a blur after that, my eyes subconsciously wandering to her desk from time to time, but I didn't get another chance to speak with her.

The next day, the same thing happened. She came up to me again, informing me about Mandira's absence. It was becoming a routine, one that I didn't mind at all. I wanted to talk to her more, to extend the conversation beyond just these small exchanges, but I didn't want to seem over-eager or unprofessional. So, instead, I played it safe.

"Is Mandira feeling any better?" I asked, trying to show concern without crossing any lines.

Jolene gave me a soft smile, pressing her lips for a moment before replying, "She's still got a fever."

I nodded, trying not to let my excitement show. "Thanks again for letting me know," I said, hoping I could find something—anything—to prolong the conversation, but she smiled politely and walked away, leaving me in the same state of quiet longing.

By the third day, I was ready for her. As soon as I saw her walking toward me, I couldn't help but smile. Before she could even speak, I smiled and said, "Let me guess—Mandira's not coming today either, right?"

I winked playfully, surprising even myself with my boldness. Jolene's eyes widened in surprise for a moment, but then she laughed—a sweet, musical sound that made my heart swell.

For the first time, I felt like I'd broken through the invisible wall that had always separated us. It was a small victory, but it felt huge. I didn't know where things would go from there, but for the first time, I felt like maybe, just maybe, I had a chance to get closer to her.

"Yes," she said, her eyes sparkling with a light that sent my heart into a tailspin.

I couldn't help but smile back, and for a few lingering seconds, we were locked in an unspoken conversation, our eyes meeting in a way that felt deeper than words. My heart raced, and it felt like everything around us faded into the background. Then, she broke the gaze, turning away with a soft smile still playing on her lips, and walked back to her seat, leaving me standing there with my mind swirling in a thousand directions.

Every time I saw her, I wanted to say something—anything—to keep that connection alive. But how could I just walk up to her when she was always surrounded by her group of friends? I had no excuse, no good reason to break through the invisible barrier between us.

One day, while I was standing at Sandy's desk, one of my good friends, we were casually chatting and sharing chocolates. Suddenly, I saw her—the girl who had unknowingly stolen my attention. Jolene walked by, her presence lighting up the space around her. As she passed, she looked my way, and for a moment, our eyes met again. This time, she flashed me a smile that could light up the gloomiest room. It was so sweet, so genuine, that it felt like my feet lifted off the ground. I didn't know what it was about that smile, but it felt like she had just given me a quiet, reluctant "yes" without even saying a word.

I was still riding that high when, a little while later, she walked back in my direction, heading toward her desk. My heart leaped at the thought of interacting with her again. As she passed by, I impulsively offered her a piece of chocolate. It was a simple gesture, but it felt like the most important thing I'd done all day. For a split second, she looked surprised—her eyes widened just a little, and the surprise was enough to make my heart race. Then, without breaking eye contact, she smiled faintly and said, "No, thank you," her voice soft but polite, before turning away with her friend.

My heart sank just a bit. Sandy, ever the joker, decided to step in. Folding his arms across his chest, he smirked and quipped in his typical Mumbai accent, "Boss, tere hi type ka maalom hoti hai ye. Tum dono ka jodi mast rahega maalom."

I laughed, trying to brush off the moment, though his words lingered. "She's probably got a boyfriend, man. A girl like her? I bet there's a line of guys waiting for their shot," I said, half-joking, though a part of me believed it.

Sandy shrugged. "That, I can't say. But you should at least try. Kya maalom? Chance mil jaye."

I chuckled, but in the back of my mind, it stung a little. Why had she refused? Was it just because she didn't like chocolate? Or was it something more? Girls rarely say no to chocolate—especially not someone as sweet as her. And yet, there it was. That polite refusal.

Trying to convince myself not to read too much into it, I headed back to my desk, mentally battling my own thoughts. The smile, the eye contact—what had that meant if she wasn't interested? And if she wasn't, why did she seem so surprised when I offered the chocolate? It was as if the whole encounter was layered with something unspoken, but I couldn't quite figure out what.

I sat at my desk, trying hard to push the moment out of my mind, to shake off the sinking feeling that her refusal had planted in my heart. But the question kept circling back, like a stubborn echo: Why did she flash that smile at me if she didn't want the chocolate?

I distracted myself with work, or at least tried to. But then, just as I was beginning to lose myself in the steady rhythm of typing and emails, I felt her presence. I looked up, and there she was, standing by my desk, her eyes sparkling with mischief.

"If someone refuses," she said, a teasing smile tugging at her lips, "then you should ask again."

Her words caught me completely off guard. I blinked, trying to process what she'd just said. "What?" I managed to say, stunned by her boldness and the fact that she had heard my unspoken thoughts.

Oh my God, how did she know? Did she somehow hear the debate I was having in my head? But in that moment, all I could do was smile, enjoying the playful energy between us. Whatever her reasons were for refusing earlier, it didn't matter anymore. What mattered was that she had come back, breaking the ice in the most unexpected way, and with it, my hope flickered back to life.

"Why didn't you ask me again for the chocolate? You should have asked again," she said with a mischievous smile. The way her lips curved up sent a jolt of warmth through me, a feeling I hadn't known I was missing until that very moment.

I chuckled, trying to play it cool. "Hey, why didn't you take it the first time?" I asked, keeping it casual, but inside, my heart was beating in a rhythm I could barely keep up with.

To my surprise, her smile faltered slightly, and she looked away for a brief second before saying, almost sadly, "I don't know, but I was waiting for you to ask again... and you didn't."

Her words hit me like a sweet melody, each syllable landing like the soft chime of jingle bells in the winter air. I never believed in the kind of love you see in movies, but as Yash Chopra's love stories had always portrayed, maybe this was how it felt—something subtle, soft, but powerful enough to leave an imprint. With each passing moment, I was getting more convinced that this—whatever this was—wasn't just some passing attraction. It was real. And it was growing.

I pulled out another chocolate, this time with a little more confidence, and handed it to her. Her face lit up, her eyes twinkling like stars, and she took it with a smile that could melt the coldest of hearts.

"Thank you," she said softly before walking away, leaving me standing there, slightly dazed, unsure of how she had somehow heard the silent conversation I'd had with myself earlier. Was I blushing? I couldn't tell, but something inside me was buzzing with a feeling that I couldn't quite explain.

Time passed, and soon, she came back, walking toward me with that same light step. "Do you have a leave application card?" she asked sweetly. "I need to take some time off."

Normally, I would have pointed employees to the box where they could find the forms themselves, but for her? Well, for her, I didn't mind going the extra mile. I rummaged through the files and handed her one, knowing full well it was the wrong file, but secretly wanting her to stay just a little longer.

"Here you go," I said, handing it over. Then, casually, I pulled out the chair next to me. "Beta, yahaan baith jaao," I said with a lighthearted tone. The word "beta" felt natural, like I was teasing a child, but at the same time, it was the affection in my tone that mattered more. She was as cute as a child, but with the grace and beauty of a woman whose presence could light up the room. And today, for some reason, it felt like every color in the universe had come together to suit her perfectly.

She wore a black top and jeans, simple yet stunning, and it wasn't just her outfit that caught my attention—it was the way she carried herself. Her signature hair clip, which was shaped like a butterfly, only added to her charm, giving her an almost ethereal quality. My eyes kept drifting to it, that small yet enchanting detail that had somehow woven itself into my thoughts.

As she sifted through the files, my gaze never left her. Her eyes, soft and mesmerizing, her lips a shade of red that I knew couldn't be from any makeup—it was natural, just like the pink blush that dusted her cheeks. Her nose, a little sharper than average, added a uniqueness to her beauty that made her even more captivating. And her smile? God, that smile. It was like a balm, soothing every bit of stress that life threw my way.

I couldn't help but think that while she might not have been the "most beautiful" girl by conventional standards, there was something about her presence, her aura, that was magnetic. She was simple, yet effortlessly captivating. It wasn't just about her looks—it was the way she spoke, the way she moved, the way she carried herself. She didn't need to be the loudest or the most outgoing. Her mere existence in the room was enough to make it feel full.

Lost in my daydream, I watched as she fiddled with her hair, trying to tuck the loose strands behind her ear while continuing her search through the file. She looked slightly annoyed by the stray locks that kept falling onto her face, but the way she kept setting them back with gentle frustration only made her more endearing.

And that's when I knew I had to say something. Anything.

"Where are you going?" I asked, trying to sound as casual as possible, though inside, my nerves were bubbling. "I mean, why are you taking leaves?"

She looked up, slightly startled by the question but quick to respond, "I'm going home. Hometown—Bahadurgarh. It's in

Haryana."

"I know it's in Haryana. I'm also from Haryana," I said, trying to keep my tone casual but unable to hide the excitement bubbling inside me.

"Really?" she asked, her face lighting up with a hint of excitement.

"Yes," I replied with a smile that I was struggling to control.

"Where are you from?" she asked, her interest piqued.

"I live in Kurukshetra now, but I was born and brought up in a small town near Rohtak," I explained, wondering if she'd know the place.

She nodded, "I've heard of Rohtak."

"Well, it's just one of those towns that people drive through and never stop to remember," I joked lightly, and she smiled. It felt good—like we had discovered a small connection, a thread that linked our worlds together. Both from Haryana, both having roots in nearby places. Maybe it wasn't much, but in that moment, it felt like something significant.

She finally found her leave application in another file, carefully pulling it out. As she started putting the other cards back into their places, I gently stopped her. "Leave that for me. I'll handle it."

She gave me a soft, appreciative smile, and then she thanked me before walking away, her presence lingering even after she had disappeared from view.

Later that evening, during our dinner break, I went outside with a couple of colleagues, just to get some air and stretch my legs. As we walked, laughing and chatting, my eyes caught sight of her, walking alone inside the office building. She looked... serene. Her slender figure moved gracefully, and for a moment, the entire world seemed to slow down.

My colleagues continued on, oblivious to the shift in my attention. I made up some quick excuse, something about forgetting something at my desk, and turned back. My heart raced as I headed towards her, my steps growing more deliberate as I neared.

"Hi," I greeted her, trying not to sound as nervous as I felt.

"Hello," she responded, her face softening into a warm smile, her eyes sparkling with that same playful light that made everything about her feel so inviting.

"What are you doing here alone?" I asked, genuinely curious.

"Nothing, just tired," she said with a small shrug, her voice laced with exhaustion but still so sweet that it almost made me forget where I was.

"Did you have dinner?" I asked, hoping she hadn't, but not sure why that mattered to me.

"No," she said simply, brushing a loose strand of hair behind her ear.

I nodded, taking in the chill of the February air that I hadn't really noticed until now. She was only wearing a thin top, and I could feel the cold creeping through my jacket, yet she didn't seem affected at all. "Aren't you cold?" I asked, concerned for her more than myself.

She smiled cheekily. "No, I'm fine. You Punjabis are the weak ones, always feeling cold."

I couldn't help but laugh, even though I was freezing. "Right, right," I said with a grin, even though my breath was turning into fog in the chilly night air. My pride kicked in, and despite my shivering body, I straightened up. "Well, I could afford a pullover, but I don't need one."

She raised an eyebrow and gave me a quick glance. "Sure, sure," she said with a soft smile.

I suddenly felt this surge of warmth. Not just from my so-called "Punjabi pride," but from something else entirely. Standing there with her, talking to her, I felt this overwhelming sensation that I had never quite felt before. The cold air biting at my skin didn't matter anymore. The excitement of being near her, talking to her, was enough to keep me warm.

I was smiling so much, I could barely control it. My heart was racing, and my hands felt sweaty even in the cold. The nervousness was kicking in, but it was more than that. It was excitement, pure and simple. I had never felt this way around anyone before.

"Stop smiling like an idiot," I told myself in my head, "What's wrong with you? She'll think you're crazy."

But even as I tried to curb my enthusiasm, my smile grew wider. She had that effect on me, like I couldn't help but be happy just being in her presence. I was shivering—partly from the cold, partly from nerves—but I didn't want this moment to end.

I was doing my best to keep my excitement in check, but it wasn't easy. Being around her, talking to her, felt like a dream, and no matter how hard I tried, my face was probably giving away everything I was feeling inside. Somehow, she already knew—she could sense it, I think, that I had come back outside just for her. There was something about the way she spoke to me, sweetly and with a kind of warmth that made my heart race.

Her voice, oh man—every time she said something, it felt like the rest of the world just faded into the background. I couldn't focus on anything else, like her voice was a soft melody and I was the only one listening. Everything about her captivated me: her smile, her eyes, and her cute clip. She had this simple beauty that made her stand out in the most understated way. Her top fit perfectly, and the way her jeans hugged her frame—it was like every detail about her just fell into place.

We chatted casually about the basics—her background, her education, my life, and where I came from. It was just surface-level stuff, but with her, even the most ordinary conversations felt special. Every now and then, my more playful side nudged me to ask her out on a date. I wanted to so badly, but the more cautious part of me held back. I didn't want to push too hard, too soon. We were just getting to know each other, after all.

Our break ended all too quickly, and as much as I wanted to keep talking, she had to go back inside. "I have to go, bye," she said softly, smiling as she left.

I watched her walk away, her long legs carrying her with that same grace that had me hooked from the start. I waved, though I'm not even sure she saw it.

Later that night, I was back at my desk, trying to focus on work, when she came over with her leave application in hand. It was signed and ready to go, and for some reason, just seeing her again made my heart do that familiar little dance.

"So, your leave got approved?" I asked, pretending to be nonchalant when, really, I was just looking for an excuse to keep her talking.

"Yes, but it's only for two days," she replied, pointing at the form.

I nodded, trying to mask my disappointment at the thought of her not being around. But then something else came to mind. It was night shift, and in our company, cabs were only provided during the late hours. In the morning, everyone had to find their own way back home. I knew this, and the thought of her walking alone in the early morning didn't sit well with me.

"How are you getting back in the morning?" I asked, keeping my tone casual even though I was already mentally preparing to offer her a ride.

"Oh, I'll just walk," she said, as if it was the most normal thing in the world.

Without thinking, I blurted out, "We'll go together."

"If you say no, this time, I'll ask again", I added with a smile.

She paused for a moment, then smiled, giving me this look—an expression that told me she had been thinking the same thing all along. My heart did that familiar jingle-bell routine again, and I tried to keep my cool as she nodded in agreement.

"Okay," she said, her smile widening just a bit.

The rest of the night was a blur. My mind was spinning with the thought of walking her home in the morning, wondering if it would just be the two of us or if her friends would tag along. Honestly, it didn't matter. Whether it was just the two of us or not, I'd still be with her, and that was enough for me.

By the time the morning rolled around, I was a bundle of nerves and excitement. Every minute felt like an hour as I waited for 7 AM to come. I couldn't concentrate on work anymore, so I wandered outside with a few colleagues, pretending to chat with them but constantly checking my watch. It was almost time.

As we started heading back inside, I saw her. She was walking out of the office, her friends with her, but she caught my eye immediately. For a second, I thought maybe she wouldn't acknowledge me, but then she raised her eyebrows in a curious, questioning way. I couldn't help but smile.

I held up two fingers, signalling that I'd be out in two minutes. She smiled at the gesture, and it felt like our little secret, communicating with each other through subtle signals that no one else could understand.

The thrill of it all was unreal—talking to her with nothing but a glance, a nod, and a small gesture. It felt like the beginning of something, even though neither of us had said anything out loud yet. But in that moment, I knew—I knew she felt it too.

She understood and kept walking with her friends.

I quickly shut down my PC, eager to meet her, and went straight to the parking area to bring my car. As I drove up, I saw her walking with her friends, a little distance away from the office. I could tell she was torn. She didn't want to abandon her friends, but at the same time, she seemed hesitant about asking them to wait for me. Still, I pulled up beside her and gently gestured for her to hop in. Her surprise was evident—she had no idea I even had a car. But more than surprised, she seemed a little confused, unsure whether to get in or continue walking with her friends.

Her friends, however, seemed to understand exactly what was happening. They smiled knowingly, waving her off, "You go ahead, we'll walk," one of them said, as if they were in on a secret we hadn't even acknowledged yet.

She hesitated for just a second before finally making the decision that I was secretly hoping for. She opened the door, still looking at her friends, and asked them once more to join us. But they declined again, playfully shooing her into the car. I was full of excitement, trying my best to hide the fact that my heart was pounding. For the first time in my life, I had a girl in my car, and not just any girl—*her*.

"They're not coming," she said, almost like she was apologizing for being alone with me.

"It's okay," I replied, trying to sound casual while my insides were doing somersaults. "I hope you're fine with just me?" I asked, though my tone was teasing.

She nodded, a small, shy smile playing on her lips, trying to hide her own nervousness.

I smiled back, glancing at her as I started driving. "So... where do you stay?"

"In Sector 7," she said, her voice soft but steady. "I'm in a PG there."

Sector 7 was just a few minutes away from where we were. But I wasn't in any rush. I slowed the car down, hoping to stretch out this brief moment we had. I couldn't drive *too* slowly though—what would she think? That I didn't know how to drive properly? I tried to maintain a good pace, all the while savoring every second I had with her beside me.

At that time, I was staying in a PG in Sector 27, a good half-hour drive from Sector 7. Normally, I'd grumble about driving that far, especially with the rising petrol prices. But today? Today, I'd have driven a hundred miles if it meant having her with me for just a little longer.

There was so much I wanted to say, but my nerves kept getting in the way. After a few seconds of silence, I finally managed to ask, "So, what do you usually do on weekends?"

She shrugged, "Nothing much. I mostly just stay at the PG."

I chuckled nervously, trying to find a way to keep the conversation going. "Don't you go out? Maybe catch a movie or something?"

"No, very rarely. We mostly just hang out at the PG with friends," she said casually, but the simplicity of her words only made me want to be a part of that little world she shared with them.

I didn't want to waste this opportunity, so I decided to go for it. Without overthinking, I said, "Well, let's spend the next Sunday together."

She looked at me, her eyes sparkling a little, then nodded with a smile. That smile—it was like the universe granting me permission to dream a little further.

As we drove closer to her PG, my thoughts were racing. I wanted to ask for her number, but I felt edgy, hesitant. It wasn't something I had done before—asking for a girl's number wasn't exactly in my playbook. When we reached her PG, she opened the car door and stepped out, pausing for a moment before saying, "Thank you," with that sweet, sincere tone that made my heart flip.

Just as she was about to close the car door, I gathered the courage and said, "I'll give you a call on Sunday before I come to pick you up."

She stopped and smiled, a mix of amusement and certainty in her expression. "You don't have my number."

Those words hit me like a wave of excitement. My heart started racing, and for a second, I felt like a nervous schoolboy. So, she was aware of what I was trying to get at! Butterflies danced in my stomach as if they had been waiting for this very moment.

"Hmmm," I managed to say, trying to hide my growing excitement.

Then, she winked—yes, actually winked—and said, "You're in HR, right? I'm sure you can find my number from anywhere."

That wink, combined with her mischievous smile, nearly knocked me off balance. I couldn't help but smile back. Her lighthearted confidence, her teasing tone—it all felt like a subtle invitation, a way of telling me she wasn't indifferent. She shut the door and walked away, but I sat there for a moment, replaying the scene in my head, flattened once again by her smile.

The date was 28th February, I was in the middle of drafting attendance, trying to focus, but my thoughts kept drifting back to her. Just then, her friend Preeti approached me, breaking the spell.

"Jolene won't be coming today. She's not feeling well," Preeti informed me.

I felt my heart sink just a little. I had been eagerly waiting to see her, to catch another glimpse of her infectious smile, but hearing this news dampened my mood.

Instantly, I felt an overwhelming urge to check on her. My mind raced with worry, and before I knew it, I was already opening the employee database, searching for her contact details. As she had teased, it wasn't a big deal for someone in HR to access employee information. In no time, I found her number.

I unlocked my phone, my fingers trembling slightly as I typed in her number. I pressed the green button to call, but just as it started ringing, I hesitated. Maybe calling her this late at night wasn't the best idea. I didn't want to come off too strong, too soon.

So, I disconnected the call before it could go through and decided to send her a message instead. I quickly typed, "What happened? Are you okay?"

I stared at my phone, waiting, and within a few seconds, her reply came: "I'm having a cold."

My heart ached a little, imagining her feeling unwell. I quickly texted back, "Have you taken any medicines?"

"Hmmm," she replied, a small confirmation that she had, but her message was short, which made me think she wasn't feeling up for much conversation.

But I couldn't stop myself from offering more. I needed to make sure she knew I cared. I typed another message, my fingers moving fast, filled with both concern and affection: "If you need anything, let me know. It's 12 AM, and I understand you might not be able to go out, but I can bring you whatever you need, okay?"

I hit send and leaned back, waiting for her response. I could only hope that, somehow, through those small words on a screen, she could feel how much I genuinely cared.

"Hmm, thanks a lot." she replied with a simple text, but that smiley at the end? It spoke volumes, sending a flutter through my chest. We started texting back and forth, and with each message, the invisible wall of formality between us began to dissolve. It felt like we had taken our first step into something... something more than just casual office acquaintances. There was an ease now, a comfort that hadn't been there before.

She opened up about her college life, her friends, and all the little details that made her who she was. The conversation flowed so naturally, but amidst the warmth of our budding friendship, I had a question gnawing at the back of my mind. A question that could either make or break everything. It took all my courage to type it out, but somehow, my fingers managed to string the words together on the screen:

"Do you have a boyfriend?"

I stared at my phone, my heart pounding. The few seconds that passed felt like hours. Each tick of the clock amplified the anxious thudding within me. What if she did? What if I was just another guy in the background, someone she'd smile at but never think about in *that* way?

I forced myself to focus on my work, but I kept glancing at my phone, my mind racing. Just as I was about to give in to my swirling thoughts, my phone vibrated.

The screen lit up, and her message appeared.

"No."

We continued exchanging texts for a while, talking about everything and nothing. But deep down, that simple "No" had changed everything for me. The possibilities seemed endless now. Still, I didn't want to push too hard, so when it was getting late, I told her to rest and take care of herself. She agreed, and we wished each other good night. But long after she had probably fallen asleep, I found myself scrolling through our conversation over and over again. I must have read it more than twenty times, just to reassure myself that I wasn't dreaming, that she was single—and that maybe, just maybe, I had a chance.

The next morning, March 1$^{st}$, felt like a fresh start, like the world was painting itself in brighter colors just for me. I reached the office with a strange kind of energy, almost like something magical had happened overnight. As I stepped onto the porch, I saw her. Her eyes met mine, and she greeted me with a smile—*that* smile, the one that could stop time, the one that seemed to make everything around her glow. She gave me a small nod, and it was like a silent acknowledgment of our shared connection.

We started texting again that day. Even though mobile phones were technically restricted for the designers, and only the management staff like me were allowed to use them, she found a way to sneak hers out just to chat with me. That thought alone made me smile.

After some back-and-forth, teasing and light conversations, she suddenly texted me something that stopped me in my tracks.

"Can I ask you something?"

Why not?

"Why did you ask me yesterday whether I had a boyfriend or not?" she asked directly, her message lighting up my screen.

I knew this question was coming, but I still wasn't fully prepared for it. My fingers hovered over the keypad, unsure of how to respond. I had wanted to ask her, needed to know if she was available, but I also didn't want to come across too eager.

"I asked it in a general way," I finally typed back, trying to sound casual, as if the question hadn't been weighing on my mind for the past 24 hours.

Her next text popped up almost instantly. "Do you like me?"

That hit me like a truck. My heart felt like it was ready to leap out of me. I stared at the message for what felt like an eternity, my mind racing. *Yes*, I wanted to scream. *Yes, I like you. I've been thinking about you nonstop, imagining us together. I like you more than I've liked anyone before.*

But my nerves held me back. Fear crept into my thoughts. *What if she doesn't feel the same? What if I say yes and it ruins everything? What if she stops talking to me altogether?* The risk of losing her, of damaging whatever connection we had built, terrified me.

So, I played it safe.

"No, nothing like that," I replied, my heart sinking as I pressed send, knowing that it wasn't the truth.

For a moment, I could almost feel her disappointment through the phone. But then her reply came: "Then it's fine."

Fine? *Was she disappointed? Or was she relieved?* My mind spun with a thousand different interpretations of that simple text. But before I could overthink it any further, we resumed our usual back-and-forth chat, diving into casual topics and office gossip. Yet, despite the surface-level conversation, the unspoken tension between us lingered.

As the night dragged on, I asked her if she wanted a lift home again in the morning. But she politely declined, explaining that she couldn't leave her friends behind, and her friends weren't comfortable with the idea of joining us. I sensed a little sadness in her message, and it mirrored my own disappointment. I wanted to spend more time with her, just the two of us, but maybe it wasn't the right moment.

The next night, March 2$^{nd}$, our texting picked up where it left off, both of us eager to continue the conversation that had started to feel like our little secret world. The banter, the teasing, the late-night thoughts—it was becoming the highlight of my day.

And then, out of the blue, she asked again. "Why did you ask me about my boyfriend?"

I couldn't dodge it this time. Before I could even formulate a vague reply, another message popped up: "Please tell, do you like me?" There was an anxious energy to her question, something raw and vulnerable that made my heart race.

*This is it*, I thought. She was giving me another chance, opening the door for honesty. *But what if...?* The fear of losing her still gnawed at me, but there was something about her persistence, her genuine curiosity, that made me feel like this moment was important.

Taking a deep breath, I typed, "What if I say yes?"

And then, the wait. Every second felt like an hour. My mind was a whirlwind of emotions, torn between hope and panic. I stared at my phone, waiting for her reply like my life depended on it. *What if she laughs it off? What if she never replies? What if...*

Finally, my phone buzzed. I snatched it up, my hands trembling slightly as I opened the message.

"I like you too."

I read it again. And again. The words felt surreal, like a dream I didn't want to wake up from. My heart soared, relief and joy flooding through me all at once. Her honesty, her straightforwardness—it stole my heart in that moment. There was no game-playing, no beating around the bush. Just pure, simple truth.

*She likes me too.*

In that instant, my world turned upside down in the best way possible.

This was what I liked about her—the perfect blend of innocence and honesty. It wasn't just appealing; it also had the power to steal my heart entirely.

Then, there was *that* moment—*Oh my God!* She likes me. I couldn't believe it. A surge of joy rushed through me, and I couldn't stop smiling. I re-read her message over and over, trying to soak in every word. Was this real? Could I have misinterpreted it? My mind raced, and my heart pounded as if I had discovered some long-lost treasure. I couldn't shake the excitement; I even considered grabbing my glasses to double-check, making sure it wasn't a figment of my imagination. The feeling was indescribable. My dream girl—the one I had admired from afar—liked me back. It was like a dream suddenly coming to life.

I sat there, feeling like the universe had aligned in my favor, as though God Himself was smiling upon me, gifting me this moment. I started bouncing in my chair, and before I realized it, a joyful *"Yahoooo!"* escaped my lips. The sound echoed in the room, and that's when I snapped back to reality. *Oops,* I thought, trying to hide my excitement. *Maybe I shouldn't let everyone know just yet.* I mumbled to myself, but it was too late—some colleagues had noticed.

"What's going on?" one asked, curiosity evident in his eyes.

"Why the excitement?" another chimed in.

I quickly composed myself and, trying to downplay everything, responded, "Oh, nothing." But in truth, I wanted to tell the whole world that I was in love. The rush of emotions made me feel like I was floating, but I had to keep it quiet. She was in the same office, and the last thing I wanted was for anyone to know about us before we were ready to tell them. So, I kept it to myself, all the while feeling like I might burst with joy.

At the time, our office had a music system running, courtesy of the IT department. They'd play different playlists throughout the day, just to make work a little more enjoyable. But today, I needed something more specific. My heart was beating to the rhythm of love, and I wanted the soundtrack to match. So, I made my way to the IT department and casually asked them to switch the playlist to something romantic. They obliged, and as soon as the soft tunes filled the air, it felt as though every song had been composed just for me, just for us. The lyrics of love songs I'd heard a hundred times before suddenly had new meaning, speaking directly to my heart.

That night, we stayed up chatting on the phone, texting back and forth for hours. I couldn't stop smiling. My heart was a kaleidoscope of emotions, and even though I should've been exhausted, I felt more alive than ever. Every message from her sent a thrill through me, and I found myself grinning like a fool at the screen. And then there were those moments at work—when we'd pass by each other, exchange a subtle smile, or share a quick glance that lingered just a bit too long. It was our little secret. To everyone else, we were just friends, but those smiles carried a weight only we understood.

Then came March 3rd. A Saturday I'll never forget. I wanted everything to be perfect, so I decided to start preparing for the day ahead—the day we would finally meet outside of work. I picked out a brand-new shirt for the occasion, something sharp but comfortable. I wanted to look my best for her. After that, I took my car for a thorough wash—something I hadn't done in five years. For the first time, I even asked the boy to dry-clean the car from the inside, making sure every corner was spotless. When the car was sparkling clean, I bought a new air freshener, lavender-scented, to add a touch of freshness for our special day. As I prepared, I also picked up some chocolates for her—her favorites, of course. Everything had to be just right. It was our first date, after all.

That night, sleep eluded me. My excitement was boundless, my mind racing with thoughts of her—of us. I kept picking up my phone, re-reading her texts, replaying our conversations in my head. It was like a movie on loop, one I couldn't stop watching. Even with closed eyes, I could see her smile, hear her laugh. The anticipation was almost unbearable.

And finally, it was March 4th—Sunday. I woke up with a smile plastered on my face, a sense of anticipation buzzing inside me. Without even thinking, I grabbed my phone and dialed her number. It rang, each second feeling longer than the last, until at last, she picked up.

"Hello..." she said, her voice soft, sweet, and shy.

There was something in her tone, a warmth that made my heart flutter. I could tell she was smiling on the other side of the line, perhaps feeling the same excitement I was.

She asked me to come to her PG, and without hesitation, I replied, "I'll be there in 30 minutes."

I hung up the phone, my heart racing with excitement. This was it. The day I had been waiting for had finally arrived.

Today, I wanted to look good—*intentionally*. I could feel the heat rising in my cheeks, realizing I was blushing like a schoolboy. But I pulled myself out of that daze, shaking off the nervous energy, and made my way to the car. My heart raced as I started my journey to her place. The anticipation was intoxicating.

When I arrived, I gave her a call and asked her to come outside. Moments later, there she was—stepping out of the building. She wore a sleek black top paired with light blue jeans that almost had a hint of white. Simple, yet effortlessly beautiful. She opened the door of my car, slipped inside, and greeted me with a warm handshake and a brilliant smile that instantly made the world seem brighter.

"Let's go," she said, closing the window.

As we pulled away from her PG, I asked her, "So, where would you like to go?"

"I just want to stay in the car," she replied softly.

We drove aimlessly, talking about everything and nothing, just enjoying the comfort of being close to one another. At one point, she casually mentioned that she was craving ice cream. I kept driving until we found a vendor on the side of the road. Rolling down the window, I asked for two ice creams after confirming her flavor of choice.

We parked nearby and sat there, savoring our ice creams while the conversation flowed. She began telling me about her PG, about Preeti and her other friends, and even though I nodded along, I realized I wasn't fully paying attention. My focus had shifted completely to her lips. They moved so gracefully, each word leaving her mouth in what felt like slow motion. The way her smile stretched across her face—it was mesmerizing. I couldn't help it. I was completely lost in the moment, captivated by the way she looked so effortlessly beautiful just sitting there, eating ice cream.

Snapping myself out of it, I forced myself to listen again, but the silence that followed told me she had noticed. I had been staring. Our eyes met, and she must have read the expression on my face because suddenly, her demeanor changed. She grew shy, her eyes darting around as though searching for something to focus on other than my gaze. She was stunning. The way her lips parted just slightly, her cheeks glowing pink from embarrassment—it was a sight I would never forget.

"Please don't look at me like that," she said, her voice soft, almost a whisper. "I feel shy."

I smiled. "Why?"

"I don't know... just don't," she said, laughing nervously, still avoiding my eyes.

It was moments like these—small, almost unnoticeable to the outside world—that made my heart swell. Our conversation flowed effortlessly, laced with sweetness and easy banter that made my day. I complimented her, telling her she looked stunning, and she responded with a sly smile, "You know, your dressing sense isn't exactly impressive."

I chuckled, fully admitting, "Yeah, I've never been good at that. But next time, we'll go shopping together. You can help me pick something out, just to make sure I look my best for you."

Her smile widened at that, and we continued talking, laughing, and sharing little pieces of ourselves. Time felt irrelevant. We spent two hours just sitting there, in the car, but it felt like mere minutes. I had always wondered how people could spend so much time together in a car—my friends used to tell me stories, and I thought it sounded silly. But now, I understood. The space didn't matter. The time didn't matter. It was being with her that made everything feel *right*.

"Whatever this is," I thought to myself, "it's amazing."

*I was smiling and let the words flow*

*..*

*I didn't see it coming, no,*
*You walked in, and now my world's aglow,*
*Every little glance, every little smile,*
*Gets me tangled up, like we're lost for a while.*

*..*

*I'm sitting here, heart's in my hand,*
*Wondering if you even understand,*
*The way your voice makes the whole room fade,*
*Like a melody, I can't escape.*

*..*

*Every touch, every beat of your heart,*
*Pulls me closer, and now we're not apart.*
*I feel the rush, I feel the high,*
*When you look my way, I can't deny.*

*..*

*You give me goosebumps, like I'm flying,*
*Can't stop this feeling, no use trying.*
*You give me butterflies, every time,*
*Falling into you, can't get you off my mind.*

*Oh oh oh, oh oh oh,*
*Falling into you, like stars align.*
*Oh oh oh, oh oh oh,*
*You give me butterflies, every time.*

..

*Late at night, I'm wide awake,*
*Thinking 'bout the chances we might take,*
*Every word you say plays on repeat,*
*Like a song I've always known, so sweet.*

..

*I'm floating through the air when you're near,*
*Every moment with you, crystal clear.*
*Wondering how this could ever be real,*
*But you make me believe, and now I feel...*

..

*Every touch, every beat of your heart,*
*Pulls me closer, and now we're not apart.*
*I feel the rush, I feel the high,*
*When you look my way, I can't deny.*

..

*You give me goosebumps, like I'm flying,*
*Can't stop this feeling, no use trying.*
*You give me butterflies, every time,*
*Falling into you, can't get you off my mind.*
*Oh oh oh, oh oh oh,*
*Falling into you, like stars align.*
*Oh oh oh, oh oh oh,*
*You give me butterflies, every time.*

..

*I'll follow the rhythm, follow the sound,*
*Every time you're close, my heart pounds.*
*No need to fight it, I'm yours tonight,*
*Falling into love feels so right.*

..

*You give me goosebumps, like I'm flying,*

*Can't stop this feeling, no use trying.*
*You give me butterflies, every time,*
*Falling into you, can't get you off my mind.*
*Oh oh oh, oh oh oh,*
*Falling into you, like stars align.*
*Oh oh oh, oh oh oh,*
*You give me butterflies, every time.*

..

*Oh oh oh, you give me goosebumps...*
*Oh oh oh, you give me butterflies...*
*Oh oh oh, falling into you...*
*Oh oh oh, falling into you...*

..

But like all good things, the moment couldn't last forever. She glanced at the time and said she needed to get back to her PG—Sundays were busy, with so many things to take care of. I didn't want her to leave. I didn't want these moments with her to end. But I knew it was too soon to ask for more. Our friendship was still fresh, still unfolding, and I didn't want to be too pushy.

So, I nodded, started the car, and began driving toward Sector 7.

The ride back was quieter, but not in an uncomfortable way. There was a weight to the silence, as if both of us knew what the other was thinking. When we arrived at her PG, I pulled over and we both just sat there for a moment, looking into each other's eyes. Neither of us wanted the day to end, but there was nothing to say. It was a feeling we both understood without needing words.

"It was nice being with you," I said softly, my voice calm yet full of emotion. As I looked into her eyes, a quiet sense of peace settled over me.

"Same here," she replied, her voice gentle, her gaze locking with mine. There was something honest, almost magical, in the way she spoke. I could see it in her eyes—the sparkle of the moments we had just shared, lingering between us like a soft glow. Neither of us wanted to break the connection, not yet.

She didn't even open the car door, as if by staying in the enclosed space, she could hold on to the time we had together a little longer. Her hesitation was clear—she wasn't ready to step out, wasn't ready to leave. It was a quiet moment, but it spoke volumes.

I smiled, sensing her reluctance. "What happened?" I asked, my tone light but knowing.

She pressed her lips together, shaking her head slightly. "Nothing," she murmured, though her eyes told a different story.

I leaned in a little, my voice soft and reassuring. "Don't worry," I said, tilting my head slightly to the right, mirroring the unspoken feelings between us. "We'll meet daily." I wanted her to know that I felt the same way. The idea of saying goodbye, even just for now, didn't sit well with me either. But this was how it had to be—for now, at least.

There was a pause, the kind that only comes when words fall short of the emotion they're trying to carry. I pressed my lips together and gently said, "Please take care of yourself." My words carried more weight than I intended, but they were filled with genuine care, a tenderness I couldn't fully express.

She nodded, her eyes softening as she slowly opened the car window. The door clicked open, and with one last look, she stepped out, turning to face me. "Bye," she whispered, her voice barely louder than the gentle breeze that stirred in the quiet street.

"Bye," I said, my heart not fully accepting the moment.

She closed the door gently, and as she walked away, a small ache settled in my chest. I watched her until she disappeared into the building. The moment lingered, even after she was gone.

14th March. The date remained etched in my mind, vivid and clear. Tomorrow, on the 15th and 16th, she would be on leave—heading home to Bahadurgarh. I knew I would miss her, even though it would only be a couple of days.

That week, our shifts had changed. She was now on the morning shift, starting at 7 AM and finishing at 3 in the afternoon. I, on the other hand, was on the afternoon shift, beginning at 3 PM and ending at 11. The shift difference meant that, for most of the week, our paths barely crossed. By the time she was done for the day, I would just be arriving, and when I finished, she would already be gone. It felt like an odd game of missed connections—her day ending just as mine began.

"I'll miss her," I murmured under my breath, the words slipping out before I could stop them. It was true, though. I already felt the distance creeping in.

So, without overthinking it, I grabbed my phone and typed out a message: "I'll drop you tomorrow at 17 bus stand."

Her reply came quickly: she mentioned she'd be taking half a day off tomorrow, a small adjustment to our plan.

"Ok then, I'll be there at 12 PM," I texted back.

With everything set, I went to bed that night thinking of her. I woke up the next morning with a sense of anticipation, and at 11 AM, I sent her a quick SMS, just to confirm the plan. I didn't want anything to go wrong today. Not today.

She called me back, and the moment I answered, I could hear it—her soft, broken voice, laced with tears. "I'm not going anywhere," she said between sniffles. "I'll talk to you in the evening." And with that, she abruptly disconnected the call, leaving me hanging in silence.

Concern flooded through me. I immediately dialed her number again, but she didn't answer. My mind raced with worry, so I tried once more, and this time, she picked up.

"What happened?" I asked, my voice filled with concern.

Her voice trembled as she explained, telling me how her request for a half-day leave had been denied by her reporting manager. She had planned to head home to Bahadurgarh, but since it was far from Chandigarh, leaving at 3 PM would have meant she'd reach home very late at night. So, she canceled the trip entirely, her disappointment palpable through the phone.

I felt a tightness spread through me. Hearing her cry, knowing she was upset—it was unbearable. I couldn't just sit there, listening to her pain. I had to do something. "Don't cry," I said softly, trying to soothe her. "I'm coming to the office. Don't worry."

"No, it's okay," she said, trying to brush it off. But I could hear the sadness still lingering in her voice.

"I'm coming," I insisted, leaving no room for debate.

Without even bothering to take a bath, I quickly changed my clothes, grabbed my keys, and rushed out of the house. I didn't care about the stares or the hurried nature of my actions. All I knew was that I needed to be there for her.

When I reached the office, I didn't hesitate—I went straight to her desk. People around me noticed, casting curious glances, but I paid no attention to them. The only thing that mattered was her. She sat there, looking despondent, her earlier tears still fresh in her eyes.

"I'll talk to your reporting manager," I told her firmly. "I'll get your leave approved. Just wait for me."

She shook her head, hesitant. "Please, don't... You don't have to do that."

But I wasn't backing down. "Wait," I repeated. I wasn't about to let her suffer like this.

As I turned to go, I noticed some of the other girls nearby, whispering among themselves, wondering what I was doing there, asking her questions. But she remained quiet, saying nothing to them.

Before I could even reach her manager's desk, I received good news—her leave had already been approved. A wave of relief washed over me. She was happy, and that's all that mattered.

Just as I was standing with her manager, my phone rang. Her name lit up on the screen. I excused myself, saying, "Just two minutes, I'm coming," before quickly ending my conversation with her manager and waving goodbye.

I headed straight to the parking area, fired up my car, and sped out onto the road to find her. As I drove, I called her again. "Where are you?"

"I'm in front of the blue building," she replied.

"Wait there," I said, my voice filled with urgency.

I arrived where she was waiting and opened the car door. She stepped in, and the moment she did, I couldn't help but scold her, my voice firm but filled with concern. "Why were you crying?" I asked, my frustration tempered by my care for her. "And why did you leave the office when I specifically told you to stay?" I emphasized the words, making sure she understood I wasn't angry—just worried.

It was a scorching afternoon, and I noticed she had been walking on foot. That only added to my worry. "And walking in this heat? What were you thinking?" I lightly tapped the top of her head, a gesture she had grown used to.

Despite my scolding, she didn't seem bothered—in fact, I could tell she appreciated it. She knew my fussing over her came from a place of genuine care, and every time I showed concern, it only made her smile a little more. I could sense it.

We drove to her PG, and once we arrived, I waited outside while she went in to grab her bags and laptop. When she returned, I got out of the car to help her with the luggage, loading it into the back. She didn't have to ask—I was already moving, making sure everything was secure.

Once we were back in the car, I glanced over at her and said, "Now, give me a smile."

She nodded, her lips curving into that soft, familiar smile. "Are you happy now?" I asked, wanting to be sure.

She nodded again, still smiling.

"Good," I said gently. "Never be sad. I'm here with you, okay? I don't like it when you're sad." My voice softened even more as I added, "I'll always be here with you."

She pressed her lips together, trying to hold back another smile. It was these moments—her silent acknowledgment, her quiet responses—that made everything worthwhile. I would do anything just to keep that smile on her face.

We talked as we drove, filling the car with conversation that flowed effortlessly. At one point, she thanked me for helping her, but I quickly waved it off. "There's no need for thanks," I said.

"It's my job to help you, isn't it? But please—never cry. I'm always here, whenever you have a problem, just tell me. Don't cry. You're beautiful when you smile, and I want to keep seeing that smile."

She nodded, her eyes reflecting her appreciation without needing more words.

Soon, we reached Sector 17 ISBT. I parked the car, stepped out, and grabbed her luggage, hoisting it onto my shoulder. "Come on," I said, gesturing for her to follow. We walked together toward the bus terminal. As we moved, the wheels on her luggage made an irritating, squeaky noise, but I ignored it, focused entirely on her.

"Which route do you take to Bahadurgarh?" I asked, trying to distract her from any lingering sadness.

"From Panipat," she replied.

We made our way to the area where the Haryana Transport buses were lined up. I asked her to sit down on a nearby bench and placed the bags near her feet. "Watch these for a minute," I said as I walked off to check the buses. I scanned each one, but none of them seemed to be headed in her direction. So, I headed over to the inquiry counter to confirm.

"Bahadurgarh depot bus will come at 2:40 PM," the man at the counter told me. That meant we had an hour to wait.

I returned to her, sitting down beside her. "The bus will be here at 2:40," I informed her.

She nodded, but I noticed she still hadn't eaten. "You should have something to eat," I suggested. "You didn't have lunch, and it'll be a long six-hour ride. You won't get the chance to eat on the bus."

She shook her head slightly. "I'm not that hungry... maybe just a glass of juice."

We strolled over to a juice corner and ordered two glasses of juice. The place was buzzing with people, all waiting for their orders, creating a soft hum of voices around us. After a short wait, our glasses were served—frosty and chilled, condensation forming small droplets on the surface. I could see the mist of cold vapors rising from the glass, and with each sip, we continued talking, lost in our conversation.

As we sipped, immersed in our moment, a small, poor boy approached us. His clothes were tattered, his face smeared with dust, and he timidly asked for one rupee. I looked at him for a moment, then bent down slightly and asked, "Would you like a glass of juice instead?"

His eyes lit up as he nodded eagerly. I turned to the owner of the juice corner and asked for another glass, but in a plastic cup, wondering if he could handle the frosty glass we were using. The owner quickly prepared it, and I handed the boy the juice. His tiny hands held it carefully, and his face brightened with pure happiness. He smiled, his eyes gleaming with gratitude before he disappeared into the crowd.

As I straightened up, I noticed Jolene watching me, her eyes twinkling with something more than just affection—a smile that spoke volumes. I furrowed my brow, giving her a questioning look. "Why are you looking at me like that?" I asked, half-amused, half-curious.

She just smiled, shaking her head slightly, her eyes still on me. "Nothing," she murmured, but her expression said otherwise. I could tell she was happy—happy with what I had done for the boy.

"I've always wanted to do something for kids like him," I told her quietly. "I hate seeing them begging. I'm not in a position to do much for them yet, but these small things... they're something, right?"

She nodded and smiled, her eyes soft with admiration. The moment felt intimate, like we were sharing a deeper part of ourselves that went beyond just words.

I slowed my pace, sipping the juice as slowly as I could, wanting to match her rhythm. I didn't want to finish mine before her—I wanted us to finish together, so she wouldn't feel self-conscious for drinking slowly.

Eventually, we both finished, and I gathered the glasses, placing them back on the counter. As I reached into my pocket for my wallet, I asked her, "Do you want to eat something else? Anything at all?"

She shook her head gently. "No, I'm good."

We walked back toward the spot where we had been sitting earlier, but by then, someone else had taken the chairs. "There, let's sit there," I said, pointing to two vacant chairs nearby.

We sat down, and as the noise of the world faded into the background, I found myself looking deep into her eyes. They were stunning—bright, warm, and full of life. She looked radiant in her yellow suit, her beauty captivating me in that quiet moment. My heart stirred, and I felt something shift inside me. I could feel it, right there, an undeniable certainty—I was falling in love with her. Sitting there, staring into her eyes, I realized that she was the one I wanted to spend the rest of my life with. I could see it so clearly, the two of us together, sharing a future.

Just as I was lost in the thought, she snapped me out of my trance by reaching out her hand. "Look," she said, showing me her nails with a sense of pride and excitement. Her nails were adorned with intricate nail art—cartoons, tiny flowers, and sparkling stones. She had clearly put a lot of care into them.

"I did this yesterday," she added, beaming. "I'm crazy about nail art, you know. I change it every week."

Her enthusiasm was infectious. I admired her attention to detail, the way she found joy in the smallest of things. Each little flower, each tiny stone was a reflection of her creativity and personality.

She leaned in slightly and asked, "Have you noticed my nails before?"

I found myself silently chastising myself for never noticing her nail art before. *How could I have missed it?* I murmured an honest, "No, sorry." Then, quickly added, "But they're beautiful," my voice soft but sincere.

When I reached out and touched her hand to take a closer look at her nails, I felt her hand start to tremble slightly, as if my touch had sent a wave of nervousness through her. But despite that, she didn't pull away. She seemed fine with it, even comfortable in a shy sort of way. She began explaining the details of her nail art, telling me about the designs she had painted. Her hand stayed resting in mine the entire time, her soft fingers placed gently on top of my skin, not moving until I was done admiring the tiny flowers, stones, and intricate cartoons decorating her nails. There was something intimate about it, a quiet connection we both felt without needing words.

After a moment, she reached into her purse and pulled out her mobile. It was a classic, girly white-colored Spice touchscreen phone—a perfect match for her personality. It looked well-loved but worn, especially the screen guard, which was old and peeling at the edges, making it harder to see the display clearly.

"Why haven't you changed this?" I asked, teasing her slightly. "You can barely see through it."

She gave me a small, sheepish smile. "I haven't had time," she said, shrugging.

She then started flipping through her phone, showing me photos of her nails, each design more intricate than the last. She scrolled further, and suddenly, she was showing me pictures from a talent show where she had walked on a ramp as a model, some from dance programs, and a few college events. I couldn't help but notice how beautiful she looked in many of them. Her elegance and charm shone through every picture, and I found myself captivated by the person in those images.

Then, I noticed something curious in a few of the photos—she had written the name "Jojo." I raised an eyebrow, intrigued. "Who's Jojo?" I asked.

She chuckled softly, her voice light with amusement. "That's my nickname. My full name is Jolene Jose, so the initials become Jojo" she said.

"Nice nickname," I complimented her, smiling. Somehow, everything about her—every little detail—was becoming more and more appealing to me. It was as if her very essence was drawing me in, making me want to know every part of her, no matter how small.

As she continued showing me more pictures, I held her mobile along with her hand, my fingers gently brushing against hers. Once again, I felt the slight trembling of her hand, but instead of pulling away, she stayed like that, content. I wasn't really looking at the pictures anymore; instead, I was watching her—her face, the way she spoke, the way her eyes sparkled when she talked about things she was passionate about.

She caught my gaze and, for a moment, our eyes met. She stopped talking, biting her lower lip as though she was holding back something unspoken. Her mouth opened slightly, but the words seemed to catch in her throat. Then, after a second, she finally whispered, "Please, don't look at me this way... I feel shy."

I kept my eyes on hers, a soft smile playing on my lips. There was something irresistible in the way she said it, her voice low and filled with a mixture of embarrassment and affection. "Please na," she said again, her voice even quieter now. "Aise mat dekho." She wasn't even able to look straight into my eyes as she spoke, her gaze darting away nervously.

I couldn't help but love the way she said it—so sweet, so genuine. We both smiled, a quiet laughter lingering between us. For a moment, we just sat there, her hand still on mine, our conversation falling into a silence that wasn't awkward at all. In fact, it was the kind of silence that spoke louder than words, the kind that carried a weight only the two of us could feel.

I glanced down at her hand, still resting on mine, and then back into her eyes. There was a deep silence, a kind of stillness that was filled with its own sound, a sound only we could hear. The connection between us was palpable, as if something unspoken had already begun to bloom, something tender and new.

She looked tired. I could see it in her eyes, the way her energy seemed to dip after a long day. I wanted so badly to tell her to rest, to put her head on my shoulder and relax, but I knew it was too soon for that. I couldn't ask her—*not yet*. Instead, I just watched her quietly, wishing I could give her the comfort she deserved.

I spotted the bus from Bahadurgarh Depot approaching, and immediately grabbed her bags. "Let's go," I said, signaling for her to follow. We walked toward the bus, and when we reached it, I quickly bought her ticket before she could say anything.

She turned to me, a little annoyed. "I didn't want you to pay for it," she protested.

But I waved her off. "Don't worry about it," I said firmly. Something inside me had shifted—I couldn't help but feel like looking after her had become my responsibility.

I led her to a seat by the window and helped her settle in. The bus wasn't set to leave just yet, so I took the seat next to her, feeling like I wanted to hold on to these last few moments together.

We sat there for a while, both of us unsure of what to say. I noticed she was staring down, avoiding my eyes. That's when I felt it—our hands, without any thought or planning, had found each other. Fingers intertwined, as if it was the most natural thing in the world. My heart started racing, the kind of nervous excitement that felt unfamiliar but thrilling.

We looked down at our hands at the same time, realizing what had happened. I smiled, and she did too. There was no need to speak; the connection between us was clear. Her hand started trembling a little, probably from nervousness. It was the first time we'd really held hands like this.

"What's wrong?" I asked softly.

"I don't know," she replied, almost in a whisper, her voice tinged with nervousness. I could see she wasn't used to this, but neither was I. Still, I knew she wanted to be with me in that moment, despite the nervous energy between us.

I gave her hand a light squeeze and asked, "Are you sure you don't need anything to eat? It's a long journey ahead."

"No, I'm okay," she replied with a small smile, though her hand stayed tightly clasped in mine.

In that moment, I had the strongest urge to pull her close, to hug her and kiss her forehead, just to show how much I cared. But I held back. We weren't in a relationship yet, and I didn't want to rush things. Instead, I settled for giving her some practical advice.

"Please don't talk to any strangers," I said, my tone becoming more serious. "And don't take anything from anyone during the trip. Just be careful, okay?" I couldn't help it—I was worried about her, like she was someone precious I needed to protect.

She nodded and smiled again, pressing her lips together as if holding back her own emotions. "Okay," she whispered, showing that she understood and appreciated the concern.

Just then, the bus engine started up, and I knew my time with her was running out. I glanced at the driver, who was getting ready to pull out, and turned back to her.

"I have to go now," I said quietly, not wanting to leave. "Bye."

She didn't say anything at first, just gave me a look that said everything. Slowly, she let go of my hand, the sadness in her eyes making it clear she didn't want to part either.

"Please take care," I added, standing up. "And call me when you reach, okay?"

She nodded again, her voice lost in the emotion of the moment. I could see how hard this was for her too, and that only made it harder for me to leave. As I stepped out of the bus, I saw a girl standing nearby, waiting for a seat, which snapped me back to reality.

As I stood up, I noticed a woman standing nearby, looking for a seat. In a courteous gesture, I offered her my spot. Deep down, I wanted a woman to sit beside her for the long journey, knowing it would make her feel more comfortable. I glanced at Jolene again, and passed her a small smile. She returned it, but I could tell it was forced—a smile that didn't reach her eyes. It wasn't because she was upset with me. I knew she wasn't happy about leaving me behind. The sadness on her face reflected the same separation anxiety I felt inside.

I stepped off the bus, feeling the weight of the moment. As I walked out, I sensed her eyes following me, not wanting to lose sight of me. Both of us were quietly struggling with the parting. Her gaze was fixed on me through the window, and I couldn't bring myself to stop looking at her either. Our eyes remained locked through the glass, both of us unwilling to break that connection. I raised my hand and placed it on the bus window. She did the same from her side, pressing her hand against the glass, meeting my touch in that small, yet powerful gesture.

I smiled at her one last time, and then, with a soft rumble, the bus began to move. Slowly, she faded from view, and I stood there, watching the bus disappear into the distance.

I had to be at work by 3 PM, and the clock was already ticking—it was 2:55. I hurried to the parking area, quickly dialing into the office to inform them I'd be late.

As I was rushing to my car, I heard the familiar tone of an SMS, but in my hurry, I ignored it. I needed to get to the office. I started the car and drove, my thoughts still lingering on her. When I finally reached work, I settled in at my desk and placed my phone beside the computer, as usual. That's when the soft, blue notification light caught my attention—reminding me that I had an unread message.

I picked up the phone and opened it. It was a message from her: *"I will miss you."*

The words touched me deeply, making my heart swell with emotion. I smiled to myself, thanking God for bringing someone so special into my life. She was everything I'd ever wanted—beautiful, tall, caring, loving, sweet, and cute, all wrapped into one perfect person.

I replied, "I'll miss you too. Please inform me when you reach home, and take care."

The rest of the day was a blur. My mind kept drifting back to her, the thought of missing her for even just two days weighing on me more than I expected. I couldn't stop thinking about her, and with each passing hour, the desire to know she was safe and sound grew stronger.

That evening, I sent her another message: *"Where are you?"*

No reply. I assumed she was still on the bus, maybe she hadn't heard the SMS tone, or perhaps she was asleep, exhausted from the long journey. I tried not to worry, but something inside me felt uneasy.

Around 10 PM, the concern got the better of me, and I decided to call her to check if she had reached home. The phone rang for a moment, and when she picked up, her voice immediately unsettled me. She sounded tense.

"I'm at a small bus stop in Gohana," she said quietly.

My heart sank. "What? What are you doing there?" I asked, my voice suddenly filled with alarm.

She explained, but I was barely processing it—I was too focused on the fact that she was alone, standing in a strange place, far from home. Panic stirred inside me, and all I could think about was how to help her.

She explained the whole situation quickly, her voice laced with worry. It turned out that the bus she had boarded wasn't the right one. Instead of taking her directly to Bahadurgarh, it was headed to Delhi first, which would have added hours to her journey. So, she got off at Panipat, but from there, no buses were going to Bahadurgarh. Desperate, she managed to find a bus headed to Gohana and decided to take it, hoping it would get her closer to home.

Now, she was stuck at a small bus stop in Gohana, waiting for her dad and brother, who were on their way to pick her up. But it would take them at least an hour to get there. Her voice wavered as she told me she was scared—there were some drunken men hanging around nearby, and she felt uneasy standing there alone.

My heart sank, hearing the fear in her voice. "Can you go to the main bus stand?" I asked, trying to keep my voice steady, though inside I was just as worried.

"I tried that," she replied, "but there was no one there. It felt even scarier, so I came back."

I quickly thought about what she could do to stay safe. "Is there any place nearby with more people? Somewhere safer?"

"There's a juice corner," she said, her voice hesitant. "But it's a little far from here."

"Go there," I urged gently but firmly. "Please, it's better than standing alone at this stop."

She agreed and began walking toward the juice corner. As she moved, I stayed on the phone with her, encouraging her and trying my best to distract her from the fear I knew she was feeling. My own worry was growing by the second, but I kept it hidden, doing my best to sound calm.

When she reached the juice corner, she found that all the other shops were closed, and the juice vendor was just about to shut down for the night too. Worse, there were no streetlights along the road, which only made the situation feel more unsettling.

"Talk to the juice vendor," I said. "Ask him if he can stay open a bit longer, just until your family arrives."

She spoke to the owner, and thankfully, he agreed to wait. I could hear the relief in her voice, though I knew she was still nervous. I stayed on the phone, talking to her non-stop, reassuring her. Her fear was palpable, but she sounded a little more relaxed knowing I was on the other end, keeping her company.

"I'm sorry," I blurted out after a while, guilt starting to eat at me. "I should've checked the bus properly. I just saw the sign and didn't confirm with the conductor."

Her response made me pause. "You don't need to say sorry," she said, her voice soft but sincere. "It wasn't your fault."

Her kindness, even in a moment like this, amazed me. She could have easily blamed me, but instead, she brushed it off, showing me once again why I was so drawn to her. Her outlook on life, the way she handled situations with grace, only made me admire her more.

As we continued talking, her phone buzzed. "It's my dad," she said. "I need to take this call."

"Okay," I replied, feeling a little better now that her dad was almost there. "Talk to you soon."

She disconnected the call, and I sat there, still feeling a knot of worry in my chest. I waited a few minutes, pacing, wanting to check in again. Eventually, I called her back to see if everything was okay, but she didn't pick up. That familiar uneasiness crept back in, and my mind started spinning with worst-case scenarios. I couldn't help it—negative thoughts raced through my mind. Was she still okay? Had something happened?

But just as I was about to call again, my phone buzzed. I quickly looked at the screen and saw her message: *"I am fine, in the car with*

*Dad. Talk to you later... Bye. Take care!"*

I let out a long breath, feeling a wave of relief wash over me. She was safe now, with her father, and my tension slowly began to fade.

I replied in kind, *"Glad you're safe. Take care. Talk soon."*

Even though I was finally at ease, knowing she was on her way home, I couldn't help but berate myself for not double-checking the bus earlier. It was a small mistake, but it had caused her so much worry. Still, her calm, forgiving nature left me feeling even more grateful for having her in my life.

She didn't call or message me for two days. I tried not to overthink it, but I was missing her more than I expected. In the back of my mind, I knew the reason—she hadn't been home in a long time, and being with her family probably made her forget about everything else. Still, it stung a little.

Sometimes, we expect too much from others, and when those expectations aren't met, it hurts—even if we know better. I tried to remind myself of that. I knew I had to be more understanding, to appreciate that she was busy with her loved ones. But even though I told myself that, it didn't completely stop the feeling of discontent from creeping in.

Finally, after two days of silence, my phone buzzed with a message from her: *"I'm on the way to Chandigarh."*

A wave of relief hit me. Without wasting time, I called her, offering to meet her at the bus stand. "I'll come pick you up," I said eagerly, ready to see her again.

But she declined. "One of my friends is already coming to get me," she replied.

I paused for a moment, then asked, "Who's this friend?"

"You don't know him," she said, her tone casual.

That didn't sit well with me for a second, but I let it go. I didn't want to seem too possessive. She came back to the city, and soon enough, we were back to chatting over messages. It felt like things had fallen back into place.

One day, while we were talking, I decided to mess with her a bit. "You said you'd miss me," I joked, "but you didn't call me even once in the last two days!"

She laughed softly and explained, "I went home after such a long time... I was just busy with my family."

I couldn't resist teasing her more. "So, what did you bring me from home?" I asked mischievously, already smiling at her response.

There was a brief pause, and then she said, "I... I've come back for you." Her voice had a lively tone, and I could picture her smiling as she said it.

We both laughed, and after that, our conversations became longer. We started talking more over the phone, less on SMS. She seemed more relaxed, but every now and then, she would admit something that made me smile.

"You always make me nervous," she said once, a hint of shyness in her voice.

I was genuinely surprised. "Me? How do I make you nervous?" I asked, trying to understand what she meant.

"The way you look at me," she replied softly. "It makes me nervous."

That confession made me pause. I hadn't realized that my gaze affected her so much, but I liked that it did. There was something sweet in the way she admitted it, and it only deepened the bond between us.

Feeling a renewed sense of connection, I asked her to meet me after the office. She didn't hesitate. "We'll meet after work," she agreed, and I could hear the warmth in her voice. She loved spending time with me as much as I did with her.

My shift had changed to 7 AM to 3 PM, the same as her now. While it was nice being on the same schedule, I didn't like that she had to walk back to her PG in the sweltering heat at 3 PM. The summer sun was merciless at that time, and it bothered me to think of her walking under it. I offered to drive her home, but she always had a group of friends to walk with, so I didn't push the issue.

Still, it didn't sit well with me. Today, as usual, everyone began to leave the office at 3 PM, but I couldn't. Right at 2:45 PM—like clockwork—my manager dumped another "priority" task on my desk. It was always me, never anyone else, who got stuck with these last-minute, useless tasks. I handed it over to Dipaansh, my colleague, and rushed out as quickly as I could. By then, I was already 10 minutes late, and she was likely close to her PG.

I sprinted to my car, jumped in, and started the engine. Without wasting a second, I shifted gears, dragged the clutch, and pressed the accelerator hard. My heart raced as I scanned the road for her. Finally, I spotted her, just about 100 feet away from her PG. I pulled up behind her, honked, and she turned around.

She smiled when she saw me, but walking beside her was her friend, Mandira. I asked her to get in the car, and though Jolene tried to convince Mandira to join us, she refused and waved us off with a smile, telling us to carry on without her.

I smiled, pulling the car over to a stop. "Here, let me show you," I said, reaching over gently. As I grabbed the seatbelt and leaned closer, I realized just how near I was to her. Our faces were only inches apart, and I could feel the warmth between us. Her eyes caught mine, and for a brief moment, I was completely lost in them—deep, beautiful, and filled with a certain nervousness. Her lips were soft and inviting, so close that I felt a gentle warmth radiate within me. She was breathtaking, even in this simple moment. "*Beta,* this is how you lock it," I quipped softly, guiding the seatbelt into place, but my attention was still on her. The closeness made my chest tighten, but I kept my composure, trying to act like this was just any ordinary gesture, even though it was anything but.

She was a little nervous at first, probably expecting me to poke fun at her for not knowing how to fasten a seatbelt, but I didn't feel that at all. In fact, I found it endearing. A sense of belonging had started to develop between us, and there was no way I could mock her for something so small. It just didn't feel right.

She was wearing a white T-shirt with an "Angry Birds" print, layered under a bright red shrug. The casual outfit suited her perfectly, and she looked effortlessly good. As we drove, I asked her, "So, where do you want to go?"

She smiled, relaxed now. "I'm fine just being in the car," she said. "Let's get some ice cream."

So, we spent some time together in the car, chatting and driving around, enjoying each other's company. It was a bit awkward for me to just sit in the car without doing much, but since she was comfortable, that was all that mattered to me. Her happiness always put me at ease.

After a while, I suggested, "How about we go to Café Coffee Day in Sector 11? It's nearby."

She agreed, and soon enough, we arrived. The café was quiet, perfect for a more relaxed conversation. We found a cozy corner near the television and sat down. I handed her the menu and asked her to choose what she wanted.

"I feel like having something cold," she said with a smile. We ordered cold coffee with melted chocolate coating the inside of the glass and a scoop of ice cream on top, and as we waited, our conversation flowed easily. She started talking about cameras and photography, pointing out the camera angles being used in the cricket match that was playing on the TV.

It wasn't exactly my area of interest—camera specs and photography details had always bored me. But as I sat there listening to her talk with such passion, I found myself paying attention. Maybe it was that feeling—*that love inclination*—that made everything she said sound interesting, even if the topic wasn't something I typically cared about.

After a few moments, the server arrived, placing our order on the table. It came in a large glass with an equally large spoon, and it looked delicious. "This is my favorite," I told her, smiling.

We took our time, not in any rush to finish. There was something about the moment—quiet but full—that made us both linger. I wanted to share it with her in a more personal way, so I picked up the spoon, scooped a bit of the dessert, and gently moved it toward her lips. "Here, try this," I said.

She opened her mouth, waiting patiently as I fed her. I watched her eyes light up the moment the spoon touched her lips. There was something about the way she looked at me, the way she took it in, that told me she loved it. It wasn't just the dessert—it was the gesture.

Then, in her usual excited way, she started showing me her new nail art, which she had done two days ago. It was intricate, a series of thick lines and designs that looked incredibly difficult to draw on such small nails. I was genuinely impressed.

"Wow, that's amazing," I said, staring at the details. "How do you even manage to draw lines that fine?"

She laughed softly, clearly enjoying my interest. I could tell she was talking to me more openly, her shyness starting to fade. The more time we spent together, the more I could feel her becoming comfortable with me. And, to my surprise, I was enjoying learning about something I'd never thought twice about before—*nail art*.

*Have you ever imagined a man starting to like nail art? Well, that man was me.*

As I examined her nails, her hand resting lightly on mine, I felt it again—her hand trembled ever so slightly. I looked up, catching her eyes. "Why are your hands shivering?" I asked, even though I already knew the answer.

"I don't know," she said, her voice a little quieter now. "But... you make me nervous."

I smiled at her honesty, squeezing her hand gently. "You don't like it when I touch your hand?" I asked, my tone soft but curious.

She shook her head quickly. "No, it's not that. I like it. It's just... I feel nervous."

I leaned in a little closer, trying to reassure her. "Don't worry. That'll change," I said with a quiet confidence. "The more time we spend together, the less nervous you'll feel with me."

She gave me a small nod, pressing her lips together as if to steady herself. Slowly, our hands found each other again, fingers intertwining naturally, and this time, neither of us hesitated. Our hands remained clasped, a quiet, unsaid agreement passing between us. There was something deeper growing between us, something unspoken but undeniably present. We didn't need to say it—we could feel it in the way we held each other's hands, in the way our eyes met but didn't rush to look away.

For the first time, I could hear the silence speaking between us—words neither of us said aloud, but words that existed all the same.

..

Few unsaid words, I could hear.
Few unsaid promises, I made.
Few unsaid commitments, I felt deep inside.
Few unsaid dreams I saw,
Few unsaid....

..

We sat there, holding hands, just knowing.

I can't even begin to describe the feeling—being unwed, yet somehow, in my heart, already feeling like I was bound to her. There was a silent understanding between us, an invisible thread that tied us together.

To my surprise, as we sat there, she began showing me pictures of a ramp walk she'd done. In one of the photos, she wore a stunning white bridal dress, delicate flowers in her hands. She looked absolutely gorgeous, like someone straight out of a dream. Her beauty in that moment took my breath away. She excitedly told me about the experience, describing every small detail—how she had bought the dress just for that event, a classic white Christian bridal gown that looked perfect on her. She seemed so happy reminiscing, sharing the little moments with me.

It was getting late, and we both realized it was time to go. We left the café, walking quietly to the parking lot. Once we were seated in the car, I didn't start the engine right away. Instead, we just sat there, the night quiet around us. I turned toward her, my heart full but my words caught in my throat. I wanted to be closer, to feel her in a way that words couldn't express.

I rested my elbow on the seat near her face and gently moved my hand toward her head. Slowly, I ran my fingers through her hair, pushing a few loose strands back behind her ear. Her hair was soft, and as I touched it, we locked eyes. Neither of us said a word—there was no need for words. We were close, yet the moment still felt full of anticipation, as if we were waiting for something that was already there.

I shifted slightly, moving my hand to her left shoulder, and gently pulled her toward me. She didn't resist, which surprised me in a way, but then again, it didn't. There was an unspoken trust between us. As she leaned in, she nuzzled her face into my neck, closing her eyes. The warmth of her against me was something I hadn't realized I longed for so deeply until that very moment.

I held her hand in mine, while with the other, I continued to play with her hair, running my fingers through it gently. We stayed like that for a while, neither of us moving, lost in the simple intimacy of being close. I didn't know how it happened, but the next thing I knew, I found myself pressing a soft kiss on her forehead. It wasn't planned—it just felt natural, like something I was meant to do. She didn't pull away; in fact, she seemed to sink deeper into my embrace, resting comfortably under my chin.

I moved my hand to her cheek, feeling the softness of her skin, and then pulled her closer into my arms, holding her tight. It was such a tender, quiet moment—one I would never forget. Everything I had dreamed of, all those quiet hopes, were suddenly real. I had her in my arms, and for the first time, I felt completely at peace.

After a while, she whispered, "I'm feeling sleepy now."

I kissed her softly again and said with a smile, "Then who's stopping you? You can sleep here in my arms, my baby."

She smiled, eyes closed, but then said, "I'm getting late, let's go."

"Are you sure?" I asked, not wanting to let the moment end just yet.

"Hmmm," she nodded, her eyes still closed for a long moment, savoring the last of our quiet time together.

Reluctantly, I started the car and began driving toward her PG. But as we neared it, I couldn't help but stop the car just a little before we reached. "Can we spend just five more minutes together?" I asked, my voice low, almost pleading.

She smiled again, that soft, sweet smile, and nodded. "Okay," she said gently, her head resting against the seat, eyes still soft and tired.

I asked her to come closer, motioning for her to unlock the seatbelt so I could hold her again. She smiled, unfastened the belt, and moved back into my arms, where she seemed to fit perfectly. I kissed her gently on the top of her head, then placed a soft kiss on her forehead. My hand found its way under her chin, and I lifted her face delicately, planting a kiss on her left cheek, then her nose. She smiled shyly, her cheeks flushing as she lowered her gaze, still smiling.

She rested her head against my chest, and we sat there, holding each other close, so close that we could feel the rhythm of each other's breaths and the rapid beating of our hearts. It was as though the air between us had disappeared, leaving just us, in the purest form of closeness.

And then, something completely unexpected happened—she lifted her face, her eyes searching mine for just a brief second, and before I could fully process it, her lips met mine. It was soft, hesitant at first, but it was as if the world around us disappeared in that single moment. A wave of warmth coursed through me, spreading from the spot where her lips touched mine and reaching every inch of me.

I hadn't anticipated it, hadn't even imagined that this moment could feel so electric, so powerful. But the second our lips met, nothing else mattered. Every thought, every concern vanished, and it was just her and me, together in this delicate yet intense kiss. The touch of her lips was both gentle and consuming, a mixture of innocence and passion that left me breathless.

At first, I wasn't sure how to respond. My heart raced, each beat intensifying as the reality of what was happening sank in. I could feel the nervousness rising in me, but it melted away just as quickly when I closed my eyes and let myself fall into the moment. Slowly, instinctively, we deepened the kiss, and time seemed to lose all meaning.

I could feel the warmth of her breath as our lips stayed together, the soft pressure of her mouth against mine. There was something pure and beautiful about it, something I had never felt before. It was my first kiss, and yet, it felt so right, as if this was what I had been waiting for all along. I could sense her own nervousness too, but we both leaned into the feeling, letting go of everything else.

The kiss grew slower, more deliberate, and the connection between us became stronger with every passing second. Her lips moved with mine, softly at first, then with a gentle urgency that made my heart race. My hands found their way to her waist, pulling her closer to me, and she responded by pressing even more into the kiss, as if she didn't want it to end either.

It wasn't just a kiss—it was a confession, a silent way of telling me what words could never express. Her lips told me she trusted me, that she cared for me, and in that moment, I knew I felt the same. I kissed her back with a tenderness I didn't know I was capable of, as if I was afraid of breaking the spell we had created between us.

I could taste the sweetness of her lips, feel the softness of her skin, and it made everything inside me come alive. Every touch, every movement, every breath was charged with a kind of magic I'd never known before. And still, we didn't stop. It was as though we were both lost, not wanting to be found, wrapped in this bubble of pure emotion and closeness that we didn't want to let go of.

When we finally, slowly, pulled apart, it wasn't because we wanted to—it was because we had to. My forehead rested against hers, our breaths still heavy, our hearts still racing. She nuzzled her face into my neck, and I held her close, as if trying to keep the moment from slipping away too quickly.

I placed my hand gently on her waist and pulled her into a hug, feeling the beat of her heart against my chest. I whispered, half-joking, but full of truth, "Every time I make you nervous, but this time... you made me."

She didn't say anything, but I could feel the smile on her lips against my neck. Her hand moved slowly up to rest on my chest, and I knew, without needing to ask, that she felt the same way I did. This was more than just a kiss—it was the beginning of something deeper, something real.

I leaned back slightly, picking up her face once more, and kissed her again, softly on the lips. It was more gentle this time, but no less full of meaning. When we pulled away, I placed her head on my chest, my fingers running gently through her hair.

"I'm feeling sleepy in your arms," she whispered, her voice soft and content.

"Then sleep here, relax, my baby," I said, hugging her a little more tightly, hoping to keep her there for just a bit longer.

But she shook her head slightly, her voice filled with a kind of reluctant sadness. "No, I have to go. Everyone will be waiting for me at the PG."

I sighed but understood. Reaching into the car's compartment, I pulled out the chocolate I had bought for her earlier. "Here, I got this for you," I said, handing it to her.

Her face brightened, and she smiled, taking it from me. "Thank you for a lovely evening," she said, her voice sweet and genuine.

With that, she stepped out of the car, closing the door gently behind her. I watched as she walked toward the entrance of her PG, disappearing from view. And then, I drove back to my room, but sleep didn't come that night.

The magic of that kiss lingered, its softness, its warmth, the way it felt to be so close to her. She had left for the day, but she hadn't truly left. She had left something behind—an imprint on my heart. I could feel her love, her feelings, and the way she had given herself to me in that moment, fully and without hesitation. I realized just how lucky I was to have someone like her who loved me so deeply.

As I lay in bed, I promised myself that I would never hurt her, that I would always be there for her, to give her happiness and everything she deserved.

Still riding the thrill of the kiss, I sent her a message: *"You made me nervous at that time."*

A few moments later, my phone buzzed. She had sent back a smile emoji.

That night, after we said our goodbyes, I wished her a good night and logged into Facebook. My heart was still racing from the evening we'd shared, so I decided to post a status to reflect how I was feeling: *"I'm in love."* It felt liberating, like finally releasing a truth I could no longer hold inside.

Curiosity tugged at me, and I immediately searched for her profile on Facebook. At first, I couldn't find her under her real name, but then I remembered the nickname she had told me about—Jojo. I typed it in and scrolled through a few profiles until one caught my eye. The profile picture was of nail art—those intricate designs she was always proud of. I smiled to myself, knowing instantly it was her. Without hesitation, I sent her a friend request.

Sleep didn't come easily that night, as I knew it wouldn't. My mind kept replaying every detail of the day, every glance, every word, every touch. I tossed and turned, restless with thoughts of her.

The next day at work, my eyes instinctively searched for her. When they finally found her across the room, our eyes met, and we both exchanged a sweet, playful smile, the kind that held unspoken words and shared secrets. It was one of those moments that made me realize how special this was becoming. Our shift ended, and as she was heading out, she waved me goodbye, her smile lingering like an invisible tether between us.

I sent her a quick text: *"I sent you a friend request on Facebook."*

She replied soon after: *"Ok, I'll accept it today."*

March 15th. It was an ordinary day. We were chatting when she mentioned that it was her friend Navita Kaur's birthday, and she was planning to buy a cake for a small celebration at their PG that night.

"Let's meet this evening," I suggested. "We can buy the cake together, and it'll give us a chance to hang out."

She agreed without hesitation, and we made plans to meet later. When I saw her that evening, she was wearing a green checkered shirt with jeans, and as always, she looked stunning—tall, slim, with a natural elegance. The simplicity of her outfit only highlighted her effortless beauty.

Instead of going to a restaurant, she said she just wanted to spend some quiet time with me in the car. There was something intimate about the idea—just us, away from the noise of the world. We decided to grab ice cream, and after picking some up, I parked on the side of the road. The windows down slightly, the cool evening air drifting in, we sat in the car, eating ice cream, and talking about everything and nothing. The world outside felt distant, as if it had faded away, leaving just the two of us in our small bubble.

After a while, she turned to me and said, "Can we go to bakery? I want to get the cake for Navita."

"Of course," I replied, starting the car again.

As we drove toward it, she grew a little nervous. "A lot of people from the office live near there," she asked with a hint of worry, glancing out the window. "What if someone sees us together?"

I could sense the anxiety in her voice. She wasn't ready for anyone to know about us just yet, and I understood that completely. We were still navigating these new, exciting feelings.

I reassured her, "Don't worry, it's late and most of the market will be closed. Only a couple of shops are still open at this time. We won't run into anyone."

She hesitated but then smiled, trusting me, and we continued toward Polka. Once there, we quickly bought the cake, candles, and a few other things for the celebration. The shop was quiet, with just a couple of people inside, as I had predicted. She seemed to relax once we left, carrying the small bag of birthday supplies.

After buying the cake, candles, and a few other things for Navita's birthday, we stepped outside into the night air. I carefully placed everything in the back seat of my car, and we drove toward her PG. As usual, I stopped a little before her place, where we always had our quiet moments alone.

I turned off the engine, and without a word, pulled her gently into my arms. She rested against my chest, her breath warm and steady. The closeness was intoxicating, and soon, our lips found each other. The kiss began softly, but it quickly deepened, becoming more intense with each passing second. I could feel her responding to me, her body softening in my arms as she relaxed into the moment.

My hands began to explore her slowly, tracing the curves of her body, feeling the warmth through her clothes. Every touch was deliberate, filled with a sense of discovery. Her skin felt like silk beneath my fingertips, and the connection between us seemed to grow stronger with each touch. She didn't resist—if anything, she pressed herself closer to me, her arms around my neck, her breath quickening with mine.

I kissed her again, deeper this time, letting myself get lost in the moment. My hand slid up her back, fingers tangling gently in her hair as we melted into each other. Her hands moved across my chest, tentative but full of curiosity, making my heart race even faster.

For what felt like forever, we stayed like that—wrapped in each other, our breaths mingling, our hearts racing. Her head eventually rested against my shoulder, and I could feel her pulse steady as she exhaled softly, relaxing into me.

I kissed the top of her head, my hand resting on her waist, the warmth of her skin against mine. Neither of us said a word—we didn't need to. The silence was filled with everything we couldn't yet put into words.

But moments like these are fleeting. Her breath hitched slightly as she pulled back, her eyes meeting mine, a soft regret in her voice. 'I'm getting late,' she whispered, as if wishing time could slow down.

I didn't let go of her just yet. I kept looking at her, my gaze searching hers, wanting to hold on to the moment for as long as I could.

"Please don't look at me that way," she said softly, her cheeks turning a shade of pink. I could tell she was feeling shy.

I smiled, teasing her gently. "You kissed me yourself and rested in my arms, but you're still feeling nervous?"

She bit her lip, looking down for a moment before replying, "I don't know."

I brushed her cheek lightly, trying to reassure her. "It's okay. Everything will be fine with time. You'll feel comfortable with me."

She nodded, her smile returning as her nervousness faded.

Before I started the car again, I asked, "What did you tell your friends about where you were?"

She smiled timidly. "I already told Preeti and Navita that I'd be with you."

Hearing that made me smile, knowing that she trusted me enough to share it with her close friends. I moved the car forward, driving slowly until we were right near her PG. Before she could open the door, I leaned in a little closer and asked, "Can I have one last hug?"

She smiled softly and leaned in, wrapping her arms around me tightly, her body fitting perfectly against mine. I held her close, feeling the weight of her in my arms, her breath steady against my chest. And then, something happened—something neither of us expected.

As I shifted slightly to hold her more comfortably, my hand accidentally slipped under her shirt, resting on her bare waist. For a split second, I froze. The warmth of her skin against my palm sent a shiver through me. I didn't mean to touch her there, and I wondered how she would react. My heart raced, a mixture of nervousness and excitement running through me. But when she didn't pull away, when she didn't flinch or seem startled, I felt a quiet sense of relief.

Instead, she stayed pressed against me, letting me feel the soft, smooth warmth of her skin. My fingers rested there for a moment, softly caressing the curve of her waist, and I couldn't help but savor the intimacy of it.

Her skin was like silk under my fingertips, soft and inviting. There was something magical about the moment, as if the touch had created an even deeper connection between us. I could tell she felt it too. She was a little nervous, her breathing uneven, but I could also sense the excitement in her, mirroring my own.

We stayed like that for a few moments, neither of us wanting to break the spell. But then, she gently pulled back, smiling as she reached for the car door.

Before she stepped out, I realized she had forgotten something. "Wait, you forgot the cake and candles," I reminded her with a grin.

She laughed softly, her face lighting up with that beautiful smile I adored. "Oh, right!" she said, her voice filled with a mix of nervousness and joy.

She grabbed everything from the back seat and got out of the car. I watched as she walked toward the entrance of her PG, her figure disappearing into the night. But even though she was gone, the memory of that touch, that kiss, and that embrace lingered with me.

It struck me then—despite everything we'd shared, despite the closeness, we had never exchanged those three golden words. *I love you.* But the truth was, we didn't need to.

Those three words—*I love you*—seemed too small, too simple for the vastness of what I felt for her. I wondered if they could ever capture the magic of these moments, the way my heart raced every time I saw her, the way I felt so complete just being near her.

he next day, I logged into Facebook, curious to see if she had accepted my friend request. But when I checked, it still hadn't been accepted. I couldn't help but smile to myself—*Maybe she's just had forgotten.* I sent her a quick message: *"You haven't accepted my friend request yet?"*

Her reply came almost immediately: *"I haven't received it yet."*

I raised an eyebrow. *Haven't received it?* I was sure I'd sent it to the right profile. To be sure, I gave her my email ID and asked her to send me a request instead.

*"I'll add you when I log in,"* she replied.

Days passed, and we didn't talk much about Facebook after that. I was more interested in spending time with her in real life, anyway. One day, feeling courageous, I asked her if she'd like to come to the lake with me. It seemed like the perfect opportunity to spend some quiet time together.

She hesitated for a moment and said, "Preeti will be alone at the PG..."

I smiled, sensing her concern. "Then bring Preeti along," I offered. "I don't mind, really. It'll be fun with all three of us."

She checked with Preeti, and later confirmed they'd both come. We planned to meet at 6 o'clock.

That evening, they arrived together, and I had the chance to meet Preeti for the first time. She was a sweet girl, polite and with an easy smile. As we greeted each other, Preeti turned to me and said with a cheeky smile, "Thank you, sir, for letting me come along with both of you."

I couldn't resist teasing her a little. "Actually," I said, pretending to be serious, "I didn't invite you. I was asking Jojo not to bring you."

Preeti's eyes widened in mock surprise. "Seriously?"

I couldn't hold back my laughter. "No, no! I'm just joking. You're most welcome," I said, smiling warmly.

She laughed too, and the mood between the three of us lightened even more. The evening had only just begun, but it already felt like it was going to be special.

We spent a peaceful and cool evening at the lake, the gentle breeze brushing against our faces. The atmosphere was serene, and the sound of the water brought a sense of calm. We laughed a lot, discussing their college days, sharing stories that felt light and full of life. Somewhere in the middle of all that, I rested my head on her shoulder. She seemed surprised at first, especially with Preeti there, but she didn't say anything—just smiled softly and let me stay there. It felt natural, like we were already in sync with each other.

As we sat there enjoying the moment, Preeti suddenly pulled out her phone, dialed a number, and asked, "Where are you?" Not long after, her boyfriend arrived, and she introduced us. We shook hands, exchanging polite greetings before Preeti and her boyfriend excused themselves, leaving us alone by the lakeside.

With just the two of us now, we moved closer to the edge of the lake and sat down, the quiet settling around us. Our conversation shifted from lighthearted stories to something more personal, more meaningful. Slowly, we began talking about us—our relationship, our future. It was the first time we really discussed where we were headed. It was the first time we really discussed what the future might look like for us—not as a vague idea, but as something tangible, something real.

She grew quiet. Her fingers idly played with the grass beside her, twisting a blade in her hand as if trying to gather the right words. I could feel the air between us grow heavier, a tension I hadn't felt before, and then she turned to me, her eyes full of something deeper, something serious. The playfulness that had colored the evening was gone, replaced by a weight that seemed to pull her down.

"I need to tell you something," she said softly, her voice barely above a whisper, the slightest tremor betraying her nerves. Her eyes flickered away for a moment, as though searching for the courage to continue. "Before we move forward, I think... I need you to know everything. About me."

She hesitated again, then finally spoke, her voice steady but fragile. "It's about Nikhil. My ex," she began, her eyes glancing at the water like it could wash away the uncertainty she was feeling. "I haven't really talked about him with anyone in a long time."

Her words hung in the air between us, tentative. I could feel her discomfort, her unease at revisiting a part of her past she'd rather forget. She was picking her way carefully through this confession, trying to be honest but also wary of how it might affect us.

"I loved him," she said after a pause, her voice catching slightly. "A lot. We were really close for a while, and it felt like he was going to be in my life forever. But then things changed. He changed. We haven't spoken for over a year now." She glanced at me to gauge my reaction, her face soft with vulnerability, almost as if she was bracing for something.

As she spoke, I could hear the strain in her words—the weight of emotions she'd never fully processed. There was sadness there, yes, but more than that, I could sense something deeper.

Her grip tightened on my hand, her thumb brushing against mine as if she were drawing strength from the connection. After her breakup with Nikhil, she had been left with a sense of emptiness—a part of her feeling lost, adrift in the aftermath of what she thought her life would become. She had been trying to fill that space ever since, trying to move on. And in many ways, being with me had been part of that healing process.

Her voice grew quieter, more sincere with every word. "I want to be with you," she said, turning to look at me with a raw honesty in her eyes. "I want us to have a future. I want to start fresh with you, and I mean that. But sometimes... sometimes it feels like I'm cheating you. Like I should be completely free of this before we decide future, but I'm not yet. Even though I'm trying."

She looked down, her words weighed with a mix of guilt and fear. She wanted to give herself to me completely, but she was scared—scared that a part of her would always be tied to the past. It was clear she wanted to love me, but there was a small part of her that wasn't sure if she could let go of those lingering memories easily.

I took her hand in mine, squeezing it gently, wanting to reassure her. "Hey," I said softly, "it's okay. I understand." She looked up at me, her eyes searching for something—comfort, maybe, or a sign that everything would be alright. "These things take time," I continued. "You don't have to force anything. I'm not asking you to forget anything overnight. I'm here for you, and I'll love you no matter how long it takes. We'll go through this together."

She smiled weakly, her eyes softening a little, but the uncertainty still lingered beneath the surface. I could see it—the fear of being left behind again, the vulnerability she was trying to hide. Gently, I pulled her closer, wrapping my arm around her as if to shield her from that doubt.

"You don't have to worry about me leaving," I said softly, my voice steady with reassurance. I tilted her chin up slightly, wanting her to meet my eyes, to really hear me. "I'm not going anywhere. Your past doesn't scare me—it's part of who you are, and I love every part of you."

I paused, caught in a moment of disbelief. How could anyone walk away from her? It was hard to fathom. She was so gentle, so pure, like untouched snow—delicate, soft, and beautiful in a way that made you want to protect her, never let her go. The thought of someone abandoning her was beyond me.

"I don't understand how anyone could have let you go," I murmured, shaking my head slightly. "You're... special, in a way that makes you unforgettable. It doesn't matter what happened before—what I see now is someone worth holding onto. You're the best thing that's ever happened to me, and I'm not going to let the past come between us."

I tightened my grip around her, wanting her to feel the weight of my words, to know I was all in. "I'm here—with no demands, no complaints. Just me and you. I'm not leaving, no matter what."

Her body seemed to relax against mine, and I could feel some of the weight lift from her. I knew it wouldn't be easy for her to let go of her past completely, but I wanted her to know that I was committed to helping her through it—however long it took.

After a while, she brought up something that had been on her mind. "I've been thinking about moving to Mumbai," she said. "I want to find a better job, chase my dreams, and build something for myself."

There was a fire in her voice, and for a moment, I just felt proud—proud of her ambition and the way she refused to settle. I admired her determination, her drive to make something more of herself. But at the same time, I felt the weight of it, knowing my path was different.

"I understand," I replied after a pause. "You deserve that. But you know I don't have plans to leave here. I want to start the business with my dad, settle down here. We'll figure it out when the time comes."

There was a brief silence, the reality of our separate plans hanging between us. It wasn't an easy conversation, but we both let it fade, knowing we weren't ready to tackle it yet. For now, we'd leave it for the future to decide.

Instead, we leaned into the warmth of the evening, letting the lake and the stars overhead guide us into lighter, more romantic talk. She rested her head on my shoulder again, and we stayed there for a while longer, just enjoying the stillness of being together.

She looked at me with a sparkle in her eyes and said, "I have some secrets to tell you."

"Really?" I asked, leaning in with a teasing smile. "What are these secrets?"

She took a deep breath and started revealing them one by one, each one making my heart swell.

"First," she began, "I knew how to lock the seatbelt in the car that day, but I wanted you to help me when we met in the afternoon."

I laughed softly, remembering how carefully I'd shown her, thinking she didn't know.

"Second," she continued, "when you sent me that SMS for the first time when I was sick, I was waiting for it. I knew you'd message me, and I was hoping for it."

I smiled, remembering how anxious I was to reach out to her, how I wondered if she'd even reply.

"Third," she said, "whenever I came to see you or talk to you, I'd always bring some kind of question or information—like that time I told you about Mandira—just to have a reason to talk to you."

I raised an eyebrow, feeling both surprised and flattered.

"Fourth," she said softly, "that night when I was walking alone and you joined me—I was walking alone *for* you. I was waiting for you to come, and when you were walking with the others, I was sure you'd come back for me."

I could vividly remember that night, the pull I felt toward her. I had no idea she was waiting for me the whole time.

"And lastly," she continued, laughing, "when you asked me to sit on the chair by saying, 'Beta, yaha baith jao,' I told my friends afterward that you must already have a girlfriend because only guys with girlfriends use 'beta' like that."

I couldn't help but laugh softly, not because her secrets were shocking, but because they were so sweetly innocent—like a child sharing their most cherished thoughts, not realizing how adorable they were. "Wait, really?" I asked, still grinning. "All that because of how I said 'beta'?"

She nodded with a gleam in her eyes, and it struck me how beautifully simple these little confessions were. These weren't secrets meant to be hidden—they were more like small, endearing moments she'd held close, things that mattered to her in a way I hadn't realized. There was something so pure in the way she shared them, like she was letting me in on the softest parts of herself.

I couldn't stop the warmth spreading through me. It wasn't just her words—it was the way she said them, the way she looked at me, like these tiny details had meant the world to her. My heart felt full, overwhelmed by how genuinely she had cared, even in the smallest of moments.

I smiled, not out of amusement but out of love—deep, simple love. These "secrets" were the sweetest things I'd ever heard, and knowing she'd held onto them all this time made me feel closer to her than ever. It was as if each one was a thread, gently pulling me deeper into her heart.

But then she tilted her head, her voice carrying a gentle complaint, though beneath it was a deeper wish. Her eyes softened as she asked, "But why haven't you proposed to me yet?"

Her question caught me off guard. I blinked, and for a moment, I was completely blank. I could feel my heart race, trying to figure out why I hadn't formally proposed to her. She had been waiting, and I didn't even realize it.

Seeing my confusion, she smiled and leaned in closer. "You know," she added, "I'm a huge fan of Shahrukh Khan. I want you to propose to me like he does in his movies—very romantic, very filmy."

I laughed, relieved but also charmed by her amusing demand. "Oh, so you want the full SRK-style proposal, huh?" I teased. "Alright, I'll do it, I promise. I'll make it as filmy as you want."

She smiled wide, satisfied with my promise. The moment was light and full of laughter, but it also deepened the bond between us.

We continued walking, until we passed a few artists sketching portraits for couples sitting nearby. I pointed toward them, an idea sparking in my mind.

"I've always wanted to get a sketch of us," I said, imagining us captured in pencil strokes on paper.

She turned to me, her expression softening. "I can make one," she said quietly.

I looked at her, surprised. "Wait—you can sketch?" I asked, amazed by this newfound talent.

She nodded confidently. "Yes, I can. And I'll make one for you... one day, when I have all the instruments."

I smiled, my heart swelling with pride as my admiration for her grew even more. "You're incredible, you know that? You walk on ramps, you dance, you do nail art, you make paintings, and now, you can sketch too? What *can't* you do?"

She looked up at me, her eyes shining with amusement.

I asked, "Why do you like me, though? I'm terrible at all these things. I don't have any talents like you."

"You are very sweet, that's why I like you," she said, smiling as she lightly tapped my nose. Her touch was gentle, but it sent a warmth through me.

I smiled at her answer but then noticed a mischievous glint in her eyes. "I have one more secret to tell," she added, drawing out the moment.

"Now what?" I asked, genuinely curious and a little amused.

She giggled and leaned in closer. "When you joined the company, you used to talk so sweetly with everyone. Whenever you came to our bay to ask about absent employees, you'd always ask so politely, and I loved that." She paused for a moment, her smile widening. "So I gave you a nickname—'*Sweet Se HR*.' And soon, all the girls started calling you that! Whenever someone needed something from HR, they'd tell me, 'Go and ask your *Sweet Se HR*.'"

"Seriously?" I asked, still surprised.

She nodded, grinning from ear to ear. "Yep."

I couldn't help but smile, feeling an unexpected warmth spread through me. The thought of her noticing my kindness—and even giving me a nickname for it—brought me a quiet joy. It was more than just amusement; it felt like being seen, like someone appreciated me for the simple way I was. My honesty, my nature—things I didn't think much about—had meant something to her.

"That's cute," I replied, feeling happier than I expected to know these small secrets.

I looked at her with raised eyebrows. "So... any more secrets I should know about?"

She laughed, shaking her head. "There are more, but I'll tell you later—one by one."

We spent the rest of the time together, feeling light and content. She pulled out her phone and asked me to pose for her photos, her excitement shining through as she adjusted her phone's camera. She loved photography, and I could tell it gave her joy to capture moments. I played along, posing awkwardly at first, but her playful comments and laughter made me loosen up. She clicked a few pictures, instructing me on where to stand and how to pose, and we both ended up laughing.

As I stood there, watching her take pictures, I could see the happiness in her eyes. It wasn't just the lake, the quiet evening, or the photography. It was *us*. She was glowing, radiating a quiet joy that came from being with me. Even in her silence, I could sense her heart speaking, her eyes full of unspoken desires and hopes.

In that moment, I made a silent promise to myself—to never hurt her, to always protect her, and to love her as deeply as I could. I wanted to be the reason for that happiness, always.

After a while, we decided to go upstairs in one of the nearby buildings to get a better view of the lake. The water stretched out before us, the lights from the surrounding area reflecting off its surface like tiny stars. It was beautiful, peaceful. I reached for her hand, and she placed hers in mine, our fingers intertwining naturally. We stood there for a while, enjoying the view, just the two of us.

Eventually, we thought it was time to leave. As we walked down the stairs, something amusing happened. There was a separator running down the middle of the stairs, and she instinctively went to the right side while I took the left. As we continued down, we noticed three boys coming up the stairs—two on my side and one on hers.

I saw her hesitate, her steps slowing. "What do we do?" she asked, her voice a little nervous.

I could see she was uncomfortable, so I spoke softly, reassuring her. "Just keep moving. I'm right here on the other side."

She nodded, her trust in me evident, and we both continued down the stairs. The boys passed us without incident, but as soon as we reached the bottom, she immediately reached for my hand, gripping it tightly.

Feeling her need for reassurance, I gently moved my hand to her waist, pulling her a little closer to me as we walked. The night was settling in, the cool air brushing against us, but in that moment, with her by my side, everything felt warm and just right.

As we walked back to the parking area, I asked her softly, "Are you feeling hungry?"

She nodded. "Yes, I am. I'd like to have dinner."

It was already past 9 PM, and we couldn't find anything open near the lake, so we decided to leave. I started the car, driving slowly, wanting to stretch the time we had together. But she glanced at the clock and said, "Can you drive a little faster? I don't want to be too late for the PG."

Smiling, I pressed down on the accelerator, picking up the pace, and soon we arrived at a small restaurant. It wasn't anything fancy, but it was quiet, and the atmosphere felt right. We sat across from each other, ordering our meals, but as we ate, something subtle happened. Our eyes kept meeting across the table. Every time I looked at her, she'd glance away, playing with her hair nervously, her cheeks flushing slightly. It was adorable, the way she'd fidget whenever she caught me staring.

There was something in her eyes, a kind of sweetness mixed with shyness. We didn't need to speak much. The quiet glances, the smiles, the way we were simply comfortable in each other's presence—it was enough.

When we finished dinner, I leaned back in my chair, my eyes meeting hers with a subtle glint. "How about some ice cream to top off the night?" I asked, not really wanting the evening to end.

She looked at me, her eyes softening as a small, tender smile played on her lips. She shook her head, her expression warm. "No, I'm full." Her voice was gentle, almost as if she too wanted to hold onto this moment for just a little longer.

"Thanks for tonight," she said softly, her words carrying more weight than just about dinner. "This was perfect."

I smiled, feeling a sense of pride and happiness that I'd made her feel that way. But then she glanced at her watch, her expression shifting slightly. "Can you drop me at my PG now?"

As the evening began to wind down, I reached out and asked for the bill. The waiter nodded politely and handed it over. Without thinking, I instinctively reached for my wallet, but as soon as I opened it, I realized—it was empty. Not a single rupee in sight.

I pressed my lips together, feeling a bit embarrassed. With a small sigh, I handed over my card to swipe instead.

She noticed right away. "No cash, huh?" she said with a knowing smile tugging at her lips.

I shook my head with a sheepish smile. "I forget every single time. Honestly, one day I'm going to get into serious trouble because of this terrible habit." I chuckled, pressing my lips together again.

She smiled softly, her eyes shining with understanding. It was a lighthearted moment, but there was something comforting about how she never judged me, always accepting these little quirks of mine with warmth. We shared a quiet laugh, the kind that comes from truly knowing each other's imperfections—and loving them anyway.

Then we drove toward her place, the car filled with a comfortable silence. As we neared her PG, I stopped one street ahead, like I always did, giving us a little extra time together.

She turned to me, her expression soft but laced with vulnerability. Her eyes, usually bright with mischief, now held something deeper—a quiet longing, a need for comfort that she couldn't quite put into words. Without saying a word, she rested her head on my shoulder, the warmth of her cheek gently pressing against me. It was as if she was searching for a moment of pure connection, for a feeling only the two of us could share.

Then, in a whisper, barely audible, she asked, "Can you hug me?"

Hearing those words made my heart swell. It wasn't just a question—it was her trusting me with her desire for closeness, for love. I felt an overwhelming rush of tenderness, knowing that all she wanted was to feel cared for, and in that instant, I realized I would give her anything to make her feel cherished. This was more than just a hug—it was her letting me into her heart, and I wanted nothing more than to hold her, to make her feel the love she deserved.

I pulled her close, wrapping my arms around her as if I could shield her from everything else in the world. She nestled into my chest, fitting perfectly against me, and I could feel the warmth of her body relax into mine. It felt intimate, natural, like we belonged just like this. My fingers gently traced her back, and I breathed her in, my chest full of love, knowing there was nowhere else I'd rather be than holding her.

We stayed like that for a while, neither of us wanting to move. The world around us faded, leaving only the feeling of her in my arms, the rhythm of her breath syncing with mine. In that perfect, quiet moment, nothing else mattered—just us, wrapped in a soft, unspoken love.

"I feel safe in your arms," she whispered, her voice barely audible but full of meaning. "I feel... satisfied in your arms."

Her words sent a warmth through me, filling me with a sense of responsibility and care. I tightened my embrace slightly, wanting her to know that I was there for her, that she could always feel this safety with me. It wasn't just about protection; it was about the comfort we found in each other, the unspoken understanding that we could be vulnerable together without fear. I silently promised myself that I'd do everything I could to keep making her feel this way—safe, cared for, and loved.

"This is how you're going to spend your whole life," I said softly, pressing a kiss on her forehead. I handed her a small, slightly melted chocolate and smiled. "I'll give you a chocolate every time we meet," I added, teasing her.

She looked down at it and giggled. "This chocolate is melted."

"I bought it in the morning and left it in the car, so it melted," I replied with a shrug.

She smiled, shook her head, and then stepped out of the car, holding the chocolate. I couldn't take my eyes off her until she finally disappeared into her PG. That image of her, waving goodbye, lingered with me long after she was gone.

A few days passed, and Saturday came. I was at work, but as usual, we were texting each other throughout the day. I asked her what she was up to.

"Bored," she replied quickly. "All the girls from my PG have gone to their hometowns, so I'm alone here."

An idea crossed my mind, and with a bit of hesitation, I asked, "Would you like to spend the night with me at my place?"

It wasn't something I usually asked, but I meant it in the purest way. We'd spent so much time meeting in public places—at the lake, restaurants, or in the car—where it was hard to truly share our feelings in peace. There was always someone around, something to distract us. But tonight felt like the perfect opportunity to find that quiet space where we could just be. I longed for a place where our heartbeats were the only sounds that filled the room.

"I promise, it's just to spend time together. I want to be with you, in peace. No distractions," I added quickly, afraid that she might misinterpret my invitation and think otherwise. I didn't want her to be uncomfortable or doubt my intentions. My love for her was pure, and I wanted her to feel that.

To my relief, she agreed. "I'd love that," she said after a few moments. She wanted the same—time together without interruptions, without the world intruding. It made me feel incredibly grateful to have someone who understood me so deeply.

Her only concern was the timing—her PG had strict rules, and she wasn't allowed out after 9 PM. It was already 7 PM, and my shift didn't end until 11 PM. But I wasn't going to let that stop us. "I'll be there at 9 PM for sure," I reassured her.

At around 8:30 PM, she sent me a quick SMS. *"Are you free yet?"* she asked.

I replied immediately, telling her I'd be leaving in 10 minutes. I wrapped up my work, handed over a few tasks to a colleague, and hurried out of the office by 9 PM sharp. I parked my car in the street next to her PG and gave her a call. "Come out. I've reached," I said.

A few minutes later, she appeared. And when I saw her, I couldn't help but feel like time stopped. She had never looked so beautiful before. She had taken a bath, and her hair was still damp, falling softly over her shoulders. I could smell the faint fragrance of her shampoo, a scent that filled the car when she approached. She was wearing a pair of blue jeans, a black top, and a black net shrug that clung to her frame. Her simplicity, the freshness in her look—it took my breath away.

She smiled shyly as she approached the car, her eyes sparkling in the dim light of the streetlamp. It was like seeing her for the first time all over again, and in that moment, I knew—this was the girl I wanted to be with, the girl I wanted to protect, cherish, and love.

"You're looking beautiful," I complimented her as she slid into the car, her damp hair framing her face perfectly.

She gave me a sly look, showing just a hint of attitude. "You always say that. Nothing new," she quipped, the corner of her lips curling into a smile.

I couldn't help but grin. "But tonight... you've never looked *this* beautiful," I added sincerely.

Her eyes widened with mock surprise. "What? I *always* look beautiful when I come in front of you!" She folded her arms and pretended to pout. "Don't talk to me." Then, with a sly glance, she added, "You haven't even proposed to me yet."

I laughed, knowing where she was going with this. "I *will* propose to you, and I know you want it to be in some grand, Shahrukh Khan-style moment," I teased back. "Give me a little time to plan something huge."

She narrowed her eyes with a hint of challenge, still not letting it go. "Forget about the proposal for now. You haven't even said the three golden words yet. I don't want to talk to you."

Her teasing suddenly hit a bit deeper. She was right—*we* hadn't exchanged those words yet, even though we'd both felt them for a long time. I realized how important it was, not just for her, but for both of us, to say those words out loud.

I reached over, gently touching her chin and tilting her head upward so her eyes met mine. For a moment, she blushed and looked away, flinching as she often did when she felt shy. But I held her gaze, my heart pounding with the weight of what I was about to say. Slowly, softly, I whispered those three golden words for the first time.

"I love you."

As the words left my lips, I could feel everything shift between us. Her eyes widened, sparkling like they held entire galaxies, and for a second, it felt like the world stopped. There was a moment of perfect stillness—like the air between us had changed, grown softer, warmer. I watched as her face lit up, her smile slowly spreading, and I could see the happiness bloom in her expression, her cheeks glowing with emotion.

It was like I had unlocked something inside her—a joy she couldn't contain. She looked at me with such love, such pure affection. In that moment, nothing else mattered. No doubts, no fears—just her and me, and the love that had been building between us for so long.

"I love you, Guddu," I added softly, using the name I had always affectionately called her by, my voice thick with emotion. Saying it felt like coming home, like everything had finally fallen into place.

She smiled wide, the joy unmistakable in her eyes, and without another word, she wrapped her arms around me in a tight hug. I held her close, feeling the warmth of her body against mine. I kissed her cheek softly, letting the moment sink in. The unspoken feelings we'd carried for so long were now out in the open, and it felt right, like something we should have said long ago.

After a moment, she pulled away slightly and reached for the small bag she had brought with her. "What's in there?" I asked curiously.

"Board, paper, colors, and a pencil," she said, smiling. "I'm going to make a sketch of you tonight."

I smiled at her dedication and creativity. She had always promised she'd sketch me one day, and here she was, carrying the tools with her, ready to turn her words into action.

In return, I handed her a small, familiar item. "Here," I said, passing her another chocolate.

She laughed softly when she took it. "Again melted!" she exclaimed with a mock frown. "Why don't you buy it fresh when you come to meet me?"

I smiled, admitting to myself that she had a point. "Well, because most of the time, our plans are spontaneous, and I never know when we're going to meet. But I never want to show up empty-handed, so I always keep a chocolate ready in the car."

She smiled at that, touched by the small, thoughtful gesture. "You're sweet," she murmured, placing the melted chocolate in her bag along with her art supplies.

I held her hand as we sat in the car, the air between us thick with unspoken words and emotions. I kissed her hand softly, unable to stop myself from looking at her. Every glance felt like it deepened the connection between us. She smiled, her cheeks glowing softly in the dim light, and then said, "Let's go to your place."

"Look at the road, not me, while driving," she added playfully, her voice filled with warmth.

I chuckled, stealing one last glance at her before focusing on the road, the warmth of her presence making it hard to do anything else. We drove quietly.

We had dinner at a small restaurant. When we reached my place at 11 PM, I noticed that the main gate of the house had been locked by the landlord. My heart sank a little, remembering the times I had been locked out and had to spend nights in my car. But this time was different—she was with me, and I couldn't let that happen.

I called a friend who lived on the same floor and asked him to come down and unlock the gate. While we waited, I leaned back into the car and looked at her. I said, "The gate is locked. Looks like we'll have to spend the night in a hotel."

Her eyes widened in shock. "What? Are you serious?" she exclaimed, a mix of surprise and panic in her voice.

I couldn't help but burst out laughing. "No, no, I'm just kidding! The gate's being unlocked now."

She sighed, realizing I had been joking, and tapped my arm. "Don't do that! I almost believed you!" she said with mock frustration, but the smile on her face said she wasn't really upset.

Soon enough, my friend came down and unlocked the gate. I thanked him, then turned back to her. "Let's go inside now," I said, offering my hand.

She took it, and we got out of the car. I led her inside, and as we walked up the stairs to my room, the playful moment from earlier faded into a softer, more intimate silence.

Once inside, I quietly locked the door, turning back to find her standing close to me. The room felt quieter than ever, with no distractions, just us. She stepped closer, her eyes reflecting the privacy of the moment. Without a word, she wrapped her arms around me and leaned up to kiss me. It was soft at first, but the kiss deepened, full of emotions we had both been holding onto for so long.

I kissed her back, holding her close. "Wait," I whispered gently. "Let me turn off the lights."

I turned off the lights, leaving the room in a soft, comforting darkness. When I returned to the bed, I extended my hand to her. She took it, her fingers sliding into mine, and we lay down together, wrapping ourselves in each other's arms. The world outside disappeared, and it was just us, finally at peace, holding each other.

Though the desire between us was palpable, I never let it overpower the respect I had for her. We lingered in the intimacy of the moment, letting soft kisses and whispered words speak louder than anything physical could. I didn't push, didn't try to take things further—there was something sacred in holding back, in honoring her boundaries and cherishing the quiet affection we shared. Her face glowed with happiness, not from passion but from the pure joy of being together, present, without needing to cross any lines.

Then I noticed something—tears rolling down her cheeks, catching the soft light in the room. Gently, I wiped them away with my fingers.

"What happened?" I asked softly, my voice full of concern.

She looked at me with tear-filled eyes and smiled. "I'm just so happy," she whispered. "These tears... they're because I've never felt this kind of happiness before. Being with you, feeling this way—it's everything I ever wanted."

I kissed her forehead softly and whispered, "I love you."

I cupped her cheek gently, pulling her closer, and placed her head under my neck. I kissed her softly on the forehead, wanting to comfort her. Slowly, I reached for her hand, bringing it to my lips, kissing it with care. "I love you, and I can't see tears in your eyes," I whispered, my voice filled with sincerity.

She lifted her face, her eyes meeting mine with that familiar warmth. She leaned in and kissed me gently on the cheek, a sweet smile spreading across her lips—an expression of love and trust that melted my heart. I could see it in her eyes—she trusted me, completely.

Wanting to lift her mood, I smiled and said, "So, tell me—how should I propose to you?"

Her smile faded, replaced by an exaggerated pout. "I don't want to talk to you. You never propose to me. Move back, don't touch me," she said, looking up at the ceiling, clearly waiting for me to make things right. She wasn't really upset—just waiting for me to please her. I adored her playful, mischievous tantrums. It was a delightful mix of challenge and charm, a side of her that drew me in even more, making me fall for her all over again with each lighthearted moment.

I leaned in, kissed her cheek softly, and said, "I'm sorry." I kissed her cheek again and added, "Sorry, again."

I kept repeating it—*a kiss, an apology, another kiss, another apology*—until I finally saw her lips curve into a smile. She tried to resist but eventually giggled, giving in to the moment.

"I'm not going to tell you how to propose to me," she said, her eyes twinkling with mischief. "That's your job. But I'm not asking for anything huge—I just want it to be special and memorable."

I thought for a moment and asked, "What if I bent down on my knees and proposed with a red rose?"

She scrunched her nose and shook her head. "Boring and old-fashioned," she said, dismissing the idea with a smile.

"Well, then, what should I do?"

Her eyes lit up as she remembered something. "Have you seen *Kuch Kuch Hota Hai*? You know, the scene where Shahrukh Khan and Kajol watch the movie on the projector?"

I nodded, intrigued. "Yeah, I've seen it."

She smiled, excitement building. "I want you to propose in a romantic and special way like that. But don't copy it," she added quickly. "Make it original. I want something that feels like *us*."

I chuckled softly, loving how she knew exactly what she wanted. "Okay," I agreed, nodding seriously.

She looked at me, her voice soft but firm, "If you don't propose, I won't talk to you anymore." Her sweet complaint was clear—this proposal was important to her, something she had been waiting for.

I decided to lighten the mood a little and teased, "You know… there's a girl in our office who likes me. She always gives me these looks, like she's super interested. If you stop talking to me, I might just make her my girlfriend."

Her eyes narrowed immediately, the smile vanishing. "Who is she?" she asked, her tone suddenly sharp, her hint of jealousy unmistakable.

I couldn't help but laugh. "You're so cute when you get jealous," I said, leaning in to kiss her again.

She folded her arms, pretending to be mad, but I could see the smile tugging at the corner of her lips. "Tell me who she is," she insisted, her eyes flashing with mock seriousness.

"I don't know her name, but I'll show you," I replied, teasing her.

She narrowed her eyes at me, making a long, exaggerated "Hmmmmm" sound, clearly not pleased with my answer, but still playing along.

Just then, my phone rang. It was on the table, a few steps away from the bed. I hesitated for a moment, not wanting to move and leave her. But she nudged me gently and said, "Go see who's calling at this time of night."

Reluctantly, I was about to get up when the call disconnected.

"Nice ringtone," she said, breaking the silence.

"It's 'Invincible,' the theme song from WrestleMania 28," I replied, shaking my head. "I love it."

She rolled her eyes with a hint of amusement, probably not sharing the same enthusiasm for wrestling, but she smiled anyway.

Then, wanting to bring the focus back to us, I asked her to share some pictures from her phone. She handed it over and transferred a few pictures to mine—some beautiful ones of her, including a couple of personal ones that she hadn't shared before. I smiled, admiring each one, feeling honored that she trusted me with these intimate glimpses of her.

We then placed our phones aside, our world narrowing down to just the two of us again. Between soft kisses and whispered words, we found ourselves lost in each other. I loved running my fingers across her face—her cheeks, her lips. I traced the outline of her smile, brushing gently over her soft skin. "I love your cheeks," I whispered, "and your lips... they make such a sweet smile."

She smiled, and we kissed again, the warmth between us growing. There was a shared longing to be closer, to break all the limitations, but we knew we had to stay within the boundaries.

She was talking, her voice soft and sweet, but I wasn't really listening. My mind was somewhere else, completely consumed by the way she looked—the curve of her lips, the softness of her cheeks, the way her hair framed her face so perfectly. Every word she spoke drifted into the background, like a distant hum. All I could think about was how much I wanted to kiss her again. My eyes fixated on her lips, eager to feel them again, my heart pounding as the desire grew stronger.

And then, without warning, I couldn't hold back anymore.

I leaned in suddenly, my face closing the distance between us in an instant. Before she could finish her sentence, I pressed my lips against hers, forcefully, passionately. She gasped, surprised, but melted into the kiss almost immediately. I pushed harder, my hands finding their way to her hair, tangling my fingers through it as I deepened the kiss. My touch became restless, moving from her hair to her cheeks, her neck, sliding down to her waist. I felt the shape of her body under my hands, my fingertips tracing every curve, like I was memorizing her in the heat of the moment.

The kiss was intense, filled with raw emotion, the kind that makes everything else disappear. My body moved with hers as we pressed into each other, rolling across the bed, the sheets twisting beneath us. I kissed her lips with a need I hadn't felt before, then moved to her cheeks, her neck, her ears. Every inch of her felt like something new, something I needed to explore, needed to feel.

That kiss held more than simple affection; it was a storm of emotions, passion and longing crashing together in a frenzy. I didn't want it to stop. It was forceful, primal, and when it ended, we both lay there breathless, staring into each other's eyes, as if we were trying to catch up with everything that just happened.

She looked at me, her eyes shining with a mix of surprise and desire. Then, with a mischievous smile, she whispered, "Do it again."

I didn't need to be told twice.

Without a second thought, I pulled her back into me, and we kissed again—this time even more intensely, if that was possible. My hands were on her, my lips exploring hers, and the world outside faded away as we lost ourselves in each other all over again.

As we lay there, catching our breath, I suddenly remembered something and said, "You haven't sent me that friend request on Facebook yet."

She laughed softly and shook her head. "I tried, but I couldn't find your profile."

I smiled. "I'll send you another request then. We'll fix that."

We talked for hours.

As I was speaking, lost in whatever I was saying, she suddenly leaned in, her body pressing against mine with an unexpected urgency. Her hands cupped my face, and before I could react, she kissed me hard, cutting me off mid-sentence. I was caught off guard but quickly surrendered, feeling the same rush of passion that always pulled us together. She pushed herself into me, deepening the kiss, her touch igniting something electric between us.

Our bodies seemed to move in unison, the world fading around us as everything narrowed to the heat of her lips, the pressure of her hands. But just as the moment began to spiral toward something deeper, she gently pulled back, her forehead resting against mine. Her breath was warm against my skin, and for a second, we stayed like that, suspended between want and restraint.

She brushed a hand softly over my chest, her eyes finding mine. "Let's not rush," she whispered, her voice tender but steady. "I want to wait. Not because I don't want this, but because I want it to mean more... when the time is right."

Her words weren't a wall—they were a promise, infused with an affection that left the air between us charged, brimming with anticipation. I smiled, feeling the connection still strong, knowing the moment wasn't lost. It was only being saved for something bigger.

In between kisses and soft words, time seemed to slip away from us. We didn't even realize when we both drifted off to sleep, wrapped in each other's arms, our hearts in sync.

At some point in the early morning, I woke up because my arm had gone numb. She was still sound asleep, her head resting gently on my arm like a pillow. I tried to move my arm slowly, hoping not to wake her, but she stirred, her eyes fluttering open as she looked up at me with a sleepy smile.

"You can come to this side," she whispered, her voice soft and drowsy. "I'll take your place."

I smiled, grateful for the suggestion, and as I started to shift sides, an idea popped into my head. Instead of just quietly moving, I mischievously passed over her, hovering above. For a moment, I stayed there, teasing her by kissing her all over her face—her cheeks, her forehead, her nose. She laughed softly, still half-asleep, trying to shield herself from my cheeky kisses..

"Stop it," she whispered, smiling, her eyes crinkling with amusement. "You're just using this as an excuse to kiss me more!"

I grinned, refusing to let her go so easily. "Maybe," I said, leaning down to steal one more kiss from her lips before finally shifting to the other side.

She was still smiling, her sleepy laugh soft as she settled into my other arm. "That's it," she said, shaking her head in mock disbelief. "No more changing sides for you. You take advantage of every little thing!"

I chuckled, pulling her close again. "I can't help it," I whispered into her hair. "You make it too easy."

Her teasing faded into a contented silence, and before long, she drifted back to sleep, her breath steady and soft against my skin. I smiled to myself, feeling the warmth of her body next to mine and the simple comfort of having her so close. There was something special about these little moments—filled with affection, joy, and the easy trust we shared.

At 6 AM, she woke me up with a gentle nudge. I opened my eyes, and the first thing I saw was her sleepy, smiling face. I leaned in and kissed her lips softly. "Good morning," I whispered.

She smiled and pushed herself up slightly, stretching a bit. The room was quiet, but there was something magical lingering in the air—the kind of magic only love can create.

She picked up her phone to check the time and then casually showed me a few pictures on her phone. As she flipped through them, I suddenly had an idea.

"Let's take a picture," I suggested.

She handed me her phone and said, "Go ahead, take it with mine."

We were still wrapped in the blanket, so I pulled her closer into my arms, covering us both snugly. She smiled and nuzzled her head under my neck, and with my arm around her, I clicked the picture.

"Not nice, it's distorted. Try again," she said, scrunching her nose as she looked at the picture.

I chuckled and clicked a few more snaps until one finally turned out just right. I showed it to her, and she smiled, pleased.

"Keep it private," I told her, leaning closer. "And don't delete it."

She laughed softly, shaking her head. "This is our first picture together. I'll keep it hidden somewhere in my laptop."

I raised an eyebrow, half-teasing. "And if someone sees it? What then?"

She looked at me with a faint smile. "If anyone finds out, it'll be big news in our company," she said, her voice full of amusement.

We both laughed, but soon, the easy conversation quieted as we became absorbed in each other again. We couldn't resist the pull, the way we kept coming back to soft kisses and lingering touches.

The world outside felt miles away, like it didn't exist at all.

But by 10 o'clock, our stomachs reminded us that love wasn't the only thing we needed to fuel us. "I'm getting hungry," I said, breaking the moment with a smile.

"Me too," she nodded, her hand still resting gently in mine.

"Let's go out for breakfast," I suggested. She agreed, but first, she wanted to get freshened up. She stood and disappeared into the washroom, leaving me alone with my thoughts for a few minutes. I sat on the bed, smiling to myself, thinking about how peaceful the morning felt.

When she came out, her hair slightly damp, she looked radiant. Instead of getting ready to leave, though, she walked over to a chair, opened her handbag, and pulled out her sketching instruments.

"Hold on," she said, giving me a half-serious look. "Stay in that position. Don't move."

I blinked in surprise but obliged, sitting perfectly still, wondering how she was going to pull off this impromptu sketch. She focused intently on her work, and I couldn't help but smile.

"Don't smile!" she scolded sweetly, her eyes narrowing at me as her pencil moved across the paper.

I fought to keep a straight face, sitting as still as I could. Every now and then, she'd glance up at me, her brows furrowing in concentration, and I couldn't help but admire her dedication.

Halfway through, she spoke up. "Uh-oh," she muttered, still sketching. "I accidentally drew your nose a little bigger. But now I can't rub it out, so... you'll have to live with it."

I laughed softly, still trying not to move. "Big nose, huh? Can't wait to see it."

I stayed in that same pose for several more minutes, imagining how the sketch might look. I could see her working with such care, such focus. Her pencil moved in precise strokes, and I could tell how dedicated she was to making it just right.

When she finally finished, she held the sketch close, keeping it hidden. "Okay, but before you look," she said with a teasing smile, "you have to promise me you won't say anything about the nose.

Deal?"

I nodded, playing along. "Deal. I won't say a word about the nose."

She revealed the sketch, and my smile widened. It was beautiful, even with the slightly exaggerated nose. Her talent shone through every stroke, and I couldn't help but admire the effort she had put into it.

I leaned in and kissed her cheek softly. "Thank you," I said, smiling. "I'll always keep this safe with me."

She shrugged. "No problem. If it gets destroyed, I'll just make another one for you."

"No," I said firmly, shaking my head. "This is the first one. I'm going to frame it and hang it on the wall."

She smiled, enjoying my insistence.

"But," I added, a spark in my eyes, "I want a sketch of both of us next."

"I'll make a sketch of both of us, but I'll need a picture of us together to do it," she said, smiling as she got up and switched on my computer.

I watched as she navigated through my files. I'd always been fond of experimenting with effects on pictures, and there was a specific demo effect I'd been struggling to apply to one of my own photos. I showed her the effect and asked if she knew how to replicate it.

She gave it a try, her fingers tapping quickly at the keyboard. She managed to create something similar but looked at me thoughtfully. "I'll try again at home and let you know once I figure it out," she promised, her smile full of determination.

As she explored my computer, she came across some photos from my college days. One caught her attention—pictures of my dance performance. She raised an eyebrow, intrigued, and I laughed before explaining the theme. "That was from a college dance performance," I said, pointing at the screen. "I was the bridegroom, and my friend Ankit played the bride. We performed as a gay couple."

She chuckled, clearly amused. "I want to see the video!" she said, her eyes lighting up with excitement.

"I don't have the video on my computer, but Ankit may have uploaded it online somewhere," I replied. "I'll download it and show you next time."

After some time, I noticed the sketch she had made of me still lying on the table. "You should take the sketch with you," I suggested. "There's no clean place in my room to keep it safe. I don't want it to get ruined."

She nodded. "Okay, I'll keep it with me for now, and when you go to your hometown, I'll give it back to you."

We both smiled, and I stood up, stretching a little. "Alright," I said, "time to get ready. Let's go out for breakfast."

She got freshened up, and soon, we headed off to a nearby restaurant. The place wasn't anything special, and the food left a lot to be desired, but we were both hungry, so we didn't dwell on it. Even though it wasn't the best meal, she didn't complain—just smiled and went along with it, as she always did.

When the bill came, I reached for my wallet and, predictably, found it empty once again. I sighed internally, pulling out my card to settle the bill.

She noticed and smiled, her eyes soft with amusement. "Still no cash?" she asked smiling, though I could tell she wasn't surprised.

I gave a small, but little embarrassed. "Yeah, I really need to work on that."

She laughed softly, shaking her head, but there was no judgment in her eyes—just that familiar warmth. She knew my habits all too well by now.

After we finished, she mentioned wanting to go back to her PG. I could tell she was happy from the night we spent together—her silence spoke volumes, her contentment clear in the way she looked at me.

As we drove toward her PG, I could feel the weight of the night before in the air, that unspoken bond between us. She didn't say much, but her eyes and soft smile said it all. The love we shared wasn't just in the words but in the quiet moments too, in the glances and smiles that passed between us.

We pulled up in front of her PG. "Here we are," I said, slowing the car to a stop.

She unbuckled her seatbelt and looked at me with that familiar smile. "Bye," she said softly.

"Bye. Love you," I replied, my voice tender.

She opened the door, waved sweetly, and gave me one last smile before stepping out. The door closed behind her, but I stayed for a moment, watching as she walked inside, her presence still lingering in the car long after she was gone.

As I drove back home, I couldn't stop thinking about her. The morning, the night we spent together—it all played on repeat in my mind. When I got home, missing her, I logged into Facebook and impulsively decided to share one of the pictures she had sent me. I uploaded it with the caption: *"She is my girlfriend."*

Almost immediately, the notifications started pouring in—funny comments, sweet congratulations, and of course, a few jealous remarks from some of the guys.

Some couldn't believe it. "Fake picture?" one person joked.

Others were more supportive. "Congrats, bro, she's so cute!" another friend commented.

I couldn't help but laugh at the mix of reactions. I thanked everyone for their comments and, in a spirited mood, added a reply: *"Don't worry, I'll upload a picture of both of us soon and clear all your doubts."*

Sitting back, I smiled to myself. Sharing that small piece of my life with the world felt good, but what felt even better was knowing that she was mine, and I was hers.

That night, I sent her a friend request on Facebook again and reminded her to accept it. A few minutes later, she did. Almost instantly, I received an SMS from her: *"My brothers and cousins are also added on Facebook with me, so please don't share my picture."*

I quickly reassured her. *"But your cousins and brothers aren't in my friend list, so they won't see anything. And I won't tag you in any picture. No worries."*

The next day, I couldn't stop thinking about the previous night. Every moment with her kept replaying in my mind, and I found it hard to focus on anything else. So, I gave her a call, and we talked for a long time. I could hear the same excitement in her voice, even though she was trying to hide it.

Later, as I was driving back home to Kurukshetra, I was still completely caught up in thoughts of her. The drive seemed like a blur—I barely noticed when I reached home or even when I'd taken a bath. I was somewhere else, still with her in my mind.

The next day, during break time, I was sitting with my colleagues in the cafeteria. I sent her a quick SMS: *"Where are you?"*

Her reply came almost instantly: *"Behind you."*

I turned around and spotted her sitting with a group of girls at another table. Smiling to myself, I typed back: *"Turn on your Bluetooth."*

*"Done. My phone's name is Spice m6868,"* she replied, ready to receive the file.

I found her phone on the Bluetooth list and sent her the video. A moment later, she texted back: *"Got it! Thank you!"*

Later that night, when I called her, her voice was filled with laughter. "I watched the video," she said between giggles. "It was hilarious! Especially you and Ankit dancing together. I've never seen anything like it."

I laughed along with her, glad she enjoyed it. "It was fun to perform," I said. "We had a blast during the rehearsals. Gaurav, one of our friends, choreographed it. We couldn't stop laughing the whole time."

She continued laughing, clearly amused by the whole thing. "You looked pretty good as a bridegroom," she said with a smirk.

"I showed to other girls in PG too. They all laughed and enjoyed the video". She said.

"You're mad," I said with a laugh, shaking my head. "I'm going to kill you for that!"

She just giggled more, her happiness infectious. I couldn't help but smile too. Seeing her so happy made everything worth it.

A few days later, I made a big decision. I planned to move to Sector 7. I'd been living with my brother in Sector 27, but since he was shifting to Hyderabad, it made sense for me to find my own place. And since Sector 7 was near her PG, it felt perfect. It would make meeting up so much easier, allowing us to spend more time together.

I found a small independent room on a quiet street, far enough that no one from our company lived nearby. It was a perfect space, and best of all, I didn't have to share it with a roommate. I liked the idea of having my own place, a private spot where I could just be myself—and, of course, be closer to her.

I had been thinking a lot lately about how I never officially proposed to her. At the very least, I figured I should give her something—something special, a gift that would surprise her. But I had no idea what to get. After some consideration, I decided on a top. I didn't know why, but I could picture her in it, and the thought of surprising her made me excited.

I turned to Google and started searching for online shopping websites with cash-on-delivery options since I wasn't using internet banking. After browsing through a few sites, I landed on Jabong, which had a great collection. I found a simple but beautiful black top—it was sleeveless and long, and I imagined how amazing she'd look in it. Without a second thought, I ordered it.

The delivery would take 3-4 days, and I planned to keep it a surprise. But the excitement was bubbling inside me, and it was hard to keep it a secret. I somehow managed to hold off, telling myself it would be worth it when I saw her face.

Four days later, the package arrived. I immediately messaged her to meet me, but our work shifts were different, making it difficult to coordinate. She asked me to wait until Sunday. That was still four days away. By the next day, I couldn't hold it in anymore. My patience snapped, and I finally told her.

"I bought a top for you," I confessed, feeling a mix of excitement and nervousness.

There was a brief pause before she replied, "I don't take gifts. You really shouldn't have bought that."

I smiled to myself, already expecting this reaction. "I bought it just for you, and you *have* to accept it," I said firmly, trying to emphasize how much it meant to me.

She hesitated; her voice soft as she tried to figure out how to respond. "No, but..."

"It's already done," I interrupted gently. "I'll give it to you on Sunday."

We shifted the conversation to other topics—work, random things. We used to talk for hours, and one of the best things about her was how easy it was to connect. She wasn't demanding, never constantly calling or texting like some might. She was genuine, understanding, and sweet—a perfect balance of everything I admired in her.

Sunday finally arrived, and we met. The moment I saw her, I smiled. "You're looking beautiful," I said.

She gave me a small, embarrassed smile. "I couldn't get enough time to get ready, and besides, you always find me beautiful," she said, a bit coyly.

I laughed, knowing it was true. No matter how she appeared, she was always stunning in my eyes. I handed her a familiar melted chocolate, which she smiled at, clearly expecting it. Then, I reached for the gift on the dashboard and offered it to her.

"I told you, I don't take gifts," she said softly, but I could see her resolve cracking.

I sighed dramatically, placing the gift on the backseat. "Fine, don't take it. I guess I was a fool for buying it."

She glanced at me, her face softening. With a gentle sigh, she reached back and picked it up, her fingers brushing over the wrapping. "Just because you bought it for me, I'm taking it," she said, touching my cheek affectionately. "Don't be mad."

She unwrapped the gift, her eyes lighting up for a moment as she held the top in her hands. "It's beautiful," she admitted, but then hesitated. "But it's sleeveless... I've never worn sleeveless before."

I could tell she was a little unsure, but I smiled and encouraged her. "Try it this time. I'm sure you'll look amazing."

She gave me a shy smile, still unsure, but she didn't say no. Just knowing she appreciated the gesture and trusted me enough to step out of her comfort zone made me feel good.

We planned to go to the lake again that night, one of our favorite places for its peace and calm. It was always serene there, especially after dark, and both of us loved how quiet and reflective the lake felt at night.

We drove through the city streets, which were unusually empty. As we approached a red light, I stopped the car, even though there wasn't much traffic.

"Let's go," she said, glancing at the other cars passing through without stopping. "Everyone's breaking the red light."

I smiled and shook my head. "Should we really learn bad habits from others?" I asked.

"Hmm, you're right," she replied, her lips curling into a smile.

These small exchanges always added to our drives, turning them into unforgettable moments. We joked, traded witty remarks, and shared quiet romantic glances between conversations. Before we knew it, we had reached the lake. I parked the car in the usual spot, getting ready to step out when she suddenly turned up the volume on the FM radio.

"It's a nice song," she said, leaning back to enjoy it.

I paused, listening. "Which song is this?"

"It's *Pani Da Rang* from *Vicky Donor*," she replied.

I had never heard the song before, but I found myself liking it immediately. The melody seemed to match the peaceful mood of the night. We stayed in the car, listening quietly until the song ended. Only then did we step out and start walking toward the lake.

As we strolled, she told me about her latest project. "I'm making a showreel so I can apply for new jobs," she said. "I was hoping to use your digital camera for it. And I might even include some of your pictures in the reel."

"Of course," I said. "You can borrow it anytime you need." I smiled at her, feeling proud of her determination and drive.

As we crossed the road to the lake, I instinctively reached for her hand, holding it gently. The lake was bustling with activity—families, couples, and children were scattered everywhere. Kids were running and playing on the grass, their laughter filling the air. We wandered around for a bit before finding a quiet spot to sit down, away from the noise, making ourselves comfortable on a bench.

Sitting there, our hands intertwined, we looked into each other's eyes, exchanging soft smiles and small romantic whispers. There was something magical about these moments, just the two of us surrounded by the stillness of the lake, yet caught up in the closeness we shared.

The conversation naturally shifted toward her career. She was feeling stuck and wanted to move to Mumbai to explore new opportunities. "I don't see any growth here," she said with a sigh. "I really want to move to Mumbai. I think it would open new doors for me." She looked at me, adding softly, "I want you to come with me."

I could see how much this meant to her, and for a moment, my heart ached at the thought. But I had my own plans too. "I'd love to, but I'm more focused on starting a business here," I admitted.

She nodded, understanding the dilemma. She was ambitious, focused on her career, and I admired that about her. Part of me was willing to go wherever she went, but we both realized that this was a decision that would need time to fully think through.

A thought crossed my mind—to drop my current plan and maybe look for opportunities in Mumbai. It wasn't a solid decision, just an idea hovering in the back of my head. *I'll think it through,* I told myself, determined to at least consider the possibility. But I kept it to myself for now, not wanting to share anything until I had more clarity.

We decided to leave that conversation for another day, as it involved long-term planning that wasn't easy to figure out in a single evening.

And then, as if to lighten the mood, she shifted back to her usual teasing, flashing a lively smile. "So, when are you proposing to me?" she asked sweetly.

"Come here," I said, placing my hand on her shoulder and gently pulling her closer.

She smiled mischievously and shook her head. "No hug, no kiss until you propose to me," she said sweetly, with a hint of mischief.

I laughed, leaning back. "I'll just search on Google and get some ideas on how to propose to a girl."

She rolled her eyes, pretending to be mad. "I'll kill you! Search it on Google or hire a consultant, I don't care. But I want you to propose to me properly," she insisted, her voice still laced with humor.

"Sure, my Guddu," I replied, chuckling.

Then, she turned her face away, still smiling but adding a bit of mock seriousness. "If you don't propose to me within the next 10 days, don't even bother talking to me."

I couldn't resist teasing her. "Then I guess I'll go to that girl in the office who likes me."

Her eyes widened with a mock glare. "Go ahead," she said with a hint of challenge. "Go propose to her."

I laughed, seeing her reaction, and leaned closer. "Okay, my Guddu, I'll propose to you in front of everyone at the office."

She turned her head back to me, her lips curving into a smile. "You're mad," she whispered, resting her head on my shoulder.

I wrapped my arms around her, holding her close as we continued talking. Despite the cheerful mood, a small doubt lingered in my mind. For some reason, I was worried she might not be truly happy with me. It gnawed at me quietly, and I felt the need to clear it up.

With a bit of hesitation, I asked, "Are you happy with me? Like, really happy?"

She lifted her head, looking into my eyes with warmth and certainty. "Of course I am," she said softly. "I'm so happy with you." Her words were sincere, and just like that, the doubt faded away, replaced by a feeling of reassurance.

I held her hand and felt a wave of vulnerability wash over me. "Can I ask you something?" I said, my voice softer now.

She looked at me, her eyes encouraging. "Of course, tell me."

I took a deep breath, feeling the weight of what I was about to say. "Listen... Please... never avoid me. It's in my nature—It's just not something I can handle. If something ever goes wrong, or if we hit a rough patch, I'll face it. I can deal with it if, for some reason, this relationship has to end... but I can't deal with being avoided, with silence. If we ever have a misunderstanding, let's talk it through, clear the air. But please, don't ever leave me hanging, wondering. It drives me insane when someone ignores my calls or messages. I just need to know we'll face everything together—whatever it is."

She looked at me with such tenderness and kissed me softly. Though her words were simple—"That will never happen"—it was the way she said them that eased the weight in my chest. There was a calm in her expression, a certainty that made it clear she understood my fears and wouldn't let them come true. In that moment, without needing to say anything more, she gave me all the reassurance I needed.

Her words felt like a balm, soothing all my worries. We continued talking, falling back into our comfortable rhythm.

A few moments later, a boy approached us, asking for a donation for a small orphanage. I had always wanted to support an NGO and help poor children, so without hesitation, I reached into my back pocket for my wallet. But when I opened it, I found only a 10-rupee note inside. I glanced at Jojo, and we both smiled at each other, realizing the situation.

"You'll never change, will you?" she said, her eyes sparkling with amusement.

I handed the boy the 10-rupee note, the only cash I had on me. He started to walk away, saying, "It's okay," but I stopped him and pressed the note into his hand.

Jojo looked at me with a raised eyebrow. "That was your last note, what are you going to do now?"

I shrugged casually, trying to play it off. "I'll just withdraw some cash from the ATM. Don't worry, I have money in my account."

What I didn't mention was that I only had 200 rupees left in my bank account as well. But I didn't want to admit that. Not right now.

She laughed, shaking her head. "When was the last time you even went to an ATM, you lazy chap? You'll never change." She started listing off a few incidents where I'd gotten myself into trouble because of my laid-back nature.

I grinned, leaning in slightly. "Perfection doesn't need to change, honey," I said with a chuckle.

She shook her head and smiled, that cute smile I'd come to love. "You and your perfection."

As we sat there, the air started to cool. The breeze was gentle at first, but I could see her shiver slightly. Without thinking, I pulled her closer into my arms, wrapping them around her. She snuggled in, trying to use my arms as a blanket, and the way she tucked herself in closer was nothing short of lovely. I kissed her softly on the top of her head.

"If you're feeling cold, we can head back," I suggested.

She nestled deeper into my arms and closed her eyes. "No, I want to sleep in your arms. Your cuddle makes me feel so comfortable... I feel safe with you."

I didn't need to say anything, just kissed her again and held her tighter. The night, the chill in the air, the closeness we shared—it was perfect in its simplicity.

I asked gently, "Do you want to nap here for a while? We can head to my place afterward."

She sighed, a hint of sadness in her voice. "No, Preeti is waiting for me at the PG. I'll have to go."

For a moment, we just sat there, quiet in each other's arms. The silence wasn't awkward—it was the kind of stillness that felt complete, like nothing needed to be said. But then, the sound of a polyphonic ringtone shattered the peace.

I reached into my pocket, pulled out my old phone, and quickly rejected the call. Putting it on silent mode, I shoved it back into my pocket.

"Where's your Xperia?" she asked, curiously.

I smirked. "My brother swapped his phone with my Xperia. I didn't like his phone, so I sold it. Now I'm using this old one."

She frowned a little, clearly unimpressed. "You should really get a new phone. This one's... well, it's not great."

I laughed, holding my old phone up. "Hey, don't insult my phone! Sure, it doesn't have a touchscreen or a music player, and it's missing ringtones, wallpapers, memory card, internet, Wi-Fi, Facebook, and a camera... but it's like my old friend. We've been through a lot together. I love this phone just like I love you."

We both burst into laughter, the shared humor filling the air. That was the thing about us—no matter how silly the moment, or how imperfect life could get, we always found a way to laugh together.

"One day, you mentioned I should walk with more attitude and speed. Why?" I asked her, as we strolled leisurely along the lake.

"Because you walk so slowly," she said, making me understand. "It's like you're always tired. You need to walk with some attitude—make people notice you, like, 'Oh, someone's coming.'"

I chuckled. "Hmm, I see."

A comfortable silence settled between us for a moment as we continued walking, enjoying the peaceful atmosphere. Eventually, as more people started leaving the lake, we decided it was time to head home too. We stood up and began making our way toward the parking area.

"So," I asked, still curious, "what should I improve about my walk?"

She glanced over at me, assessing my stride with mock seriousness. "Your walk is fine," she said. "But you should walk just a little faster."

"Hmmm," I hummed in response, pretending to be deep in thought.

As we drove away from the lake, I asked her where she wanted to have dinner. "I'll have dinner at the PG with Preeti," she replied casually.

On the way, she mentioned she wanted to learn how to drive. I said, "Sure, I'll teach you next week."

But then, with a glint in my eye, I added, "There's one condition though... while teaching you, you'll have to sit on my lap."

She shot me an amused glance, immediately catching onto the joke. "No, no," she said, laughing. "In that case, I don't want to learn. Besides, I have you as my driver, so why would I need to?"

"Your driver?" I asked, raising an eyebrow.

She smiled, amused. "Yeah, all men say that after marriage, they end up becoming their wives' drivers."

I laughed. "But we haven't even married yet."

She smiled, a twinkle in her eyes. "Yeah, I know. And we won't get married either because you'll never propose to me. And I'll never marry you until you do." She was joking now, her tone light and easy.

I let out an exaggerated sigh. "O my maa," I said sweetly, pretending to be exasperated. "I'll propose to you, I'll propose to you, I'll propose to you!"

She laughed at my dramatic reply.

As we drove along, I took her hand and gently placed it on the gearshift, my hand covering hers. "Alright, let's start your first lesson," I said playfully. I guided her hand as we shifted gears together, my hand never leaving hers.

"So this is your flirty driving, huh?" she asked, raising an eyebrow.

I couldn't help but smile. "Yes, I love it."

For a moment, we both fell into a comfortable silence. My mind drifted as we drove, and she must have noticed because after a while, she asked, "What are you thinking about?"

I smiled, remembering an old memory. "I was just thinking about this one time with my friend, Rohan."

Her curiosity piqued immediately. "What happened? Tell me, I want to know!"

"Well," I began, "Rohan and I were on a night out in my car. We drove around the city, and we ended up near this haunted house—people say it's cursed. It was a pretty eerie place, and we got freaked out when we saw it."

Her eyes widened in excitement. "I want to see that place!" she said eagerly.

I laughed. "Are you sure? It's just a creepy old house with a spooky story attached to it. People say there's a spirit there, but honestly, I don't buy it."

But the more I told her, the more curious she became. She practically begged me to take her there, so I turned the car in that direction, unable to resist. As we drove, I told her the tale Rohan had shared with me about the so-called spirit, adding a bit of dramatic flair to make it sound more mysterious.

By the time we reached the haunted house, the night had gotten even quieter. I stopped the car right in front of it. The place looked abandoned, dark, and unsettling, with overgrown weeds creeping toward the entrance.

She stared at the house, her face serious. For a moment, she didn't say a word, completely absorbed in the sight before her. The silence between us grew thick, and I could tell she was fully immersed in the eerie atmosphere.

That's when I decided to pull a little prank. Leaning in slightly, I made a sudden, spooky *"Wooohhh!"* sound, mimicking a ghostly wail.

She screamed, completely startled, her whole body jerking in shock. For a second, she was frozen in place, her eyes wide with fear. I burst out laughing, unable to contain myself.

Her expression shifted from fear to realization as she started to beat me softly with her hands. "Why would you do that?!" she yelled, her voice a mix of laughter and frustration. But I could still see the trace of fear on her face, her body trembling slightly.

Still laughing, I pulled her into a hug, wrapping my arms around her to calm her down. "I'm sorry, I'm sorry," I said, kissing her forehead gently. "Don't worry, I'm here. You're safe. Sorry, Guddu." Another kiss on her cheek followed, and she began to relax in my arms.

"Can I go outside and take a picture of the house?" she asked, her eyes gleaming with curiosity. "But you need to come with me."

I couldn't say no to that. We both stepped out, and while she hurriedly clicked a picture of the eerie, old house, I noticed a security guard standing outside the neighboring high-profile house, eyeing us suspiciously.

"Let's get back in the car," I urged, laughing softly. "The guard might come over and stop us."

She quickly obliged, and we jumped back in the car, laughing as we sped away from the scene. On the drive back to her PG, we couldn't stop chuckling about the prank I had pulled earlier, and she lightly hit me a few more times in mock protest.

"You scared the life out of me!" she said, still grinning, while giving me a light punch.

"I couldn't help it," I laughed. "But you have to admit, it was funny!"

Soon, we reached her PG. I parked the car but didn't want her to leave. She leaned over, slipping into my arms, and kissed me softly, again and again. After a few lingering kisses, she finally stepped out, holding the gift I had given her.

"I'll see you soon," she whispered with a smile before heading inside. I watched her disappear into the building before driving off toward my place.

Later that night, after dinner, I gave her a call. "Did you try the top?" I asked, eager to know how she felt about it.

She sighed gently. "You know I don't wear sleeveless."

I tried to convince her. "But it's beautiful! You should at least try it once. I'm sure you'd look amazing."

"I really liked it," she said, her voice soft, "but I just don't feel comfortable in sleeveless clothes."

Seeing her hesitation, I suggested, "Why don't you give it to a friend then?"

She hesitated. "I could, but... you're not going to buy me another one, right?"

I smiled to myself. "Of course not. But if you don't want it, you can return it to me, and I'll exchange it for something else."

She didn't know that there was no exchange option, but I lied to make sure she would accept another gift. A week later, she returned the top to me.

A few days passed, and my brother Karan and sister-in-law, Heena, had returned from Hyderabad and moved to Zirakpur. I mentioned to Jojo that they'd love to meet her, but she seemed nervous about it. I reassured her, saying she didn't have to meet them unless she felt comfortable, but she eventually agreed.

One day, I received an SMS from Heena, asking when I would visit. I replied that I would come with Jojo, and she eagerly said she'd wait for us.

I called Jojo. "Get ready, we're going to meet my brother and his family," I told her, sensing a bit of hesitation on the other end of the line.

"I'd love to meet them," she said, her voice tinged with nervousness, "but I'm a little anxious."

I smiled, trying to ease her nerves. "You'll be fine. I'll be with you the entire time."

"What should I wear?" she asked, uncertainty creeping into her voice.

"Wear something simple, maybe a suit. You always look amazing in suits," I suggested.

She agreed and began getting ready while I made a mental note to pick up two chocolates—one for her and one for my niece, Priyanka. But in the rush, I completely forgot to grab them.

Soon, she called to let me know she was ready. I drove to her PG and gave her a quick call to let her know I was outside. A few moments later, she emerged, dressed in a beautiful maroon suit. She had done her hair in a new style, and as she walked towards the car, my eyes couldn't help but linger on her.

She looked stunning—more beautiful than I had imagined.

As she slid into the passenger seat, I couldn't stop staring at her.

"Please don't look at me like that," she said shyly, a smile tugging at her lips.

Feeling a surge of happiness, I shifted the car into gear. "Alright, let's go," I said, stealing glances at her as I drove.

On the way to my brother's place, I could sense Jojo was feeling nervous. It was her first time meeting them, and she hadn't even spoken to them over the phone before. I reached over, held her hand, and gave it a reassuring squeeze, hoping to calm her nerves. To distract her, I gently placed her hand on the gearshift, knowing she liked it when I did that. She smiled, her mind momentarily diverted.

After about 40 minutes, we arrived at their society. As we pulled into the parking area, I spotted my sister-in-law, Heena, and my niece, Priyanka, walking in the park. The moment Priyanka saw my car, her face lit up, and she started shouting, "Chachu has come!"

I parked the car and stepped out, introducing Jojo to both of them. Priyanka, however, wasn't interested in talking to Jojo—she rarely spoke to strangers at first. We made our way inside the flat and settled on the bed in the living room. Heena asked us to make ourselves comfortable and then disappeared into the kitchen.

Jojo sat quietly, still looking a bit shy. I noticed her smile at me, a little nervous but trying to ease into the moment. A few minutes later, Heena returned with watermelon juice. I had never had watermelon juice before, and I immediately liked it. After serving us the juice, she brought out some fruit and a glass of grapes' juice. I motioned to Heena to sit with us, encouraging everyone to chat.

Jojo, though initially a little nervous, started feeling more comfortable as the conversation flowed. Suddenly, Priyanka, who had been observing Jojo's nail art, broke the ice by calling her *Chachi*. Both Jojo and I exchanged surprised looks, not quite sure how to react. We all just smiled, pretending to ignore it for the moment. But soon enough, Priyanka and Jojo became fast friends. Priyanka admired her nail art and excitedly asked Jojo to do the same for her.

Later, my brother Karan returned from the office. When he walked in, I was sitting with Jojo, while Heena was still busy in the kitchen. I introduced them, and Karan greeted her warmly, immediately striking up a conversation.

For four hours, we chatted, shared stories, and laughed together. Heena, in her usual gracious way, kept serving snacks and drinks, not letting anyone's glass or plate stay empty for too long. At one point, I jokingly asked her to make more watermelon juice because I had enjoyed it so much. Jojo gave me a small, amused smile, clearly signaling she was too full to have anything more. I touched her cheek gently and whispered, "Don't worry, you don't have to eat if you're full. You can leave it."

Heena returned with two more glasses of watermelon juice. Jojo looked at me, her eyes pleading, and I quickly spoke up, "Bhabhi, she's had enough. I'll take both glasses instead." I laughed and happily finished the juice for her.

Later in the night, Heena prepared a simple yet delicious dinner of rajma, rice, and chapati. As we were getting ready for dinner, Jojo and Heena started setting the table, placing plates and bowls on the bed, while my brother and I were casually watching TV, and Priyanka was engrossed in her book. I glanced over and saw her working alongside Heena, effortlessly fitting in. There was something about the way she moved, her ease and warmth, that made it clear—she was perfect for the family.

When we finally sat down to eat, I couldn't help but smile as Jojo served me rice with her own hands. There was something incredibly sweet and intimate about that small gesture, and it filled me with warmth.

After dinner, we continued talking, sharing stories, and enjoying the comfort of each other's company. The night was filled with laughter, conversation, and a sense of belonging, making it one of those moments I knew I'd always cherish.

Priyanka, who had been shy at first, warmed up to Jojo as the evening went on. She wanted Jojo to help her read and even asked her to color her nails just like hers. It was clear that Priyanka had really taken a liking to her, and Jojo was more than happy to oblige.

After spending more time talking and playing, I gently asked Jojo if it was time to leave. She nodded, and I turned to Heena. "We should get going now," I said.

We stood up and made our way to the door, but, as is often the case, the conversation didn't end there. The women lingered, chatting with a few last-minute exchanges at the door. I smiled and said, "You know, you can continue talking in the lift too!"

Everyone laughed as we made our way downstairs. Once in the car, we waved goodbye to Heena and Priyanka, who both asked Jojo to visit again soon. I started the car, and we left.

As we drove away, I glanced over at Jojo. "So, how do you feel after meeting them?" I asked.

She smiled brightly, her eyes glowing. "I'm so happy," she said. "I really loved Priyanka. But I realized I should have brought something—chocolate or a teddy bear for her."

I chuckled softly. "I thought about that too, but I forgot at the last minute."

She gave me a light nudge. "You always bring chocolate for me, but you had to forget it today of all days!" she said with a teasing smile. "I hope bhabhi doesn't think poorly of me for not bringing anything on my first visit."

"Don't worry about it," I reassured her. "She wouldn't think that. And besides, next time we go, we'll bring plenty of chocolates and toys for Priyanka."

"Hmmm," she murmured, still thoughtful, but now more at ease.

Suddenly, she changed the subject, her face lighting up with excitement. "You know, I've always been fond of love stories. Have you read any good ones?"

I laughed and admitted, "I've only read one—just one, but it was a sweet one." Then, I confessed honestly, "I don't really have a habit of reading novels."

She smiled and began to tell me about her love for reading, especially romantic stories. She even recommended a particular love story, based on real life, and asked if I'd give it a read.

"I'll read it once I get the time," I promised, and we continued chatting, exchanging light-hearted jokes and a few romantic compliments along the way.

Before long, we reached her PG. She was about to get out of the car but paused, leaning toward me. I wrapped my arms around her, giving her a warm hug, followed by a soft kiss on her cheek. She smiled, her face glowing with happiness.

"Bye," she said sweetly, waving as she stepped out of the car.

I watched as she walked toward her PG, her model-like walk never failing to impress me. She always carried herself with such grace and confidence, and I couldn't help but admire her as she disappeared from sight.

Later that night, after I returned to my room, I couldn't stop thinking about the evening. I sent her a simple SMS: *"Thanks for a lovely evening."*

In truth, I wanted to write something more—*"Thanks for making me feel complete"*—but I hesitated, stopping my fingers from typing out the full depth of what I felt.

She replied to my message, *"I should thank you for the evening. I loved meeting everyone, especially Priyanka."* I smiled to myself. Jojo loved children, and that meant a lot to me. My little niece Priyanka was precious, and I always wanted my girlfriend to adore her the way I did. And that was Jojo—sweet, caring, and effortlessly fitting in.

The thought of her loving my family made me feel complete in a way. I had always hoped to find someone who would not only love me but also treat my family with kindness and respect. Jojo wasn't just a guest tonight; she blended in so naturally, as if she was already a part of the family. The way she interacted with everyone, especially Priyanka, warmed my heart. I could see how happy my family was with her presence, and in that moment, I caught myself imagining a future where she wasn't just visiting but truly a part of it.

But I stopped myself—maybe it was too soon to let my heart run wild with these thoughts. Still, it was hard to resist the feelings that came rushing in like a scene from a movie.

The next day, I couldn't get the thought of her out of my mind, and one thing kept nagging at me—I needed to make up for the sleeveless top she didn't like. I really wanted to get her something she'd love and feel comfortable in this time. So, I registered on an online shopping website, determined to find the perfect gift.

As usual, when I first logged in, I got distracted by all the good stuff on the home page—tempting things for myself. But I mentally slapped my wrist. *No, focus! This is for her,* I reminded myself.

With some effort, I found the filter for women's products and dove into the sea of choices. I'd never really done this before—shopping for a girl. It felt like a test, and I wanted to pass with flying colors. My cursor hovered over the *apparel* section, and when I clicked it, I was bombarded with so many options: tops, dresses, jeans, suits... *Will she wear a dress?* I wondered, clicking on the dress section.

"Yeah, she'd look stunning in this," I thought, admiring a sleek dress. But then I paused. *No,* I told myself. I didn't want to choose something she might not be comfortable wearing. I wanted her to feel good about what she wore, not just look good in it. So, I moved on, shifting back to tops, determined to find something that would make her happy.

I was scrolling through different styles, my mind completely focused, when suddenly the ringtone of my phone startled me. It was lying on the bed next to me. I glanced over and smiled. It was her. *She must have a long life,* I thought with a smile, remembering the old saying, as I reached for the phone.

"Hello," I said sweetly, trying to suppress the excitement I felt from picking out something for her.

"What are you doing?" she asked, her voice light and curious.

I paused for a second. I couldn't tell her I was shopping for her—it would ruin the surprise. So, I decided to keep it simple.

"Nothing much, just sitting at the computer," I replied, doing my best to sound casual.

As I continued talking to her on the phone, my eyes kept scrolling through the tops on the website. My mind was more focused on imagining how each piece would look on her. She was speaking, but my replies were mostly "hmm," as my attention kept drifting back to the screen. In the back of my mind, I could hear the melody of *Mere rang mein rangne waali,* as if she were the muse inspiring my shopping spree.

Finally, I came across a top that stopped me in my tracks. I could picture her in it so clearly, and in that moment, I knew—*Yes, this will suit her perfectly.* Without thinking twice, I placed the order.

I tried my best to hold back and keep the surprise to myself, but I was no match for my excitement. Before I knew it, I blurted out, "I bought a new one!"

She chuckled on the other end. "Did you exchange the old one, or is this a new order?"

Not wanting to admit the truth, I quickly lied, "I returned the old one and got this instead."

She sighed softly, but her concern was palpable. "You should've bought a phone for yourself instead. You really didn't have to spend this on me." Her words, full of care and affection, sank deep into my heart. It wasn't about the gift—it was her genuine concern that touched me.

Two days later, while I was in the office, I got a call from the courier guy. My room was locked, so I asked him to leave the package with my landlord. The entire day, I couldn't stop thinking about the top, eagerly waiting for my shift to end so I could go home and see it in person.

When I finally reached my building that evening, I practically ran to my landlord's place to grab the package. With excitement bubbling up, I dashed upstairs and tore open the courier.

And then... disappointment hit me like a brick.

The top looked nothing like the picture. In fact, it was pathetic. It was one of those moments where the reality of online shopping truly bites. I stared at it in disbelief, feeling both annoyed and angry at the website for showing such a misleading image. I could almost hear myself cursing the website's owner under my breath.

I didn't even want to tell her about it. The thought of giving her this top—something so far from what I had imagined—was out of the question. In a fit of frustration, I decided it wasn't even worth returning. Instead, I repurposed it as a cleaning cloth for dusting the table. A part of me couldn't help but laugh at how ridiculous the whole situation was.

But, like a fool, I still took a chance on the same website. The deals were tempting, and I figured, *Maybe this time will be different.* So I ordered another top for her and a wristwatch for my brother.

When the next package arrived, I opened it cautiously, half-expecting another disaster. Sure enough, the top was just as bad as the first—pathetic wasn't even the right word to describe it. But at least the wristwatch was perfect, and I proudly gifted it to my brother.

By then, I had made up my mind: *Never again will I buy clothes from an online store.* I shared the entire saga with Jojo, and she couldn't stop laughing. Her laughter was infectious, and soon enough, I was laughing too.

"Don't waste any more money," she said between giggles. "You being in my life is already more than enough of a gift."

Her words, as simple as they were, filled me with warmth. It reminded me that the gestures, no matter how grand or small, weren't what mattered most to her. It was us, our connection, that meant everything.

A few days later, I was working the night shift, and as I was wrapping up some tasks, I got a message from Jojo saying she was leaving the office. We ended up bumping into each other in the office building, where she was with her friend Preeti.

Her friend, Preeti, left her with me and went to the cafeteria. We chatted for a while, and then I asked her about her cab situation.

"Preeti will call me when the cab arrives," she said.

I smiled and told her, "You're looking beautiful."

She smiled back, teasing me, "I always look beautiful to you."

I reached out and held her hand. She hesitated for a moment, glancing around nervously to see if anyone was nearby. Her eyes darted between our hands, then up to meet mine. "Please leave my hand, someone might see us." she requested softly, clearly not wanting anyone to catch us holding hands like that.

Understanding, I guided her to a quieter spot where we wouldn't be seen so easily. Once we were there, I leaned in closer and whispered, "I want to kiss you."

She looked into my eyes, and I could see she wanted to kiss me too. Slowly, we moved closer to each other, the moment feeling perfect—until a sudden noise in the yard startled us both. We pulled back immediately, laughing nervously.

She quickly called Preeti, scolding her over the phone, "I'll kill you, why didn't you call me when the cab came? I asked you to call me."

When she hung up, I asked, "What happened?"

"The cab has gone and she didn't call me," she replied, frustrated.

"But why didn't she call you?" I asked.

"She thought I would be coming with you," she said, shaking her head. "Now what should I do?"

"I'll drop you, don't worry," I reassured her. "Wait here, I'll just bring the car from the parking area and give you a call when I'm at the main gate."

"Ok," she said, as I cupped her cheeks softly.

I quickly retrieved the car and called her when I reached the main gate. She came down and slid into the passenger seat.

"Sorry, you had to come with me. I know your shift has started," she said, her voice tinged with guilt.

"It's okay. Anything for you," I replied with a smile, meeting her eyes as I started driving.

We reached her PG, and as I parked the car, I shifted a little closer, opening my arms. She smiled softly and leaned into my embrace, resting her head on my chest. I kissed her gently on the cheek and whispered, "Now I have to go."

She smiled again and nodded, giving me one last look before stepping out and waving goodbye as I drove away.

She nodded with pressed lips as she got out of the car. After dropping her off at her PG, I returned to the office. Later, she sent me a thank-you SMS, and I replied with a smiley.

The following week, our shifts changed. One day while I was in the office, I called her. She told me she was going for a haircut and would be busy the entire day, so we wouldn't be able to talk much. That day, we didn't get a chance to connect.

Later, as I was about to leave the office around 11 PM, I noticed Sunaina walking around in the yard, waiting for her shift to start. I decided to join her, and we started talking about work and some of the people in the office. As we walked, a guy and a girl passed us, walking together. Sunaina, observing them, said, "There are so many couples in our office."

Then, out of nowhere, she turned to me with a suspicious look and asked, "Is Jojo your girlfriend?"

I was taken aback. *How does she know that?* I thought to myself, feeling a wave of surprise wash over me. I wasn't ready to share the details of my relationship with Jojo, especially since Sunaina was a new friend, and my relationship with Jojo had just started. So, I dodged the question with a little white lie. "We're best friends," I said. "We hang out outside the office sometimes."

As we continued walking, I found myself glancing at my phone more often than usual. Sunaina noticed and asked, "Are you expecting a call or something?"

"No, not really," I replied, trying to play it cool. But my face must've given me away because she could sense something was up. Then, suddenly, my phone buzzed with an SMS. I unlocked it at lightning speed, eager to see who it was from. It was Jojo. Her message simply read, "Where are you?"

I smiled and told Sunaina, "It's her—she's asking where I am."

I quickly replied to Jojo's text, "I'm in the backside area, come here."

A few minutes later, Jojo arrived. I was still with Sunaina when she came. The two greeted each other with polite smiles, and Sunaina even complimented Jojo. "You're looking beautiful," she said.

Jojo had straightened her hair and was wearing a white shirt paired with blue jeans. I also complimented her, saying, "You are looking amazing."

But, if I was being honest, I didn't really like her new hairstyle. Her face was long and thin, and the straight, silky hair didn't quite suit her as much as her natural look. Still, I couldn't say that to her, especially since I knew she had spent the entire day at the parlor, all for me. She had done this to look beautiful for me, and I respected the effort she put in.

"Thank you," she smiled. "I went to the parlor today, like I told you."

Sunaina was called away by someone just then and left us alone. As soon as she was gone, Jojo relaxed visibly, her smile widening. There was a certain sparkle in her eyes, a warmth I hadn't noticed earlier. Being alone with me seemed to make her more comfortable, and that made me smile too.

"It's beautiful. And you bought this shirt newly? I've never seen this before," I said, admiring her as we stood there.

"No, it's old. But I never wore this to the office before."

"It's nice," I added, then leaned in a little closer and whispered, "I want to kiss you."

She flashed her eyes at me, her expression a mix of shock and amusement. "Here?"

"Yes," I said, unable to hold back a smile.

"You want it to be big news?" she asked, raising an eyebrow. "Not here. Everybody's around." We both laughed, realizing how absurd it was to even think about it there.

Her shift was about to start, and mine was ending. She gave me one last smile before heading inside. Just as I was getting ready to leave, I got a call from Vinay, the HR of her shift. He told me he'd be running late and asked if I could handle sending the shift's attendance report, which had to be sent within the first 30 minutes.

I agreed, went back inside, and waited for the attendance sheet to be signed by everyone. As I sat with my colleagues, I spotted Jojo walking towards me. She nodded slightly, signaling me to follow her to my desk.

Once there, she looked at me, a little shy but clearly in need of help. "Are you free?" she asked, her voice carrying a hint of nervousness.

"Yes, what happened?" I asked gently, wanting her to feel comfortable.

"I forgot my pair of spectacles at the PG," she said, making a sad face. "I can't work without them."

"Let's go. We'll bring them," I said immediately, not even thinking twice about the attendance task. Her comfort was more important to me at that moment.

"Are you sure?" she asked, her face lighting up with hope.

"I'm totally free. Don't worry, I'll send the attendance once we get back."

She hesitated for a moment, then said, "But I can't just leave with you directly from the office. Too many people will notice."

I nodded, understanding her concern. "Okay, I'll go get the car and bring it to the main gate. You can join me there."

She smiled and agreed. I went to the parking area, got the car, and called her once I was near the main gate. However, when she came out, she was still hesitating. There were quite a few people standing around since the shift had just ended, and she didn't want to be seen getting into my car.

A moment later, she called me and asked, "Can you move the car a little away from the gate? There are too many people around."

I chuckled and said, "Okay," before moving the car further down the road, out of sight.

She got into the car quickly and, with a hint of urgency, asked, "Move the car fast before anyone from my shift sees us."

I laughed softly, sensing her nervousness, and pulled away from the gate. We headed to her PG, and she ran inside, returning in what felt like seconds. As we drove back to the office, she said, "So, your wish has come true."

I looked at her, confused. "Which wish?"

"Kiss," she said, her eyes gleaming, her tone light and inviting.

I smiled, leaned over, and kissed her lips while keeping one eye on the road. It was brief but sweet, and we both laughed softly afterward, the moment feeling light and spontaneous. Just then, my phone rang—it was my manager. I knew she was calling about the attendance, but I let it ring, not wanting to deal with it just yet. I had no explanation for the delay.

We reached the office, and I stopped the car at the gate. Jojo gave me a quick smile before slipping out and heading inside. I parked the car haphazardly on the footpath, knowing I wasn't supposed to park there but too rushed to care. I sprinted inside, feeling the pressure to catch up on the task I had neglected. When I reached my desk, I found out that my manager had already called the office twice, looking for me. I quickly dialed her back and lied, saying, "Sorry, I was in the cafeteria and my phone was on silent, so I didn't hear the call."

She sounded a bit skeptical, but I assured her that I was sending the attendance immediately. I scrambled to gather everything and managed to delay it just enough to avoid too much trouble. A few minutes later, I sent the report, and soon after, Vinay arrived.

After everything settled down, I found myself glancing toward Jojo's seat. She sat in the corner of the bay, where I could easily catch her eye whenever I passed through to visit the IT department or check on someone else. Whenever our paths crossed, we exchanged secret smiles. As I was leaving to wish the IT team good night, I passed by her seat again. She was smiling at her screen, completely absorbed in her work, but I couldn't resist teasing her.

"Chashmeesh," I whispered as I walked by, referring to her glasses. She gave me a quick smile without looking up, and everything seemed perfect in that small, shared moment.

But over the next few days, I started noticing that something was bothering her. There was a subtle change in her mood, a hint of sadness that lingered behind her usual smiles. I asked her several times if something was wrong, but she brushed it off, insisting, "Kuch nahi, everything's fine."

Still, I knew her well enough to sense that something was off. I figured we needed to spend some time alone so she could open up to me. With our shifts being different, it was hard to find a moment, but we agreed to meet on the upcoming Sunday.

As the weekend approached, I thought about buying her a gift—something that might cheer her up. But after my last online shopping disaster with the clothes, I was determined not to take any chances with that again. I wanted to get her something thoughtful and useful, so I remembered her love for nail art. That's when the idea hit me—I could buy her a Nail Art Kit.

I searched online, found a good website with decent reviews, and ordered the kit for her. It was delivered within a week, and I couldn't wait to surprise her with it.

When Sunday finally arrived, I called her and asked if she could meet me. I was still worried about her sadness and wanted to find out what was bothering her. She agreed to meet in the evening.

We met, and as we sat together, I could see she was still carrying some of that weight. But before diving into the serious conversation, I wanted to lift her spirits a bit.

"I have something for you", I said.

As I reached into the back seat to retrieve the gift, I could feel Jojo's eyes glued to me, brimming with excitement. She was practically on the edge of her seat, her gaze following my every movement, waiting eagerly for my hand to return with the surprise. The gift wasn't even wrapped, but as I handed it to her, the sparkle in her eyes brought a warmth to the air, making the moment feel unforgettable.

Her face broke into the most beautiful, genuine smile I'd seen all day. "Oh my God!" she exclaimed softly, clearly touched by the gesture. She looked at the Nail Art Kit in awe, as if it was the most precious thing anyone had ever given her.

A cute smile danced on her lips, and before I knew it, she leaned over and kissed me. "No one has ever given me such a wonderful gift," she said, her voice filled with emotion. She was visibly touched, her eyes softening as if she was holding back something more than happiness.

"It's the sweetest gift I've ever gotten," she continued, now getting a little emotional. "I've received so many gifts in my life, but no one has ever given me something I'm actually fond of."

She leaned in again, hugging me tightly, her warmth spreading through me. "You've given me something that matches my love for nail art, for what I'm passionate about," she whispered before planting another kiss on my cheek. "Thank you. I'm so happy."

Her eyes remained glued to the kit as if she couldn't get enough of looking at it. She tilted her head slightly to the right, gazing at the gift with an ever-widening smile, excitement bubbling inside her. It was obvious she wanted to open it right then and there but was trying to control her emotions.

After a moment, she turned to me, her smile softening into a look of concern. "Why don't you ever buy anything for yourself?" she asked, giving me a once-over. "You wear such simple clothes. You should buy something stylish, something cool."

I shrugged, giving her a smile. "I'm very simple, and my choice is also simple," I replied. Then I added, half-seriously, "Will you help me while shopping?"

She got excited by the idea. "Of course! Call me whenever you want to buy clothes. I'll definitely come." Then, narrowing her eyes teasingly, she added, "But will you actually wear the clothes I pick for you?"

In my head, I thought, *Of course, I'd wear anything for her*, but I couldn't resist teasing her a little. "No... Naaahever," I said dramatically, drawing out the word just to see her reaction.

She slapped me softly on the arm, her mock pout turning into a wide smile. "You will." she said, smiling.

We talked for a bit, sharing our usual banter, but then I turned the conversation to something that had been bothering me for a while. "But really, tell me... why were you so upset the other day?"

She hesitated for a moment, avoiding my gaze. "It's nothing serious," she said, but I could sense the sadness lurking behind her words.

"I can see something's bothering you," I said gently, my hand moving up to caress her cheek. "I'm with you, not only in happiness but also in your sorrows and problems. You don't have to face anything alone."

I wrapped my arms around her, pulling her into a warm embrace. I wanted her to feel safe, to know that no matter what, I was there for her. "I'll never let go of your hand," I whispered softly. "In any situation."

She rested her head against my chest for a moment, breathing deeply as if drawing comfort from my presence. But then, in a quiet voice, she said something that caught me completely off guard. "I feel like I'm cheating you."

I pulled back slightly, surprised by her words. I looked into her eyes, trying to understand what she meant, but my mind started racing with possibilities. *Is she engaged to someone else? Is she hiding something?* My thoughts spiraled out of control, a flood of *what if's* rushing through my head.

"Why do you feel that way?" I asked gently, trying to keep my voice steady despite the uncertainty gnawing at me.

"Nikhil called me, but I'm ignoring him. Still, I miss him sometimes, and I feel like I'm cheating you," she confessed, her voice trembling as she tried to hold back her emotions. "I'm with you, but sometimes my thoughts wander to Nikhil."

Her words hit me hard, leaving me momentarily breathless. My chest tightened, and a sadness spread through me, even though I tried to keep my expression neutral. I could sense the honesty in her words, and that honesty, while painful, also made me realize something—maybe I hadn't yet managed to make her truly fall in love with me, not the way I loved her. I was giving her everything, but maybe, in her heart, it wasn't enough.

At that moment, even though I was hurting, I knew I had to be there for her. I pushed aside my own feelings and focused on comforting her, easing her guilt. I stroked her hair gently and said, "It's okay. I understand. It's not easy to forget someone you cared about, but you're with me now, and that's all that matters to me. Don't think of it as cheating. Everything will settle with time."

I could see the turmoil in her eyes easing slightly, as if my words brought her some relief. She rested her head against my chest, burying her face under my neck, and for a few moments, we stayed like that, quiet and close. I rubbed her back softly, offering comfort the only way I knew how. Her body slowly relaxed, and I could tell she was feeling a bit better.

After a while, I suggested softly, "Would you like to come to my place? We could spend more time together, and maybe you'll feel better."

She nodded gently. "I'll come on Saturday."

It felt like the right moment to shift the mood, to lighten the weight of the conversation, so I smiled and tried to bring up something less heavy. "How about some ice cream?" I asked, trying to sound casual.

She saw right through me, giving me a mock angry look, her eyes narrowing as if she were truly upset. But then, she couldn't hold it and broke into a smile. "Ice cream, huh? You're just trying to change the topic!"

We laughed together, the tension easing, and soon we found ourselves at a small ice cream shop. The coolness of the night mixed with the sweetness of the treat, and for a little while, we forgot about the harder parts of our conversation.

We spent the next few moments joking with each other, sharing laughs between spoonfuls of ice cream. It was a relief to have this lighter moment after such an emotionally charged talk. As we sat there, it felt like our bond was growing stronger, even if the doubts still lingered in the back of my mind.

I finished my ice cream way faster than her, and she still had more than half of hers left. My eyes darted to her cone, and without thinking much, I leaned closer and took a bite.

She quickly pulled her ice cream away, pretending to pout. "Mmm, it's mine!" she said, laughing as she moved her hand away, protecting her treat.

"I'm yours too, right?" I teased, pulling her hand back toward me. "So, shouldn't you share with me?"

She smiled, eyes gleaming with a hint of challenge. "Nope, this ice cream is all mine! And I'm going to eat it slowly... right in front of you!" she said, her voice full of mock defiance as she brought the spoon to her mouth, savoring the bite while watching me closely.

After our little battle over the ice cream, we were left with just a small piece, clinging to the spoon. We both eyed it hungrily, each of us wanting the last bit for ourselves. Finally, we came up with a mischievous solution—we'd eat it together, each taking a bite from opposite sides. As we leaned in, our faces grew closer and closer, our lips brushing softly against each other as we both went for the ice cream. Neither of us backed away, enjoying the moment as much as the ice cream itself.

When the ice cream was finished, our lips lingered, and the lighthearted mood turned into something more intimate. She smiled softly, and I smiled back. Our lips touched again, this time with intention. She closed her eyes, leaning in for a kiss. I followed her lead, pressing my lips gently against hers in what we later named our "ice-cream kiss."

The kiss felt like it lasted forever, sweet and unhurried, and when it finally broke, it left us both smiling like kids.

After a while, she broke the silence, her voice soft. "That ice cream was delicious," she said with a wink. "I might have to get another one soon."

I smiled, starting the car but purposely driving slowly, hoping to savor a little more time with her. She leaned in, resting her head on my shoulder, and I couldn't resist planting soft kisses on her forehead every few seconds. It was like she wanted to be close, and I wanted to keep her there, wrapped up in our quiet little moment.

When we finally reached her PG, she looked at me with a hint of sadness in her eyes, like she didn't want to leave. I gave her a tight hug and kissed her gently on the cheeks, but she wasn't done. With her eyes closed, she leaned in again, offering me another kiss, this one longer, softer, and full of warmth. Our lips lingered, the world around us fading away until we finally had to say goodbye. We waved to each other, knowing we'd relive that evening in our minds for the rest of the night.

The next day, I couldn't help but ask if she'd tried the Nail Art Kit I'd given her. "So, have you used it yet?" I asked, eager to hear about her experience.

"I haven't used stamping before, so I don't really know how," she admitted. "But I'll try to figure it out."

"I can download a video from YouTube for you," I suggested, trying to be helpful.

She smiled. "I can just check the instructions and follow them," she said, though I could tell she wasn't entirely confident. But I still insisted on finding a tutorial, just to make things easier for her.

The next day, I downloaded the video and told her about it later that evening.

"Thanks, but I already found one and tried it," she said, sounding disheartened. "It's not working like I thought it would. I was so excited, but it's kind of disappointing."

Her words stung a little. She had been so thrilled about the gift, and now that excitement had turned to frustration.

"One more disaster gift," I muttered, feeling a bit defeated.

"Now please don't buy anything else," she said, though her voice carried a gentle tone, as if trying not to hurt my feelings. "It's okay, really."

"But I feel bad," I said, sighing. "That's the fourth time I've bought something for you, and none of them have worked out."

She laughed softly, her eyes twinkling. "Now don't buy any more calamity gifts," she said. "Instead, buy yourself a new phone. Seriously!"

"Hmmm..." I mumbled, pretending to consider it.

The next day, I wasn't really in the mood to go to the office, so I called in sick, though truthfully, I just wanted a day off. In the evening, Jojo called me. "Where are you? Let's meet up," she said with a sweetness that I could never refuse.

"Give me an hour," I replied, knowing I had to freshen up a bit if I was going to see her. I quickly took a bath, threw on a nice shirt, and spritzed some cologne. Once I was ready, I gave her a call. "I'm on my way."

When I reached her PG, she came out, dressed in a simple t-shirt and a comfortable skirt, much more casual than I was used to seeing her. Usually, she would dress up whenever we met, so her laid-back look took me by surprise.

"You usually come dressed so nicely. What's going on today?" I asked, raising an eyebrow but smiling.

"We're not going anywhere fancy. I just came to give you this," she said, holding up a non-plastic bag she had brought along.

"What's in the bag?" I asked, curious.

"I made Khichadi for you. You're not feeling well, right?" she said, her voice filled with so much care and sweetness, it made my heart melt.

"How did you know I wasn't feeling well?" I asked, genuinely surprised that she had found out about my fake sick day.

"You didn't come to the office today, and I heard you were feeling sick. So I rushed home after work and made this for you. I know you don't like the food from your tiffin service, so I thought you'd need something homemade. Just take it, and please take care of yourself," Her voice was gentle but filled with an undeniable sincerity, a care that pierced through me. She looked at me with such genuine concern that for a moment, I couldn't find the words.

I stared at the bag she held, realizing what this meant. She had come home, tired from work, and instead of resting, she had spent her evening thinking about me—about what I might need, about how she could help me feel better. It wasn't just about the food; it was about the love, the care, the thought behind it.

She handed me the bag, and I took it, feeling the warmth of the container inside, but also feeling something even warmer inside me. A lump formed in my throat. I wasn't really sick. I had just wanted a day off, a break from the routine. But now, standing there with her, holding this simple bag of food, I felt an overwhelming sense of gratitude and guilt. She had done this for me—out of love, out of care—and I didn't want to ruin that beautiful gesture by admitting the truth.

I gently cupped her face in my hands, my thumb brushing against her soft skin. "You are so sweet," I said, my voice quieter than usual, filled with something deeper. "I'm so lucky to have you."

She smiled at me then, the kind of smile that lit up her whole face, the kind of smile that reached her eyes and made everything around us seem a little brighter. "I made it in enough quantity for dinner," she said, carrying that undercurrent of love. "So don't waste it, okay? It's still hot, so eat it as soon as you get home before it gets cold."

I couldn't stop smiling, though a subtle ache lingered within me. She had done all this for me, and here I was, standing in front of her, pretending I was sick when all I wanted was a day off. But how could I tell her now? I didn't want to spoil the moment, the effort she had put into making me feel cared for.

"I promise," I said, still holding her face in my hands. I leaned in and kissed her forehead, feeling the warmth of her skin against my lips, a gesture of thanks for her care, her kindness.

She stepped back, adjusting the strap of her bag on her shoulder. "And don't forget," she added, "if you don't eat it all, I'm going to be mad."

I nodded.

Her voice had a touch of nervousness when she added, "And I'm not a good cook, by the way. I never tried making Khichadi before. It was my first time. I had my sister on the phone the whole time, giving me instructions while I followed step-by-step. So, if it doesn't taste great, just... you know, don't sleep hungry." She giggled shyly at her own words, but I could hear the genuine concern behind her funny tone.

I was overwhelmed by her effort, by how much care and love she had poured into something so simple. At that moment, I almost wished I had been truly sick, just to experience the fullness of her care without the guilt of my little lie. She was so precious, so thoughtful. Her gesture made me feel so deeply cherished. I smiled, leaning in to kiss her gently before she left. "Thank you," I whispered against her cheek, the warmth of the moment wrapping around us like a soft blanket.

When I finally reached my room, I didn't even have the patience to wash the spoon. I immediately opened the bag, and the warm aroma of the Khichadi filled the air. It smelled delicious. I took my first bite, and to my surprise, it was really tasty. Her humble words about not being a good cook didn't do justice to what she'd made—it was perfect. Every bite carried her love, her effort, and her desire to make me feel cared for. I savored each mouthful, thinking about her the entire time.

Just as I was finishing, my phone rang. It was her, checking up on me. "Did you eat it?" she asked, her voice full of anticipation. I could picture her sitting there, waiting for my answer, her eyes twinkling with a hint of nervousness.

"Yes, I did, and it was delicious," I replied, meaning every word.

"Really? You liked it?" she asked, a mix of surprise and happiness filling her voice.

"Of course! It was perfect. I think you've found a hidden talent in cooking," I joked, hearing her soft laugh on the other end. She sounded so relieved, so happy. I could tell that my enjoyment of her Khichadi meant more to her than I realized.

The following week, we made plans to spend the weekend together. She had to work on Saturday, but I had the day off. I waited for her call, knowing she would finish by 3 PM. Right on time, she called me after returning to her PG. "I'll be ready in a bit," she said sweetly.

"Okay, take your time," I replied, though I was already eager to see her.

An hour passed. I called her again. "Almost ready?" I asked, expecting her to say yes.

"Give me a little more time," she said apologetically. I could hear her fumbling with something in the background, maybe still getting ready.

Another half an hour went by. I called again, trying to mask my growing impatience. "Are you ready now?" I asked, my voice more controlled than I felt inside.

"Not yet! Just a little longer. I'm so sorry!" she replied.

By the third hour, I was starting to feel impatience. But just as I was reaching my limit, my phone rang again. "I'm ready now, come over," she said, her voice soft and apologetic.

I took a deep breath, calming myself down. She was finally ready, and I knew it wasn't worth holding onto the irritation. When I pulled up near her PG, she stepped out, and all my frustration melted away in an instant.

She was wearing the same outfit she had on when we first met—a white top with Angry Birds printed on it and a red shrug. The sight of her in that outfit brought back so many memories. It was like seeing her for the first time all over again, and I couldn't help but smile as she walked towards the car.

She got in and looked at me, her eyes filled with an apology before she even spoke. "Sorry, I made you wait for so long," she said softly, the guilt evident in her voice.

I was about to ask her what took so long when I noticed the bag she was carrying. "What's in the bag?" I asked curiously, pointing at it.

"I made dinner for you," she said, her voice warm and tender. "Chapatti and Aloo Sabzi."

In that moment, whatever irritation I had left just vanished completely. It was like she had an invisible power over me, where every small act of hers softened my heart. I smiled, my heart swelling with affection. "You made dinner for me?"

She nodded with a shy smile. "I felt bad for making you wait, so I thought I'd cook something for us."

I couldn't help but feel completely touched by her gesture. Here she was, after a long day at work, and instead of resting, she had cooked for me. All the waiting seemed so trivial now, and the only thing I could feel was gratitude. I reached over and gently squeezed her hand. "You're amazing. Thank you."

She looked at me, her eyes full of warmth and a hint of relief that I wasn't upset. "Let's eat together later," she said softly.

And just like that, the day that had started with impatience and irritation turned into something beautiful, filled with her love, her thoughtfulness, and our shared moments of tenderness.

I reached for the dashboard and picked up the chocolate I had bought earlier. Handing it to her with a grin, I said, "Here, I bought it just now. It's not melted this time!" She smiled, unwrapped it, and without hesitation, started feeding me pieces of chocolate while I was driving. Each bite felt sweeter because it came from her hand.

But then, I couldn't resist—I gently bit her finger as she was feeding me, a small, cheeky gesture.

"Ahh!" she yelped in mock protest, pulling her hand back instantly. "Eat it yourself!" she scolded with a pout, tossing the chocolate into my lap.

I couldn't help but laugh. I took her hand, kissed it gently, and said with a teasing smile, "The whole life, you'll have to feed me with your hands, and the whole life, I'll keep biting your fingers."

She looked at me with a raised eyebrow and a trace of a smile. "Then find someone else! You should go to that girl in the office who likes you," she teased, scrunching her nose and making funny faces. "You're not even my choice!"

Her words, though teasing, filled the car with a lightheartedness that made the evening even better. We laughed, trading playful jabs and enjoying the simplicity of the moment. It was one of those times when nothing mattered but us and the joy of being together.

As the evening went on, I decided to take her to my new room for the first time. Before she even stepped inside, I gave her a fair warning, with an awkward smile, "Now don't expect too much cleanliness. It's a small room, and everything's kind of... uh, creatively organized."

She rolled her eyes and laughed, "I know. I didn't expect any different. I'm pretty sure you can't even clean it properly."

When we arrived, I opened the door, and she stepped inside, scanning the room. I could see her eyes flick between the bed and the chair, which had a small pile of clothes draped over it. She was clearly weighing her options on where to sit. I chuckled softly as I closed the door behind us, and after a second of deliberation, she made her decision, walking over to sit on the bed.

I sat down beside her, our shoulders almost touching.

"Do you want to eat now?" she asked, her voice soft and caring, knowing that I hadn't eaten since we met up.

I shook my head lightly, "We'll eat later."

For a moment, neither of us said anything. It was one of those peaceful silences where words weren't necessary. We just looked at each other, letting the quiet between us say more than our voices ever could. The closeness of the room, the intimacy of the moment—it all felt perfect.

Breaking the stillness, I gently reached for her hand, my fingers curling around hers. I leaned back, resting against the wall, and slowly pulled her toward me. She followed my movement effortlessly, her body responding to my gentle tug. She slid closer, her gaze never leaving mine. My hand found its way to her cheek, my fingers grazing her soft skin. She leaned in further, her head now resting on my stomach as we settled into a comfortable position.

My fingers slowly traced patterns in her hair, and I found myself lost in her presence. She looked up at me with those eyes that always had a way of igniting a flutter in my stomach. I couldn't help but admire her—the way her cheeks flushed ever so slightly, the softness of her lips, and the warmth that radiated from her. My thumb brushed over her lips, a silent gesture that seemed to express everything I was feeling.

Without saying a word, I gently lifted her up, pulling her closer until her head rested on my chest. She seemed so at peace, so content in that moment, and it made me want to hold her even tighter. Our conversation turned soft, almost like a whisper, as if the world outside didn't exist. It was just us, wrapped up in each other.

I placed my hand under her head, guiding her gently to tilt her face up toward mine. Our lips met in a kiss, slow and tender. The world around us blurred into nothingness, and all I could feel was the softness of her lips, the warmth of her breath, and the way her heartbeat seemed to sync with mine. It was the longest kiss we had shared, and I didn't want it to end. It was like our lips were speaking a language only we understood, one where time didn't matter and the only thing that existed was the feeling between us.

As the kiss deepened, I found myself lost in her completely. But eventually, I pulled away slightly, our foreheads resting together. "Let me go turn off the light," I whispered, smiling as I gently caressed her cheek.

She gave me a soft nod, her eyes still half-closed, and smiled, "Okay."

I reluctantly moved away, already missing the warmth of her close to me. I switched off the light, the room now bathed in the soft glow of the streetlight filtering through the curtains. I returned to her side, and as I lay back down beside her, pulling her into my arms once more, I knew there was nowhere else in the world I wanted to be.

We were completely lost in each other's arms, surrendering to the moment as the passion between us surged. Her blush began to bloom, softly rising from her neck to her cheeks, warming her face with a gentle flush that made her look even more radiant and irresistible. I could feel her enjoying the way I loved her, the warmth in her touch, the way her body responded to mine. She looked up at me with eyes that sparkled with affection and whispered, "You really know how to love a girl."

Her voice was soft but carried the weight of her emotions, and I could tell she was overwhelmed by the pleasure and comfort of being in my arms. As I caressed her neck with my fingertips, she shivered slightly, feeling the intensity of the moment. When I leaned in and kissed her neck, the heat of her breath on my skin sent a wave of desire through me. She responded with gentle movements, her body silently telling me where she wanted to feel my love the most.

Her slim waist felt delicate under my hands, and she pulled me closer, crossing her arms over my back and drawing me in. Her gestures were full of temptation, almost daring me to break every restraint. Our breaths grew heavy, and our hands roamed more freely, our lips meeting in a kiss that felt endless, as if they never wanted to part.

That night, I truly understood why people crave love. If this was what love felt like, then it was pure, intoxicating bliss. We were teetering on the edge of crossing boundaries, but then, as if pulled back by her inner grace, she gently shifted the mood. With a soft, sweet smile, she said, "Let's have something to eat, I'm hungry."

I immediately understood what she was doing, changing the topic to keep us grounded, and I respected her for it. She had a way of knowing when to stop, and I admired her strength, her decency, her values.

We sat up, the air between us still thick with unspoken passion. I wrapped her in her red shrug, tenderly covering her shoulders as if shielding her from the lingering heat of the moment. Then I reached for the tiffin she had packed. The food was cold now, but there was no way I could let her know. She had made it with love, and I wasn't about to say a word about the temperature. I ate two chapatis, savoring every bite, knowing that it was the effort she put in that made it special. I started feeding her, too, offering small bites, but I could tell she was doing the same as me—eating it more for my sake than because she was hungry.

After a while, we decided to stop. "Don't eat any more," she said softly, noticing that I was pushing through just to make her happy.

We smiled at each other, a silent understanding passing between us. This was love too, in the quiet moments, in the little things like eating cold food because it was made with affection.

Then she told me she had brought some pictures for me. I had asked for her photos earlier, and now she had them stored on a pen drive. She reached for her bag to retrieve it, while I moved to my desktop and powered it on. She sat on the chair next to the desk, and I knelt beside her, resting my head against her arm, feeling the softness of her skin against my cheek. I kissed her arm gently, a quiet thank you for everything she had done.

She plugged the pen drive into the computer and began copying the pictures onto my desktop. As the images popped up on the screen, she started showing me each one, telling me stories behind them—family gatherings, college memories, moments with her friends at her PG. I loved hearing the little details, the way her voice would change with each memory, bringing it to life.

But then, suddenly, she scrolled through a few photos a bit too quickly, trying to hide something. Curious, I immediately reached for the mouse to go back, but she pulled my hand away, pleading softly, "No, don't look at those."

Her sweet voice only made me more curious. I couldn't resist a small smile as I pressed the back arrow key, determined to see what she was trying to hide. She panicked and quickly tried to cover the screen with her hands, but I managed to catch a glimpse of the photos—ones where she was wearing something smaller, more revealing. She looked absolutely stunning, but I could see she was feeling shy about showing me.

Her face turned red, and she gave me a sheepish look. "Please, leave them," she said, her voice soft and a little embarrassed.

I admired, loving how cute she looked when she was trying to hide her bashfulness. "Come on, let me see them properly," I teased, moving closer to the screen.

"No!" she protested, laughing lightly. "Just forget it."

I held her tight as she tried to delete those pictures, but I quickly pulled her hand away, stopping her. "Don't delete them," I pleaded, smiling. "I love those pictures."

She glanced down, a bit flustered, and I couldn't help but smile. "You know, you're absolutely stunning," I said softly. Then, leaning in a bit closer, I added with a touch of humor, "And, pretty damn hot, too."

Her cheeks flushed even deeper as she gave me a light swat on the arm and smiled that naughty little smile I loved.

"Okay, mister," she said smiling. Then she turned back to the computer, "I want to show you something." She opened another folder on her pen-drive, and clicked on a movie titled *UP*. It was a cartoon movie, and as she double-clicked it, I watched curiously. She skipped ahead to a specific scene she loved, her eyes full of emotion as she waited for me to see it.

In that short scene, the two main characters were children who became friends and, as they grew up, got married. The clip captured the essence of life together—love, dreams, sacrifice, and even heartache, all in just a few minutes. I watched in silence, completely absorbed, feeling a tug at my heart with every frame. When it ended, I was left speechless, only managing to say, "Wow."

She smiled, pleased by my reaction, and copied the movie along with some other films and video songs onto my computer. "You *have* to watch the whole movie," she said, her voice sweet but insistent.

"I will, for sure," I promised, pulling her in for a kiss.

We moved back to the bed, where we fell into more conversation, more laughter, more kisses. I couldn't help myself as my fingers brushed gently over her lips. Her lips were soft, red, and inviting, and I couldn't look away. We lost ourselves in each other again, the room filled with nothing but the sound of our whispered words and quiet kisses. Slowly, without realizing it, we drifted off to sleep, wrapped in each other's arms.

The next morning, I woke up first. I couldn't help but smile as I kissed her gently on the forehead, my mind replaying all the beautiful moments we had shared the night before. Her sleepy smile appeared, and she wished me a soft "Good morning" with a kiss of her own.

She snuggled deeper into my arms, her head resting under my neck. It felt like she didn't want to leave the warmth of my embrace just yet. I softly ran my fingers through her hair, trying to lull her back into a little more sleep. But after a while, she sighed, knowing she had to leave. With a pout, she looked up at me and said, "I have to go," her eyes filled with the same reluctance I felt.

"Don't go yet," I whispered, holding her closer, feeling the warmth of her body against mine. "Stay a little longer."

She sighed softly, her reluctance clear in her voice. "I have to go now," she said, but the way she lingered told me otherwise.

I reached up and pressed her nose gently, trying to delay the inevitable. "Alright, let's get ready then," I said, watching her as she shifted on the bed, lifting herself so I could free my arm that had gone numb under her weight.

As she moved, I couldn't help myself. I leaned in, kissing her lips with a sudden intensity that surprised even me.

She blinked in surprise but smiled, teasing, "I think I should've sat up before you—might've avoided that *hard* kiss."

Laughing, I reached out, cupping her cheeks, and kissed them too. "Oh, no. This is just the beginning," A smile crept onto my face. "Every morning, I'm going to wake up before you, just for these kisses. They'll be *even* harder. Every single morning, for the rest of our lives."

Her smile deepened, her eyes sparkling in that way that made my heart flutter. We both got up slowly, savoring the last moments of quiet intimacy. After she freshened up, she looked radiant, even in the soft morning light.

I moved toward her, unable to resist, sliding my hand around her waist, pulling her gently to me.

She rolled her eyes with a laugh. "Oh, not this again," she said, gently pushing me away with that irresistible smile. "Come on, let's go."

I loved how she could be playful and serious at the same time, balancing her care with a sense of fun. As I picked up my bag of clothes to take to Kurukshetra, she grabbed her tiffin with a soft chuckle. We stepped out into the hallway, the cool air from the staircase brushing against our skin.

I spotted the landlord downstairs, watching us for a brief moment. My heart raced, wondering if he might ask about her, but thankfully, he just gave a polite nod as we walked past him. We reached the car, placing the bag and tiffin in the backseat, and then I drove her to her PG.

The drive was quiet, but comfortable. As we neared her place, I felt the familiar weight of goodbye hanging between us. I stopped the car, turned to her, and saw the same sadness reflected in her eyes. She leaned toward me, offering me one last kiss, her lips warm and soft against mine.

"Take care," I whispered, kissing her cheek. "I'll miss you."

She smiled, but it didn't quite reach her eyes this time. With one final wave, she stepped out of the car and disappeared behind the gates of her PG. I sat there for a moment, staring at the empty seat beside me, already missing her presence.

I changed my plan to go by car. I went to my place again to grab my bike. I was just about to leave when my nosy neighbor, a retired colonel, marched over with a scowl on his face. He launched into a rant about how I had parked my car in front of his garden the previous day, blocking his view of some flowers or something equally insignificant. I nodded along, half-listening, but my mind was elsewhere—still replaying the sweet goodbye I had just shared with Jojo.

Finally, after what felt like ages, I excused myself and rode off, eager to leave the colonel's complaints behind.

Later that evening, I shared the whole incident with Jojo over the phone. "All retired army guys are so grumpy," I joked, chuckling at the memory of my neighbor's rant about his precious garden.

There was a sudden pause on the other end of the line. Then, with a sharp but sweet tone, Jojo said, "You do know my dad's a retired army man, right? And my brother's serving too?"

"Oh My God, no!" I laughed nervously, realizing what I'd just said. "I was just saying that some of them get a bit sarcastic after retirement!" I was laughing but also kicking myself internally for not knowing about her family's background sooner. Why had I never asked her about her family before? I felt like such an idiot.

"Haan haan, I know exactly what you're saying," she said, clearly enjoying my awkward scramble to explain.

"No, no, I respect your dad!" I quickly added. "I mean... I was just talking about my neighbor. Seriously, it's just him!"

She cut me off with a lighthearted tone, "Chhodo chhodo, I get it. But just wait till you meet my dad—then you'll understand. He's very strict." She was laughing now, and her teasing made the whole situation easier to bear.

We shared a laugh, and I told her, "I'll be back by evening." She smiled through the phone and said, "I loved yesterday night with you. I can't stop thinking about it." My heart melted a little hearing her say that. "I miss you," I said softly. "I've been thinking about it too." We exchanged some more sweet words before saying goodbye, but even after hanging up, I could still feel her with me. Her hand in mine, that warm smile, her presence lingering in the air.

Later in the evening, as promised, I called her while I was on my way back to Chandigarh. She reminded me about the movie, asking me to watch it as soon as I got back. I assured her, "I promise I'll watch it tonight."

When I got to my room, I gave her a call, but she didn't pick up. I figured she was busy, so I didn't call again. Instead, I turned on my desktop and started going through the folder she had made for me with all her pictures and movies. As I scrolled through her pictures, I smiled, admiring every one of them. One picture in particular stood out, and I immediately set it as my wallpaper. Then, as I continued, I found an even more beautiful one—this became my new background.

And then, I got to *those* pictures—the ones she was trying to hide from me, the ones where she wore smaller clothes. One picture, in particular, made me pause, my lips curving into a small, admiring smile. I couldn't help but think—*this is so hot..* She was shyly covering herself with her hands, and it was adorable. I couldn't help but smile, thinking about how she'd tried to keep these hidden from me. This one was definitely going to be my wallpaper now.

As I scrolled through her photos, I found myself wanting to know more about her—her family, her life, her quirks, her favorite pastimes, the little details hidden in her world. Each picture felt like a glimpse into who she was, and I loved going through them

Finally, I moved to the folder with the movies and played the cartoon movie she had insisted I watch. I sat through the entire thing, completely engrossed. It was exactly as she described—emotional, heartwarming, adventure, and full of love. When it ended, I immediately gave her a call.

"So? Did you watch it?" she asked excitedly.

"Yes," I said. "It was lovely."

"Hmmm," she replied with satisfaction. "I love that movie. That's why I wanted you to see it."

"I'll love you just like the character in that movie," I said softly. "And I'll help fulfill all your dreams, just like he did."

"So sweet," she whispered, her voice filled with warmth.

We lingered in that sweet silence, both of us knowing that our connection, just like the movie, was filled with dreams, promises, and love.

Somehow, I couldn't get over the memories of that beautiful night we had spent together. Everything felt like heaven, and the thought of her stayed with me. I couldn't stop thinking about her—the way she smiled, the way she held my hand, and how safe and warm it felt when she was close. The urge to see her again was overwhelming.

I request her, "I miss you a lot... Can we meet again soon?"

She replied. "I'll come when I get some time, don't worry."

And so, the days passed, and finally, the next week, we managed to meet again. I was waiting for her outside her PG, feeling the excitement and anticipation bubbling inside me. To pass the time, I glanced around, just taking in the usual sights, when I noticed two girls walking on the road. One of them caught my attention—she was undeniably attractive, and the way she carried herself was impressive. Her confidence, her style, everything about her had a certain allure that made it hard not to stare.

For a brief moment, I watched her, appreciating her presence. I even found myself imagining how Jojo would look with that kind of style, maybe dressed a little differently, trying on something new. But then, I caught myself—what the hell was I doing? I shook my head, lightly smacked myself on the forehead, and reminded myself to focus on what really mattered: Jojo.

"*Jojo's on her way. No one else matters.*" I muttered under my breath with a grin.

And just like that, as if the universe was reading my thoughts, I spotted Jojo coming out of her PG. The moment I saw her, my world snapped back into focus. She was beautiful. Stunning, even. And I realized that no one, no matter how stylish or confident, could ever compare to her in my eyes.

I smiled to myself, shaking my head at the earlier distraction. "*Jojo doesn't need to be anyone else,*" I thought. "*She's perfect just as she is. I love her just the way she is.*"

She approached my car, and I quickly rolled down the window. Her eyes met mine, and she flashed me that sweet, warm smile—the one that always melted my heart. As she slid into the passenger seat, I couldn't help but say, "You're looking beautiful."

She smiled again, this time with a hint of shyness, and I handed her the usual chocolate, as was our little tradition. She looked at it, then back at me, noticing that it was slightly melted—again. But instead of saying anything, she just gave me that familiar smile, the one that said, "*Really? You did this again?*"

We didn't feel like going to any crowded places that day. We both just wanted to be alone, somewhere peaceful, so we could talk and enjoy each other's company. She suggested we stay in the car and talk, and I agreed. I drove to a quiet spot, parked, and turned off the engine.

But as we sat there, I noticed something different about her. She wasn't herself, and there was a tension between us that I couldn't ignore. Her usual energy and smile seemed dimmed, and I could tell something was on her mind.

"Jojo, what's wrong? You've been quiet." I finally asked, concerned.

At first, she shook her head, brushing it off, but I insisted, gently urging her to tell me what was bothering her. After some coaxing, she sighed, looking down at her hands. Her voice was small, almost shaky, when she finally spoke.

"It's Nikhil," she admitted, her eyes filled with uncertainty. "He called me after a long time, and... I couldn't avoid him."

Her words hit me like a slow, spreading ache, a heaviness settling deep in my chest. I felt the sting of it, the quiet pain of realizing she still hadn't completely moved on. No matter how distant he was, the fact that he still lingered in her mind hurt more than I wanted to admit. I stayed silent, swallowing the hurt, letting her continue. Even though it pained me, I knew I had to listen—to understand what still held her back.

"I didn't want to talk to him, but when I heard his voice... I don't know. I couldn't stop myself," she said, her voice breaking slightly. "And now I feel like... like I'm cheating you. But I don't know what to do."

She kept looking down, unable to meet my eyes. I could feel the weight of her guilt, the confusion she was battling inside. And as much as it hurt to hear her talk about Nikhil, I knew this wasn't easy for her either. She was torn, caught between a past she couldn't fully let go of and a present she wasn't sure how to navigate.

I sighed deeply, my heart heavy. But more than anything, I felt for her. I loved her, and I could see she was struggling. This wasn't just about me—it was about her trying to figure out her own feelings.

As I sat there listening to her, I could see the inner turmoil she was dealing with. It was clear she was struggling to open up, torn between her past with Nikhil and her present with me. I sensed her hesitation, the weight of sharing something so personal and painful. But I knew I had to let her talk. I gently moved my hand to her cheek, tilting her face slightly so our eyes could meet.

"Beta, it's okay," I whispered softly, trying to ease her mind. "You can tell me, don't worry."

She hesitated for a moment, but then, as if she needed the comfort, she leaned into me, resting her head under my neck, her hand finding its way to my shoulder. I could feel the tension in her body, the weight of the story she was about to share. She sighed, and slowly, she began to speak.

"I... he..." she started, struggling to find the words. I held her hand, giving it a reassuring squeeze, encouraging her to continue.

"Hmmm... and?" I gently prompted.

"He wasn't giving me time," she said in a rush, almost wanting to get the words out as fast as possible. "He used to talk to me so rudely. Eventually, I couldn't take it anymore, and I decided to break up with him."

"I miss him sometimes," she admitted, her voice barely a whisper. Her eyes flickered with something I couldn't quite place—regret? Longing? "But I don't want to. I don't want to miss him, and that's the worst part. It's like... my heart doesn't know what it wants. You're here, you're good to me. I feel something real with you, but I can't lie and say I don't think of him too."

She looked down, biting her lip as if trying to hold back words she wasn't sure she should say. "Maybe it's guilt... or maybe it's the memories. We had so many plans, you know? But that's the past. You're my present. I just... I need more time to sort through these feelings."

For a moment, I just sat there, letting her words sink in. My mind was racing, trying to process everything she'd just told me. A tightness spread through me, an uncomfortable mix of emotions—hurt, confusion, and that dreaded twinge of envy. She was here with me, yet part of her still seemed to cling to someone else.

I sighed softly, but I knew I couldn't let her see how much her words had affected me. I had to be the strong one right now, the understanding one. She was being honest with me, and I respected that, even if it hurt to hear. But behind my calm exterior, a whirlwind of thoughts were swirling. *"Is she really happy with me?,"* I wondered. *"Does she still love him? Why is she still thinking about him after all this time?"*

I tried to push those thoughts aside, telling myself that her happiness mattered more than my own insecurities. *"She's with me now,"* I reminded myself. *"But does she really want to be?"*

I needed clarity. I needed to know where she stood, not just for her sake, but for mine too. Relationships are built on mutual understanding and love, and I couldn't help but wonder if her heart was truly in this with me.

I asked her quietly, "Why wasn't he giving you time? Was he ignoring you? Or was he just too busy to manage time for the relationship?"

She stayed silent, staring down at her hands, clearly wrestling with her thoughts. I gently placed my hand under her chin, lifting her face so she could meet my eyes. I kissed her forehead softly, hoping to comfort her, to let her know that I was here for her, no matter what.

But instead of leaning into my embrace, she pulled back, creating distance between us. She looked down again, her voice quieter now, but more certain. "I loved him so much," she said, the pain in her voice unmistakable.

She went on to tell me the story of Nikhil, how much she cared for him, and the tragedy that struck his family. Nikhil's father had left their home one day, without a word, without a trace. No one knew where he went, or even if he was alive. The family was left in limbo, and Nikhil was forced to take over his father's failing business. He didn't know how to manage it, and the stress of it all consumed him. Every time she tried to talk to him, he pushed her away, avoiding her, drowning in his own problems.

She became sad while telling me about him. I pulled her into my arms, trying to make her feel better. I softly touched her cheek and reassured her, "Beta, he wasn't avoiding you on purpose. You weren't the problem." I paused for a moment, gathering my thoughts. "He must've been going through so much pressure. His father leaving... it wasn't easy. He wasn't just dealing with a breakup, Jojo—he was dealing with his father's disappearance, with family responsibilities, and a business he didn't know how to handle."

She stayed silent, listening carefully, her head resting against my chest.

"I'm sure he wasn't avoiding you out of choice. It was probably guilt, or even shame. When someone close to you disappears like that, it messes with you." I was surprised at how mature I sounded—where was all of this coming from? But maybe my love for her had matured me in ways I hadn't realized. "In those situations, people don't always have the energy for a relationship. He wasn't able to focus on you. He was fighting his own battles."

Jojo nodded slightly, as if absorbing what I said but still unsure of how to feel. I could tell she was conflicted. A part of her still held on to the past with him, but she was also with me now, trying to move forward.

We talked about it for over an hour, going over their relationship, the break-up, and everything in between. I kept reassuring her that what happened with Nikhil wasn't her fault. She was stuck between guilt and confusion, unsure if she had made the right decision. She kept looking into my eyes, trying to understand why I was supporting Nikhil, almost as if she expected me to be upset. But deep down, I wasn't. I understood her feelings, her conflict.

I smiled softly and wiped a tear from her cheek. "You were both on the same side in that situation," I said gently. "You were both struggling. And maybe, instead of demanding more from him at the time, you could've supported him. But we all learn from these things."

She kissed me on the cheek and placed her head under my neck, resting for a moment. It was like she was silently thanking me for understanding her. But inside, I was struggling with my own feelings. My heart ached, hearing her talk about him. I couldn't deny it—I was jealous. I was trying so hard to be the one she needed, but I could feel that part of her still belonged to him.

"Why the kiss?" I asked, trying to lighten the mood.

"For understanding me," she replied, smiling through her tears. "I was thanking you with this kiss."

I smiled back, though my heart felt heavy. She had no idea how much that honesty hurt me. But I kept my emotions locked away. This wasn't about me—it was about her, about making her feel better.

I sighed deeply, trying to hide the pain behind my smile. "You should talk to him when you get back to your PG," I suggested.

She looked at me, a bit surprised. "What about us?" she asked quietly, almost afraid of the answer.

"I'm happy if you're happy," I replied softly, though every word felt like a lie. The truth was, I didn't know if I could be happy if she was still thinking about him. But I couldn't say that—not now.

Jojo stayed silent after that, lost in her own thoughts. I could see the confusion in her eyes, the struggle between the past and the present. But I didn't push her. Instead, I held her close, hoping that one day, she'd find clarity—not just for her, but for both of us.

She said she wouldn't be able to call him, that she had no idea what she would even say to him. I suggested she could start by forwarding any simple SMS to him first—something small to break the ice. She nodded, though her expression was still filled with uncertainty. Then she asked me to drop her at her PG.

I started the car, and this time, neither of us bothered with our seat belts. She leaned her head gently on my shoulder, her hand resting on my chest, and I drove slowly, almost aimlessly. My mind was racing, a storm of thoughts swirling around. *What am I doing?* I kept asking myself. *Why am I holding on to someone who's still inclined towards another man?* But as I glanced down at her, feeling the warmth of her resting against me, I knew this wasn't the time to question everything. All I ever wanted was her happiness.

When we finally reached her PG, there was a moment of quiet before she left. Usually, I'd kiss her on the lips before saying goodbye, but this time I pressed a kiss on her hand instead. She smiled, but it was a nervous, uncertain smile, and as she stepped out of the car, she gave me a small wave. I watched her walk into the building, my eyes following her until she disappeared inside.

Back in my room, the thoughts swirled uncontrollably. I sat there, trying to process everything, but no matter how hard I tried, the same name kept echoing in my mind—*Nikhil*. The fear of losing her to him was overwhelming, so I found myself requesting God and Nikhil to leave her for me.

..

*Nikhil, Nikhil, I'm on my knees,*
*Please don't take her from me; I'm begging you, please.*
*You know your charm could win her back,*
*But I'm pleading with you, don't put me off track.*

..

*Nikhil, Nikhil, please don't take my love,*
*I know you have a pull, like the stars up above.*
*You could have anyone, but I'm asking you this,*
*Please don't take her from me, I can't bear the abyss.*

..

*I see her light up when you walk in the room,*
*And I'm fighting these feelings, drowning in gloom.*
*She talks about moments, the laughter you shared,*
*While I'm here in silence, feeling so scared.*

..

*Nikhil, Nikhil, please don't take my love,*
*I know you have a pull, like the stars up above.*
*You could have anyone, but I'm asking you this,*
*Please don't take her from me, I can't bear the abyss.*

..

*You've got your charm, I know it's a fact,*

*With just a word, you could easily attract.*
*If you truly care, just let her be,*
*She means the world to me, can't you see?*

..

*Nikhil, Nikhil, I'm here on my own,*
*I'm begging you now, please don't take her home.*
*You could have it all, but I'm asking you clear,*
*Nikhil, don't take her; I need her right here.*

..

But I knew I couldn't control what came next. All I could do was hope, and wait.

I called her the next day and asked if she had thought about it. She sounded more nervous and confused than ever, her voice tinged with sadness.

"I just need some time," she said quietly.

"Take all the time you need," I reassured her, trying to sound calm and understanding, even though my heart was aching. "Whatever decision you make, I'll be with you."

But deep down, I knew I had to give her space. This was a life-altering decision, one that couldn't be rushed—not even for me. She needed time to clear her head and think about what she truly wanted, and I had to be patient, even though every passing moment felt like a lifetime.

For two days, we let the heavy conversations rest. We didn't talk about Nikhil or the confusing emotions surrounding our relationship. Instead, we were just us—laughing, flirting, sharing small, romantic moments like before. It felt good, and for a while, it was as if nothing had changed. Then, one evening, she finally told me that she wanted to be with me, not Nikhil. She said it with a certain softness, but there was conviction in her voice. It wasn't just words, and although part of me still hesitated to fully believe, the larger part of my heart relaxed. I wanted to trust her, to believe in us, and in that moment, I chose to.

I smiled, feeling that weight lift off my shoulders. "Everything will be fine with time. Just be with me," I said, hoping those words would push away any lingering doubts.

That evening, I asked her to meet me, and she agreed. I felt like a kid, eager, anxious, and full of excitement. I got ready early, put on a fragrance that I hoped she'd find irresistible—something with a touch of playfulness and just a bit seductive. I was already imagining our evening together, and honestly, I was imagining a whole life together. Visions of a future flashed before my mind: us being together, her laugh filling the house, two little kids running around—crazy, innocent daydreams. I smiled at the thought and felt so content that I accidentally dozed off in the car, sitting outside her PG.

Suddenly, there was a soft knock on the window. I jumped, startled, and saw her smiling through the glass, her face lighting up the evening. I rolled the window down, and before I could say anything, she stepped into the car and wrapped her arms around me in a warm hug. This hug—it was different. It felt more certain, more comforting. I didn't want to let go. I could have stayed in that moment forever.

She laughed, teasing me, "Ohh Hoo, enough hugging for now! We can't stand here forever—someone from my PG might see us!" She smacked my shoulder.

I chuckled, reluctantly releasing her from my arms, but not before cupping her cheek and giving her nose a soft press. "Okay, okay," I said, smiling as I finally let her go. She gently pushed against my chest, telling me with her eyes that she was ready to leave.

As we drove away from her PG, she asked, "So, what did you do today?"

I grinned. "I watched the WWE Special Event on YouTube."

She rolled her eyes dramatically. "WWE again? Don't you like anything else?" she asked, half-joking, as if the idea of my skinny self being a fan of wrestling was some kind of paradox.

"I like you, but unfortunately, you're not on any TV channel," I quipped, glancing over at her with a smile.

She fixed me with a half-serious glare. "Hmmm."

We laughed, and then I remembered something. "Oh, I saw this WWE t-shirt of C.M. Punk online today. I really like his stuff. His t-shirts are cool."

"Then buy the t-shirt!" she said, as if it were the most obvious solution in the world.

"I tried a lot, but I couldn't find it. Not even on any online shopping website," I replied, feeling a bit disappointed.

"Why don't you try in Sector 22 market?" she suggested.

"Hmm, can we go now?" I asked, feeling hopeful.

"Yes, no problem, we can go now," she said, her eyes lighting up with interest. We had talked about going shopping together before, and it seemed like the perfect chance to explore the market.

As I started driving towards Sector 22, I asked, "Have you ever been there before?"

"No, but I've heard about it. People say you can get stuff at cheaper rates," she replied.

"Yes, but the quality can be hit or miss," I said. "Women usually find better stuff there. For men, though? Not so much. Sector 22 is like a ladies' paradise—dresses, jewelry, shoes everywhere. It's total chaos for guys, but for my girl, all is fine with me." I smiled, knowing I would endure anything if it meant seeing her happy.

While driving, I placed her hand on the gear shift and then rested my hand gently on hers. I couldn't help but glance at her every few seconds. She was wearing a hairband today, one of those simple but cute ones that made her look even more adorable. I always loved when she wore them because it made her look like a little girl, full of innocence and charm. Sometimes, she would wear butterfly or Barbie doll-shaped hair clips, and they suited her so perfectly. That playful, childlike side of her only made her more beautiful in my eyes.

"Look at the road!" she said, smiling as she gently scolded me.

I chuckled, deciding to tease her a bit. I left the steering wheel for a moment, leaning slightly towards her, pretending to lose focus.

She immediately pushed me back, her eyes widening in mock horror. "Are you crazy? Focus on the road!" she shouted, though I could see the amusement in her eyes. She knew I was just messing around, but still, she wanted to make sure I didn't push my joke too far.

"You are mad!" she said, hitting my arm gently.

I laughed. "Oh, wait. I forgot to give you the chocolate," I said, reaching into my pocket and pulling out the treat, hoping it hadn't melted this time.

She took it from my hand, inspecting it with a smile. "Thank God! It's not melted this time," she said, laughing as she unwrapped it.

As she fed me a piece, I couldn't help but think that these were the little moments that made everything worth it—the small jokes, these laughter, the way she looked at me with those twinkling eyes. Moments like these, even in the midst of an ordinary drive, felt like magic.

After about 20 minutes, we arrived at Sector 22 market, the energy of the place buzzing around us with the usual evening crowd. I spotted a decent parking spot and slowly maneuvered the car in. As I parked, I turned to her. "Hey, be careful when you open the window. It's a tight squeeze here—don't want to hit the car next to us."

She gave me a mock serious look, but I could tell she was amused. Slowly and deliberately, she cracked open the window like it was some high-stakes operation. As she stepped out, she flashed me a teasing smile, clearly proud of herself for following my 'instructions' so perfectly.

I got out too, and as we met at the front of the car, our hands found each other naturally, fingers lacing together like they always belonged that way. There was something about the simplicity of that gesture, the warmth of her hand in mine, that made everything feel right.

"This is Sector 22," I said, gesturing to the bustling maze of shops and stalls ahead. "Nothing fancy, but people swear by the bargains here."

She looked around, taking in the chaos, the lights, and the mix of vendors hawking everything from clothes to accessories. "So, where do we start?" she asked, her eyes flicking between the different stalls.

"Anywhere," I said with a shrug, pointing towards a way that looked promising. "They're all sort of mixed together. Let's just dive in."

We wandered through the narrow lanes, sidestepping other shoppers and dodging motorbikes that seemed to appear out of nowhere. Every now and then, I'd glance at her, hoping she'd spot something she liked. "If you see anything for yourself, just say the word," I offered again.

She shook her head, smiling softly. "I'm good. I don't need anything."

"Seriously though," I pressed, slipping my arm around her waist as we strolled. "If something catches your eye, let me know. We will buy it."

She just smiled again, nodding in that way she does when she's both amused and a little shy. But, in truth, neither of us found much worth buying. The t-shirts I wanted weren't there, and even though she didn't say it, I could tell she wasn't impressed with the quality of most of the clothes.

As we walked through one of the narrower alleyways, a group of guys approached us from the opposite direction. I felt her grip on my arm tighten, and without thinking, I pulled her closer, wrapping my arm around her shoulders protectively. "It's alright," I whispered, gently guiding her past the group. She didn't say anything, but I felt her relax, a subtle shift in her body language, trusting me to shield her.

After what felt like hours of browsing and searching, we decided to call it a day. "Not a great day for shopping," I chuckled, trying to lighten the mood. She nodded, looking a little tired, but still content.

As we headed back to the car, we passed a gol-gappe vendor. My eyes lit up immediately. "Gol-gappe?" I asked, trying to hide the excitement in my voice.

She smiled but shook her head. "Not today, I'm not in the mood."

I feigned disappointment but let it go, not wanting to push her. Instead, we made our way to the parking lot. Once we were both inside the car, the energy between us shifted. The world outside—the noise, the crowd—seemed far away, leaving just the two of us in our own little space.

I reached over, placing my hand on her arm, tracing small circles with my thumb. She leaned in without hesitation, resting her head on my shoulder.

I brushed a strand of hair away from her face, tucking it behind her ear. My fingers lingered there for a second longer, grazing her skin before I leaned in and pressed a soft kiss to her cheek. Her eyes fluttered closed, and she smiled—a real, genuine smile that warmed my heart.

For a second, I just watched her, taking in the way her face softened in the dim light. Then she opened her eyes and looked up at me. "You're sweet, you know that?" she whispered.

"I know," I said, teasing, but my voice was soft too.

She laughed and gave me a light nudge. "Don't get too full of yourself."

Then I moved my hand to her waist, gently pulling her closer towards me, and kissed her lips. In that moment, it felt like we were lost in our own world, as if nothing else existed but the two of us. The connection was deep, magnetic, and for a brief moment, it was like time had stopped.

Suddenly, a loud honk from a nearby car snapped us back to reality. We opened our eyes, smiled at each other, and reluctantly parted our lips. She bit her lip and smiled, "You better start the car now."

I smiled, shifted back into the driver's seat, and started the car. As I drove, she leaned her head softly onto my shoulder, making herself comfortable. She reached out and placed her hand on mine over the gear, her fingers intertwining with mine. I was driving slowly, almost savoring every second of this intimate moment.

Then, my phone buzzed in my pocket. I pulled over to the side of the road to answer the call. It was Ankur, one of my close friends.

"Hey bro, what's up? You up for some drinks tonight? We can meet at your room," he said casually.

"Yeah, sure," I replied, not thinking too much about it. "I'll grab some ice, cold drinks, and snacks on my way."

After wrapping up the call, I slipped my phone back into my pocket.

"So, are you going to drink tonight?" she asked, a little curious but sounding indifferent.

I mumbled, "Hmmm."

"Do you drink often?" she asked, her tone now a little more inquisitive.

"Not really," I said quickly, trying to reassure her. "Just occasionally, when I'm with my friends."

She didn't seem bothered at all, smiling softly as she rested her head back on my shoulder. "It's okay, I don't mind." She paused for a moment, then added, "I've never had a drink before."

There was a brief silence, then she casually dropped, "I want to try it sometime."

I glanced at her, surprised. "Now?"

She chuckled and shook her head, "Not now, silly. But someday... I want to know what it's like."

I laughed lightly, then I turned a little serious. "I'll kill you if you ever do that," I said but with an edge of protectiveness.

She pouted a little, pretending to be offended. "But I want to try," she said softly, as if testing my reaction.

I sighed, pretending to be stern, "No. Absolutely not."

"If you don't let me, I'll just drink with my other friends," she teased, flashing me a mischievous grin.

I shot her a dramatic look, raising my hand to my chest like I'd been wounded. "Other friends? Who are these so-called friends? I need names and addresses. No one's allowed to steal my drinking buddy."

She giggled, but I couldn't help feeling protective. "Just promise me you won't go all 'party animal' without me. I've seen what happens when people lose their minds after a drink."

She smiled, resting her head back on my shoulder. "Don't worry. I'll save my wild side just for you."

We kept talking about her wish to drink with me, but somewhere in the midst of the conversation, we didn't realize that we had already reached her PG. As always, the thought of parting from her left me with that familiar ache of separation. But, as usual, she knew exactly how to soothe me. She leaned in and gave me a soft, sweet kiss—her way of saying everything would be okay. With a wave goodbye, she stepped out of the car.

I drove back home, trying to push aside the heaviness of leaving her behind. Later, after Ankur and I had finished a couple of drinks at my place, I gave her a call. We talked like we always did, catching up on the day, sharing small moments.

"I just got the new ID cards for all the employees today," I mentioned casually. "I'll be distributing them tomorrow."

"Oh really?" she said. I could hear the smile in her voice.

"I'm in your shift tomorrow. So, when it's your turn, I'm calling you as Jojo—not Jolene—in front of everyone," I said, casually hinting at my plan.

"No, please!" she almost panicked. "Girls already talk a lot about us, about you and me. If you call me Jojo in front of everyone, they'll gossip even more."

I watched her reaction, amused by how easily she got flustered. "Nope, I'm definitely calling you Jojo," I said playfully, enjoying her reaction.

She was genuinely serious and nervous now. "Please, don't. I mean it."

We continued talking for a while, but every now and then, she'd circle back to her sweet plea, reminding me not to use her nickname. I kept playing with her, though, teasing her right up until the end of our call, where I cheekily assured her that I had made up my mind.

The next day, I was in the office, distributing the ID cards. The floor was busy, but my voice boomed out loud and clear as I called out names one by one, making sure my voice reached even the farthest corners of the room.

While handing out the cards, I caught her eye across the room. She was watching me with that nervous expression, probably wondering if I'd actually go through with my teasing. I gave her a look, raising my eyebrows as if to say, *Get ready, I'm calling you Jojo.* Her face immediately filled with concern, her lips pressing into an anxious smile.

I couldn't help but chuckle. I kept her card aside, saving it for last just to keep her on edge a little longer. With every name I called, I could see her fidgeting, clearly unsure whether or not I'd actually do it.

When there were only a few cards left, she couldn't take it anymore. She hurried over to me, her expression pleading but polite.

"Sir, my ID card," she said, almost in a whisper, trying to avoid any unwanted attention.

I looked at her for a second, pretending to consider it. Then I handed her the card, resisting the temptation to call her Jojo.

When she saw her ID card, her face immediately fell. She held up the card, examining it closely, and then made a sad, disappointed expression.

Later, she came to my desk and said, "Look at this picture! It's so black," she complained, her frustration evident. "I don't want it."

I couldn't help but burst out laughing when I saw the photo. It was true—while she was fair and beautiful, the picture on the card was horribly underexposed. It didn't do her justice at all.

"Stop laughing!" she said, her voice rising in mock annoyance. "I *really* don't want this ID card."

But the more I looked at it, the funnier it seemed, and I couldn't contain my laughter. I tried to cover my mouth, but the whole situation was too hilarious.

She looked around the office, clearly tempted to hit me, but we were at work, and she restrained herself. Instead, she glared at me.

"It's okay, guddu," I said between laughs. "When we make new ID cards, I'll personally make sure to get a better picture for you. I promise. But please, just take this one for now."

"No," she protested, her forehead creasing in frustration. "All the girls were laughing at me because of this picture. It looks like it was taken with an ancient webcam! I look so dark." She crossed her arms, refusing to budge.

I took a deep breath to compose myself, then said more seriously, "Beta, I swear, when the new cards are made, we'll use your favorite picture. A proper one this time. But for now, just take this one. Please?"

She hesitated for a moment, still clearly unhappy with the card. But eventually, she relented, grabbing the ID from my hand with a sad pout. "Fine," she said, "but I'm not wearing it around my neck! And you better not ask me to wear it either, like you always do with everyone else."

"Okay, okay, I promise," I said, still laughing. "You can keep it in your pocket. Now please, go to your seat. The girls are watching us."

She rolled her eyes and headed back to her desk, still looking a bit sulky, but I could tell she was mostly over it.

Later that evening, she gave me a call.

"I have to ask," I said. "Why did you come up yourself to get the card? Why didn't you wait for me to call your name?"

There was a pause before she responded with a cheeky grin in her voice, "I couldn't trust you! I just knew you'd call me Jojo in front of everyone, so I came before you could embarrass me."

I chuckled softly, shaking my head. "You know me too well, huh?"

"Always," she replied, her voice light, and I could practically hear her smile over the phone.

She told me that girls in her PG often talked about us. They had seen her getting into my car a few times, and she didn't like the unnecessary attention it brought. I could sense the discomfort in her voice.

"I hate when they talk about us like that," she said. "I don't want them gossiping or thinking wrong things."

I tried to calm her down, offering the usual advice, "Don't worry about them, just ignore it. People always talk, but that doesn't mean it matters."

"I know," she sighed. "But it still bothers me sometimes."

The conversation shifted as I told her I had some urgent work at my hometown in Kurukshetra and needed to go there the next day. She sounded disappointed, but she understood. I reassured her it wouldn't take long and I'd be back by evening.

The next day, after finishing work in my hometown, while driving back to Chandigarh, Jojo called and asked where I was.

"I'm looking for an ATM. I don't have cash for the toll," I admitted, feeling a little embarrassed.
She laughed warmly. "You don't even have Rs. 30? You really need to start carrying cash!"

Her laughter made me smile, despite the situation. Before hanging up, she softened, "Call me when you get home. I miss you. And seriously, keep some cash on you," she added, scolding me gently, but with a lot of love in her voice.

"Miss you too," I replied, feeling the warmth in her voice linger as I stepped inside the small room to finally get the cash.

I withdrew the cash and left the ATM, feeling slightly relieved. As I made my way back to the car, I told Jojo I'd have to hang up since I was about to drive. After paying the toll and heading back toward Chandigarh, my mind was preoccupied with one thought: I needed to see her. The moment I got back, I called her, eager to meet. But to my disappointment, she apologized, her voice tinged with genuine regret, explaining that her schedule was packed, and she couldn't meet me. I sighed but tried to hide my disappointment, telling her it was okay, even though I really wanted to be with her.

The days passed, and out of the blue, she called again, this time asking if we could meet. I was at my friend's place, glued to the TV, watching the IPL final—the climax of weeks of cricket, an unmissable match for any fan. But when Jojo said she was feeling down and wanted to talk, I didn't hesitate. The match could wait. She was more important, always.

I chuckled to myself, shaking my head. But there was no resentment in that memory—just a reminder of how relationships worked. I told her I'd be there in a few minutes and said goodbye to my friends. Their teasing was inevitable as I stood up to leave, but I didn't care. I had more important things on my mind.

I rushed home, went through the usual routine—got freshened up, put on a clean shirt, sprayed her favorite fragrance, and grabbed my car keys. But my mind was racing, wondering what was bothering her. As I made my way to the car, I noticed it was covered in a layer of dust. The cleaner hadn't shown up for two days, and the car looked like it had been through a storm. I sighed, knowing I didn't have time to worry about it. I got in and texted her as I drove, letting her know I was on my way.

When I finally pulled up near her PG, I sent another message, telling her I had arrived. A few moments later, I saw her coming toward me, and I couldn't help but pause for a second. She was wearing a brown shirt, and her hair was styled differently than usual. She looked stunning—no, *hot*. I found myself staring for a second longer than I should have.

She opened the door and slipped into the passenger seat, her usual sweet fragrance filling the car. It was intoxicating in the best way possible, and my mind immediately started wandering, fighting the urge to let those thoughts take over. I had to keep myself in check. With a gentle smile, I reached over and touched her cheek softly, offering my usual compliment. "You're looking beautiful today."

She smiled, her eyes twinkling slightly, but her reply came with that familiar teasing tone, "I always look beautiful to you, don't I?"

"Because I love you," I said.

"Let's get out of here before someone sees us together," she urged, her voice quiet but tense.

I started the car and asked where she wanted to go. She shrugged, saying she just wanted to spend time with me, that anywhere was fine.

I handed her the chocolate I'd brought. Of course, it was melted—again. *Great job,* I thought, silently laughing at myself. She looked at me as she unwrapped it, her eyes soft but searching, while I avoided her gaze, smiling awkwardly. It was always the same story. She never asked me to bring chocolate, yet whenever I did, I somehow managed to mess it up. Still, she smiled at me as she took the sticky mess in her hands. That's what I loved about her—no complaints, no irritation, just that sweet smile of hers, accepting it in any condition.

We drove on for a while in silence. Eventually, I glanced over and asked, "What's bothering you?"

Her face tightened, and after a moment, she said, "Nikhil called. He wants to meet up. He's been pushing me about it."

I could see how much it upset her, how hard she was trying to shake him off. *Here we go again,* I thought *"saala meri romantic movie me yeh zaroor aata hai?"* Still, all I wanted was for Jojo to be happy, no matter what that meant.

"Dekhlo yaar, jo apko thik lagta hai," I said, keeping my voice calm, though a tension was building inside me. A part of me suspected that maybe she wasn't happy with me anymore, so I thought it was better to let her go if that's what she needed. I added. "You two should talk things out."

Her expression grew serious. "There's something I haven't told you."

My heart skipped a beat. "What is it?"

She hesitated, then spoke, her words sharp in my ears. "When I came back to Chandigarh from my hometown, and you called me to pick me up at ISBT... I told you a friend had already come to get me. That was Nikhil. I was with him that day."

It hit me hard, like a cold wave crashing over my thoughts. But I forced myself to stay calm, to hide the possessiveness burning beneath the surface.

I swallowed my feelings and, as gently as I could, said, "It's okay. Look, if you still have feelings for him, you should go. Don't lie to yourself, and don't lie to me. Don't put three lives on the line just because of pride. Let go of your ego and go to him if that's what you want. I know... I know you still love him."

She looked at me, her eyes filled with uncertainty. "What about you?" she asked quietly.

"I believe I have no right to your love," I said quietly, my voice barely rising above the hum of the engine. "Because it's already spoken for, and we both know first love always holds priority."

"I'm still in love with him," she admitted, her words raw and unfiltered. "But I don't want him in my life anymore. I want to be with you... but I've failed to love you with the intensity you deserve." Her eyes softened as she spoke, but there was an unshakable sadness in them. "I don't want to talk about this anymore."

Her confession left me in uncharted territory, a place where I didn't quite know how to navigate. I held her hands gently, trying to steady the tremor of uncertainty in my chest.

"Do whatever feels right to you," I said softly, squeezing her hands just enough for her to feel my sincerity. "But don't make any decisions that will hurt us both. Don't stay confused—make a firm choice."

I asked her what she wanted to eat.

She murmured a faint, "Anything,"

I sighed, realizing that her mind was still elsewhere, tangled in thoughts of Nikhil and me.

We let the conversation drift away after that, like the way loose threads untangle when you stop pulling on them. By the time we reached Sector 35, the mood had lightened; she seemed calmer, at least on the surface.

The streets were clogged with traffic, and my car wasn't running smoothly. Each jerk of the engine only added to the frustration building in me. But it wasn't just the car—it was everything. Her confession still weighed heavily on my mind, and no matter how hard I tried, I couldn't find peace. The thought of Nikhil lingered, gnawing at me, and I gripped the steering wheel tighter, feeling the tension between us simmer just beneath the surface.

"Come on, run properly, you idiot!" I snapped, hitting the steering wheel as if that would somehow help.

"You used to love your car," she said gently, noticing my frustration. "Now look at you, yelling at it. Very bad."

"It's not running efficiently," I muttered, trying to justify my irritation.

"Yes, yes, I know," she said with a smirk, clearly enjoying this.

"You can see for yourself how it's acting up," I grumbled.

She leaned back in her seat, clearly relishing the chance to rag on me. "Say sorry to the car," she demanded, barely stifling a laugh.

I chuckled. "Okay, fine. Sorry."

She wasn't done. "Say it humbly."

I couldn't help but laugh again, and for her sake, I exaggerated my apology. "Alright, sorry, dear car. I beg your forgiveness."

Her face lit up with triumph, her laughter ringing through the car.

"You're still using this phone?" she asked, glancing at my old mobile lying on the dashboard.

"I'll get a new one soon," I said, brushing it off with a smile.

We entered the market, but most of the shops were closed since it was Sunday. As we wandered through, I spotted an ice-cream corner and turned to her. "How about some ice cream?"

She nodded and gestured for me to park. "Let's get some."

We stepped into Baskin Robbins and scanned the display of flavors. I picked two scoops in a cone, while she opted for a wide cone, filled with a mix of her favorites.

Outside, we started on our ice creams, enjoying the cool, creamy sweetness as we strolled around. A group of people had gathered near a TV showroom, eyes fixed on a big screen hanging from the second floor, watching a cricket match. We decided to join them, leaning casually against a parked car as we savored our cones.

"Here, try mine," she said, holding her cone out to me. "It's so good."

I took a bite. It was delicious, but when I offered her mine, she wrinkled her nose. "No thanks, yours isn't as good as mine," she said, mocking me.

We stood there for a while, chatting between bites, enjoying the relaxed atmosphere. When we were done, I asked, "Ready for dinner?"

She nodded. "Yeah, I'm getting hungry."

I took the napkin and spoon from her, tossing them into the nearest dustbin. As I headed back to the car, I unlocked it with the remote and called out, "You can get inside."

We moved from there and headed to a nearby restaurant for dinner. Once inside, we decided to sit in the basement. All the tables were full, so we waited for a bit, chatting about my cousins and our families until a waiter came over and led us to a newly available table.

We settled into our chairs, and I slid the menu over to her. "You pick," I said, but we both ended up staring at it, unsure of what to order. After a few minutes of indecision, she finally made a choice, and we handed the menu back to the waiter.

We fell into a comfortable silence for a while, just enjoying the moment.

Then I leaned in closer and whispered, "Your shirt... one of the buttons is open."

She glanced down quickly, then looked back up at me, cheeks flushing slightly. "I can't button it here," she said quietly. "People will see. I'll do it in the car."

I couldn't help but smile.

"Stop smiling," she said, trying to suppress a grin of her own.

I leaned back in my chair, teasing her. "Why button it in the car?" I murmured, letting my gaze linger. "I was thinking we could just open the rest."

She hit me lightly on the arm, then darted her eyes around the restaurant, trying to hold back a laugh. Her lips curled into that mischievous smile I loved, and she kept glancing everywhere but at me.

Our eyes met again, but before we could say anything, the waiter arrived with our food. We each took a bite, then exchanged a look. The food was bad—worse than we'd expected from such a well-known restaurant—but we were hungry, so we made the best of it, finishing what we could.

"Thanks for ruining my date," I wanted to say to the manager, but instead, I just sighed. For such a popular spot, the food had been a major disappointment.

Once we stepped outside into the parking lot, we stood by the car, laughing about the food. "Do you want to get something else?" I asked, hoping to make up for the terrible dinner.

She shook her head. "I'm full. Let's just head back to my PG."

As we stood there, I couldn't resist reminding her. "Hey, don't forget about your button."

She glanced down, suddenly remembering, and gave me a shy smile as she quickly buttoned her shirt. She was avoiding my eyes, her fingers fidgeting with her hair, which I knew meant she was feeling shy. It was adorable.

I smiled back, stepping closer. Gently, I placed a hand on her waist and pulled her into a hug. Her body relaxed against mine for a moment, then she pulled away, still smiling but a little embarrassed.

"Let's go now," she whispered, her voice soft and a little breathless.

We got back into the car and headed toward her PG. The conversation drifted back to Nikhil, but she quickly shut it down. Neither of us wanted to go down that road again.

I pulled the car to the side of the road, turning off the engine. Without saying a word, I unfastened her seatbelt and gently pulled her toward me. She leaned in, resting her face against my neck, her breath warm against my skin. I tilted her face up and kissed her softly, my hand slipping under her neck. Our lips seemed to linger, unwilling to part.

Slowly, I moved my hand down, undoing the first button of her shirt. Then the second. With each touch, her skin warmed under my fingers, sending a rush of excitement through me. I kissed her neck deeply, feeling her heartbeat quicken. Her breathing grew slow but heavy, filling the quiet of the car. She wrapped her arms around my neck, pulling me closer, her hands running through my hair. She wanted more, and so did I.

I slid my hands down her waist, pulling her gently onto my lap. Time seemed to blur as we lost ourselves in each other, every kiss deeper than the last. We were both caught in the moment, in the intensity of our need for each other.

But then, she whispered, her voice soft and reluctant, "I'm getting late... the gate will close. Please, I have to go."

I kissed her neck again, not ready to let her leave. "Stay with me tonight."

"Not tonight, please... let's go now." Her voice was soft, reluctant, almost as if she was torn between her words and what she truly wanted. I could feel the weight of it—she wanted to stay, but she had to go.

"One last kiss?" I asked, my voice a whisper, hoping to hold onto the moment just a little longer.

She leaned in, and our lips met again, slow and warm. It wasn't about passion or desire now—it was about the things we couldn't bring ourselves to say out loud. It lingered, full of tenderness, like the final breath before goodbye. I could feel her reluctance in the way her hands softly gripped me, neither of us wanting to let go.

But against both our wishes, I had to drop her off. We drove the short distance to her PG, the car silent except for the quiet hum of the engine and the echo of that last kiss still hanging between us.

When we arrived, she turned to me, a sad smile on her lips. We shared one final hug, her arms wrapping around me in a way that made me feel like maybe, just maybe, things could stay the same. I touched her cheek gently, feeling the warmth of her skin beneath my fingers, and I smiled softly as she turned away, walking toward the entrance of her PG. The moment felt heavy, as if something was slipping through my grasp.

I watched until she disappeared inside. Then, with a sigh, I drove back to my room, the silence of the night wrapping around me. I lay down on my bed, staring at the ceiling, still feeling the imprint of her touch, her warmth.

# CHAPTER II

# When It All Faded

I never imagined that the kiss we shared would be our last. That night felt so full of promise, so full of everything we'd built together. But now, looking back, it feels more like a final chapter—one I didn't know I was writing. I didn't know that the love she gave me was already gone.

It's strange, isn't it? How people change. How feelings change. One day, someone is everything, your whole world wrapped up in a single person, and the next, they're a stranger, slipping away right before your eyes. It's something we all know can happen, but we never believe it will happen to us. Maybe it's natural. People evolve. What we love one day, we might lose the next. Our hearts are never as steady as we think.

That's what happened to her. Somewhere along the way, her feelings for me changed. Maybe it was slow—too subtle for me to notice at first—or maybe it was all at once, but either way, her love had already faded, and I was left in the dark.

The next day, I called her. Of course, I did. I wanted to hear her voice again, to see if she felt the same ache, the same pull toward me. But she didn't pick up. No big deal, I thought. Maybe she's busy. I sent a message—a simple "Hey" to let her know I was thinking of her. But no reply.

Still, I didn't worry. People get caught up in their day. They forget to respond. It happens. But by the second day, I couldn't shake the feeling that something was wrong. I missed her, missed the way things used to feel so easy between us. So, I scrolled to her name in my contact list, stared at it for a few seconds, then called again. It rang. And rang. And rang. But no one picked up.

I texted again. Just to be sure. *Are you okay?* Simple. Concerned. I thought maybe something was up. Maybe she wasn't feeling well, or maybe there was something on her mind.

But there was no reply.

I started to worry. We were in different shifts at work, so I couldn't just see her or ask her directly what was going on. Instead, I did the only thing I could think of: I checked her attendance at work. I needed to know if she was okay, if she was still... there. To my relief, her name was marked as present.

She was fine.

So why wasn't she responding? The knot in my chest started to grow tighter. I reassured myself. *She's busy. She'll get back to you when she can.* But that small doubt had already taken root, creeping into my mind, whispering that something wasn't right. The silence was starting to suffocate me.

A few more days passed. The calls went unanswered. My messages left unread. No matter how many times I checked my phone, hoping to see her name pop up, it never did. Each passing day felt heavier than the last, like a weight slowly pressing down on me. A week went by, and nothing. Not a single response.

I was breathing, but I felt hollow, like a light had gone out inside me. My face in the mirror looked faded, the faint glow I once had now just a memory.

Now, I couldn't ignore it. Something had changed, and I had no idea why. My mind raced with every possible scenario, each worse than the one before. *Had she gone back to Nikhil?* The thought gnawed at me, twisting my gut in knots. *Was there something I did wrong?* I replayed our last moments together over and over in my mind, searching for some clue, some mistake I'd made. *Or maybe there was a misunderstanding,* I thought, clinging to the hope that we could still fix things if we just talked.

But the silence didn't end.

Night after night, I lay awake, staring at the ceiling, my mind chasing answers I would never find. I couldn't escape the sense of dread that had settled into my bones. *What a fool I've been,* I thought. *How could I have let myself fall so hard, so fast?* But no matter how much I tried to rationalize it, the pain didn't go away. The worst part wasn't even the silence—it was the uncertainty. Not knowing why. Not knowing what went wrong. It was torture.

A thought crossed my mind: should I reach out to our Preeti, see if she knew what happened? Maybe she'd have answers, something that could explain this endless silence. But I shoved the idea aside almost as quickly as it came. It felt wrong—like opening the door to drama, or worse, setting myself up for an insult I wasn't ready to hear. And what if it made things messy for her too? I couldn't bring myself to risk it.

*Saala, baat kya hai?* I cursed myself, running over every possibility in my head. *Did I push too hard? Did her feelings for me just... change? Or am I just being paranoid?* But as the days stretched into what felt like an eternity, one thing became clear: she was avoiding me.

I remembered a conversation we'd once had, her voice steady as she told me how much she understood my fear of being shut out, how she would never put me through that. She'd looked right at me, her gaze unwavering, and said, *"This will never happen."* I'd believed her, let those words sink deep, like a promise I could rely on. And yet, here I was, left with nothing but that same silence she once promised I'd never feel.

My friends noticed the change. They told me I looked like a ghost, like I hadn't slept in days. And the truth was, I hadn't. Every night I was haunted by the same questions, the same thoughts of her, of us, of what we were and what we were becoming. The charm I used to carry, the spark that made me feel alive, was gone. I was fading, and everyone could see it.

Finally, I couldn't take it anymore. I sent her a long message, one that I hoped would get through to her:

*Please don't avoid me. I asked you before—don't ever ignore me, no matter what. If you want to leave me, just tell me. I'll understand, but please... talk to me. If there's a misunderstanding, we can fix it. But this silence? This avoidance? It's driving me insane. Please, just let me know.*

I sent the message and waited.

And waited.

Nothing.

No reply. No call. Just the same empty silence that had been slowly eating away at me for days.

I called her again. And again. I lost track of how many times I hit dial, how many times I listened to the phone ring with no answer. I kept telling myself, *Maybe this time she'll pick up. Maybe this time I'll hear her voice.* But every time, my hope was met with the same hollow void.

Eventually, my worry started to turn into something darker. I was angry now. Angry at her for leaving me in this limbo, for making me feel like I'd been used, like I didn't matter. How could she just disappear like this, without a word, without any explanation? I couldn't make sense of it. I didn't know what to do with all the hurt, so I let it turn into frustration, into rage.

The messages I sent started to reflect that anger. The words were sharper, more desperate, tinged with bitterness. I couldn't stop myself. I needed an answer, even if it was one I didn't want to hear. But the longer she stayed silent, the more I felt like I was shouting into the void.

I was unraveling. I could feel it.

Finally, after what felt like an eternity of silence, she called.

Her voice was colder than I remembered. "I need some time," she said, without preamble. "I want to be alone for a few days. I'll call you after that. But stop sending me those messages—they're just making me angry. That's why I'm not responding."

And with that, she hung up.

I stared at the phone in disbelief, the dial tone ringing in my ears. Her words echoed in my head, but none of them made sense. *Some time?* Time for what? Why had she shut me out like that for days without a single explanation? If she was upset, why hadn't she told me earlier? If she was avoiding me, why wouldn't she just tell me the reason? The coldness in her voice lingered long after the call had ended, turning over and over in my mind, refusing to let me rest.

I had so many questions, so many things I wanted to say. Concerns, confusions, words that had been piling up inside me. But the chill in her voice cut through all of it, leaving me silent. It was as if the sharp edge of her tone had taken away my right to ask anything at all.

*Fine*, I told myself. I'd give her space. As much as it hurt, I thought maybe that was what she needed. I wouldn't message her. I wouldn't call her. I'd do what she asked—wait. But waiting felt like torture. Each passing minute stretched into an hour, and each day felt like a week. My mind wouldn't stop racing. I was trapped in this anxious limbo, second-guessing everything.

Three days passed. Then four.

By the fifth day, I couldn't hold back any longer. The silence was gnawing at me, the uncertainty consuming every waking moment. I caved, sending her a simple message: *What's wrong? Why won't you just tell me what's happening?* I stared at the screen for what felt like forever, hoping for a reply, any kind of response.

But there was nothing.

Again.

I threw my phone across the room, watching it bounce on the floor with a dull thud. A heavy feeling settled within me, my pulse racing. The not knowing—the total absence of any real explanation—it was like a weight I couldn't lift, crushing me from the inside. My emotions were a tangled mess—anger, frustration, fear, and love all colliding in a chaotic swirl.

I sent her message after message, trying to capture all the different emotions flooding through me. One moment I was pleading with her, asking for some kind of clarity, for a chance to talk things through. The next, I was furious, demanding to know why she was ignoring me, why she was doing this to me. And in the midst of it all, I sent messages telling her how much I still cared, how worried I was, how I didn't want to lose her. But each message fell into the same void. No reply. Just silence. Endless, unbearable silence.

I tried to focus on work, but it was impossible. My mind wasn't in the office—it was with her, replaying every conversation, every text, every memory. I couldn't concentrate on anything. She was all I could think about. It felt like my whole world had come to a standstill, like nothing mattered if I couldn't fix this.

I kept calling, desperate for her to pick up, desperate for any sign that she still cared. And finally, after what felt like an eternity, she answered.

"What happened? Why won't you talk to me?" I snapped, my voice tinged with frustration and hurt. "Is it Nikhil? Are you with him now?" The question came out more harshly than I intended, but I couldn't help it—the thought had been eating away at me for days.

Her voice, when she spoke, was flat. Emotionless. "I don't want to talk. I don't want you or Nikhil. I don't want anything."

Before I could respond, she hung up again.

I stared at the phone, the words echoing in my head: *I don't want you or Nikhil.*

And there it was—the final blow. The confirmation of what I had been dreading all along. I had lost her. There was no saving us now. No fixing whatever had gone wrong. It was over.

I was dumped.

The realization hit me like a wave, sudden and overwhelming. A heavy pressure built up inside me, my breathing turning shallow. The pain surged up inside me, unstoppable, like a dam that had finally broken. I couldn't hold it in anymore. Right there, in my office, I started crying—big, helpless sobs that I couldn't control. It felt like the weight of everything I'd been holding onto had finally come crashing down on me. The love, the hope, the endless waiting... all of it shattered in that one moment.

For a long time, I sat there, my head in my hands, tears spilling onto the desk. My colleagues passed by, but no one said anything. Maybe they could see it, the pain written on my face, or maybe they just didn't know what to say.

Eventually, the tears slowed. My eyes stung, my chest felt raw, but I wiped my face and tried to pull myself together. I forced myself to get back to work, even though everything inside me felt like it was falling apart.

But nothing was the same. The pain lingered like a dull ache in the background of everything I did. I had loved her—really loved her—and now it was over. Just like that. It felt surreal, like something out of a bad dream, but I couldn't wake up. I had lost her, and the emptiness she left behind was consuming me.

This was the pain of first love—this unbearable, crushing grief. The realization that no matter how much you love someone, sometimes it's not enough to make them stay.

..

*No one should know the weight of first love.*
*No one should taste the sweetness of first love.*
*No one should give their heart to first love.*
*No one should waste time chasing first love.*
*No one should dream of forever with first love.*
*No one should bare their soul to first love.*
*No one should lose themselves in first love.*
*No one should endure the pain of losing first love.*
*No one should cry alone for first love.*
*No one... first love.*

..

For days, I walked around like a ghost of my former self. Everyone noticed the change, even if they didn't know the reason. I used to be the guy who was always laughing, always joking, always the first to say hello. But now, I barely had the energy to acknowledge anyone. It felt like I was moving through the office in slow motion, trapped inside my own mind, drowning in my thoughts of her.

People would ask why I was so silent, why I looked so sad. I could hear them sometimes—my colleagues, my friends—but it was like their voices came from far away, like they were speaking underwater. Many times, I didn't even notice when someone was standing next to me, trying to get my attention. All I could think about was her. I was consumed by the silence she'd left me in, by the absence of her love.

Nights were the worst. I'd lie in bed, staring at the ceiling, the darkness pressing down on me. Sleep felt like a distant memory. Instead of rest, I spent my nights with tears in my eyes, my chest aching from the weight of the heartache I couldn't escape. I wanted so badly for my wishes to come true, for her to come back to me, for everything to go back to how it was. But those wishes had turned into nightmares—dreams I never wanted to face. Every hour, I'd sit up, too restless to lie still, wiping the tears that wouldn't stop. My eyes burned, swollen and red from days without sleep.

It had been four days since I last ate. My stomach growled with hunger, but I couldn't bring myself to eat. Food felt pointless, just another reminder of how hollow everything had become. I was weak, and my body felt like it was shutting down. One day, while I was in the office, I felt my legs buckle. Before I knew it, I was on the floor.

"Hey, are you okay?" one of my colleagues asked, rushing over. They knew I hadn't eaten in four days. I was skipping all breaks in office.

"You need to eat something", Ashish said.

I waved them off, embarrassed. But I knew they were right. My body was giving up, even if my heart hadn't. Yet, even when I forced myself to eat, nothing felt right. My mind was too busy, too tangled up in thoughts of her. Every bite tasted like ash in my mouth.

No matter what I did, I couldn't stop thinking about her. She was everywhere and nowhere at once. I could see her in the office sometimes, but there was no longer any warmth in her smile for me. She didn't even look at me. One day, I saw her working late, sitting just across from me. I wanted to believe that maybe—just maybe—she would look up, meet my eyes, and see what she was doing to me. That maybe she'd remember how things used to be.

But she didn't.

She kept her head down, her gaze deliberately avoiding mine, as if I were a stranger she'd never known. As if everything we had shared, everything we had been, didn't matter anymore. The silence between us stretched, thick and unbearable. It made me want to weep right there, in front of everyone. I swallowed the lump in my throat and forced myself to hold it together. But inside, I was breaking. How could she not feel the same way? How could she just... erase me?

I kept calling her. I kept hoping for some sign, some glimmer of the love we once shared. But the more I tried, the more distant she became. She didn't pick up. No texts. No explanations. Just nothing. It was as if I had become a toy—something she could pick up, play with when it suited her, and discard when she was done.

The thought gnawed at me, making me feel small, used, and broken. I couldn't stop the cycle of sleepless nights, red eyes, and aching headaches. I felt like I was spiraling, slipping further and further away from who I used to be.

One morning, I couldn't take it anymore. I made an appointment with a doctor. When I sat in his office, I couldn't bring myself to tell him the real reason for my tension. Instead, I told him it was work, that I was stressed about my job. He looked at me with concern but didn't press me. He suggested I take sleeping pills, get proper rest, and make sure I was eating.

I took his advice. But the pills didn't work. I'd sleep for a few hours, but then I'd wake up, heart racing, mind spinning with thoughts of her. Four hours of sleep was all I could manage most nights, and it wasn't enough to pull me out of the hole I was in. I kept getting weaker—my body, my mind, everything felt like it was slowly shutting down.

The hardest part was the loneliness. Not just the physical loneliness, but the emotional void she left behind. I couldn't stop replaying her words, her silence, her absence. I was trapped in the memories of what we had, and the growing realization that she wasn't coming back.

Every day, I tried to convince myself to let go, but the love I had for her was stubborn, relentless. It clung to me like a shadow, always there, always reminding me of what I had lost. The pain was sharp, constant. I was desperate to hear her voice, to feel her close, to lose myself in her embrace just one more time. Nights were the worst, filled with the ache of missing her—the warmth of her hug, the softness of her kiss, the comfort of knowing she was there.

And even though I wanted to move on, a part of me still hoped that she'd come back, that she'd realize the mistake and that we could start over. But that hope felt more and more like a ghost I was clinging to—a last shred of her that wouldn't let me rest.

One evening, I got a call from the tiffin service owner. Her voice was hesitant but concerned. "Why aren't you eating the food? I've been taking the tiffins back untouched for days now."

I didn't know what to say. "I'm not well," I muttered, trying to avoid the full truth.

It wasn't a lie—I wasn't well. I was taking sleeping pills without eating, which only made things worse. But it wasn't my health I was thinking about. All I could think of was her—my love, the girl who had left me in the dark, like I didn't matter anymore.

By then, it had become painfully clear that she would never come back to me. I needed to get away from her, far enough so I could start to forget. The thought of seeing her every day in the office was suffocating. I decided to quit my job. No explanations, no farewells—I would just disappear.

Before leaving, I sent her a message: *I've left the company. You won't see me again. I wish you all the best in your life.* It was short, almost formal, but what else was there to say?

An hour later, she called.

"Don't leave the company," she said. Her voice was sharp, almost angry. "If you leave, I'll hate you for it."

That single sentence shattered the fragile resolve I had built. Against my better judgment, I went back to the office the next day. It felt like giving in, like losing a battle with myself. I still tried calling her, but as usual, there was no answer. The silence burned through me.

Frustration boiled over. I couldn't hold it in anymore. I sent her a string of messages, pouring out all the anger I had bottled up inside. I used words I never thought I'd say to her—ugly, bitter words. I was tired of being ignored. I felt like I had been discarded, used, and dumped. The love I once had for her had twisted into something darker. All the respect I once held for her had now curdled into hate.

But in spite of all that anger, there was one last thing I wanted from her. I sent her another message, this time pleading: *Meet me once, just once. I want the sketch you made of me that night we spent together. I'll never contact you again, I promise. But that sketch... you made it with so much love. It means something to me, even if it doesn't to you anymore. Please, just give it to me.*

I wasn't even sure why I wanted the sketch so badly. Maybe it was a symbol, a last link to what we had before everything went wrong. Maybe, deep down, I thought that if she gave it to me, it would bring some kind of closure. But her silence remained. Her avoidance was killing me from the inside out, gnawing away at what little was left of me.

I couldn't handle the emptiness, the constant ache. That's when I turned to alcohol. Every night, I drank until I couldn't feel anything anymore. I drank until I passed out, hoping that, for a few hours, I could forget the pain. But each morning, I woke up with a hangover and a heavy heart, and it all came rushing back. The crying, the loneliness, the endless questions.

People started to avoid me. Friends I once laughed with kept their distance. They told me I wasn't myself anymore, that I'd become someone else—someone bitter, broken, lost. Maybe they were right. But what was I supposed to tell them? How could I explain that the girl I had loved, the girl who had once meant everything to me, had walked out of my life without a word, without a reason?

One day, an old friend, Ritu made a call to invite me to her marriage. She wasn't just any friend—she was my best friend, the one person who had been there for me through thick and thin. She could hear something was wrong just from my voice. I told her everything—the silence, the unanswered calls, the heartbreak that had left me hollow. She listened patiently, and after a long pause, she offered to help. "Give me Jojo's number," she said gently. "I'll talk to her. Maybe I can convince her to speak with you."

I hesitated, but I was desperate. I gave her the number, but made her promise not to tell Jojo I'd asked her to call. Ritu agreed, and later that evening, she reached out to Jojo.

A few hours passed, and I received a message from Jojo. It wasn't personal—it was a forwarded message. But it was something. I called her immediately, unsure if she would answer. But this time, she did. Her voice was calm, even kind. For the first time in what felt like forever, we talked.

But nothing changed. She was still avoiding me, and I could feel the coldness settle back in the next day. The fleeting hope I had felt after our brief conversation faded fast. Frustration bubbled up inside me. I kept calling her, over and over, hoping she'd pick up just once, but every call went unanswered. The anger was starting to burn through me, consuming the last bits of patience I had left.

I needed a distraction. Something—anything—to take my mind off her silence. In a fit of desperation, I logged into Facebook, hoping it would help me forget, even if only for a moment. Without thinking, I typed out a status: *"I'm missing Jolene. She left me."* I posted it without considering the consequences, driven purely by frustration. Deep down, I knew it was a mistake. I knew it was disrespectful to put her name out there like that, to share something so personal with the world. But in that moment, all I wanted was for her to realize what I was going through.

She saw the status almost immediately. I knew because, within minutes, she had removed me from her friend list. That hurt more than I expected, like a final blow. I had pushed too far, crossed a line I couldn't take back. I shouldn't have mentioned her name. I knew it was wrong, but it was too late. My frustration had gotten the better of me, and now, I'd made things worse.

My status quickly gathered attention. Comments started flooding in from friends, many of them turning my pain into lighthearted jokes. For a brief moment, I found myself laughing at the banter, my frustration momentarily forgotten. The comments pulled my mind away from the ache, giving me a brief sense of relief—if only for a while.

But once I logged off, reality came crashing back. Nothing had changed. The laughter faded, and the hollow feeling inside me only deepened. The truth was, no amount of jokes or Facebook likes could fix what I was going through. No one could bear the weight of my pain for me. I was still alone with it, and it was growing heavier by the day.

That night, like so many before it, I turned to alcohol. I sat in my room with a bottle in hand, drowning my thoughts in liquor. It was the only thing that dulled the pain anymore. I wasn't eating, I wasn't sleeping, I was just drinking—chasing some kind of peace in the bottom of every bottle.

The next morning, the hangover hit me hard. My head throbbed, my stomach churned, but the worst part was the ache in my chest. I called her again. No answer. I sent her a message, practically begging for a response. *Please, just talk to me. Say something. Anything.* But she remained silent, as she had for so long. I couldn't understand how so much love could turn to this—this empty void. How did it all change so suddenly? How did I become nothing to her?

I was stuck, confused, and angry, but more than anything, I felt lost. The pain inside me was growing, consuming me from the inside out. I tried to convince myself to move on, but I didn't know how. Every day felt like a battle I was losing, and I didn't even know what I was fighting for anymore.

The next day, I reached out to Sunny. He had been a good friend of mine for years—someone I could trust, someone who always knew how to bring a bit of light into the darkest situations. I called him up and asked if he could come over. When he arrived later that evening, I could see the concern on his face the moment he walked in.

"What the hell happened to you?" he asked, his eyes scanning my faded expression, my red, bloodshot eyes. "You look like you haven't slept in days."

I sighed, sinking into my chair. "I haven't. It's a long story."

Sunny sat down across from me, his eyes full of quiet concern. "Tell me."

So, I did. I told him everything—about Jolene, about the avoidance, the frustration, the drinking, and how I felt like I was spiraling out of control. He listened patiently, nodding every now and then, but mostly letting me get it all out. I didn't realize how much I needed to talk until I started. The words just kept pouring out, and when I was done, I felt a little lighter, though the pain still lingered. I was begging for help.

After a moment of silence, Sunny leaned forward. "Listen," he said, his voice firm but kind. "I know this is killing you, but you've got to stop drowning in it. You need to move on. You're letting her take control of your life, and it's not worth it. You're worth more than this."

I looked at him, a knot of doubt forming inside me. "I don't know how."

"You start by living again," he said, offering a small smile. "Let's go to the club tonight. You need to get out, let off some steam. Let the music drown out your thoughts for a while. Dance, laugh—just let go for one night. You can't fix everything right now, but you can start by having a little fun. You need it."

I wasn't convinced, but Sunny was persistent. "Trust me," he said. "Let's go. I promise it'll help, even if it's just for a few hours."

"Will this really work?" I asked, not just to Sunny, but to myself, as if hoping the answer would be enough to convince me.

"Of course it will," Sunny responded confidently, flashing that cocky grin of his. "I mean, if those stupid ideas of yours—drinking alone and popping sleeping pills—can keep you going, then this? This is gonna work way better. Trust me."

I wanted to believe him. I really did. So, I nodded and let him lead the way to the club.

We joined the line outside, waiting our turn to get in. The night was alive with the beat of distant music, and people around us were buzzing with excitement. As we stood there, Sunny, of course, couldn't help himself. He nudged me, pressing his arm into mine.

"Bhai, check her out," he whispered, his eyes glued to the girl standing a few feet away. "She's hot."

I glanced at her, rolling my eyes. "Relax, man. Her boyfriend's standing right next to her."

Sunny, being Sunny, shrugged, unfazed. "Boyfriend hai toh chhhoot jayega, relation hai toh toot jayega," he said with that overconfident attitude of his, like he was invincible. His gaze lingered a little too long on her waist.

"Just try to keep your eyes in your head, alright?" I muttered, half-laughing. He was impossible.

Our turn finally came, and we stepped inside the club.

The ambience hit me immediately—the flashing lights, the pounding bass that vibrated through the floor, the crowd lost in the rhythm of the music. The atmosphere was electric, and for the first time in a long time, I felt a tiny spark of something that wasn't sadness or anger. We found a spot by the slab, settling onto the high chairs as we took it all in.

"See? This is what you needed," Sunny said, nodding with a satisfied smile as he looked out at the dance floor. "Forget the past, man. Just live a little."

I ordered drinks for us, the cold glass feeling foreign in my hand after so many nights of drinking alone. As I took a sip, I noticed the dance floor was packed with people, mostly groups of girls twirling and laughing in their short skirts, carefree and full of energy. It was obvious Sunny was in his element. He kept elbowing me, pointing out every girl who caught his eye.

"You know that's the only reason you dragged me here," I laughed, shaking my head.

"What can I say, bro? I'm a man of simple pleasures," he said, winking.

As I watched the crowd, I caught sight of a group of boys standing near the dance floor, their eyes glued to the girls, watching their every move. It reminded me of old times—those carefree, reckless days with my friends when we'd joke around, act stupid, and just enjoy life. For a moment, a smile tugged at my lips, and I turned to Sunny to bring up the memories. But then I noticed him—eyes locked on the girls' legs, just like the guys I'd been observing.

I smacked his arm lightly. "Enough, man."

He looked at me, pretending to be innocent. "What? I'm just... appreciating the view."

"Right." I laughed, but this time, it felt real.

As the night went on, I ordered another round of drinks. My mood was shifting, little by little. The music pulsed through me, and the drinks started to ease the depression that had been building up inside me for days. I could feel the tension in my body start to fade as the alcohol did its work, warming my skin and quieting the anxious thoughts that usually wouldn't let me breathe. My foot started tapping to the beat, and before I knew it, I was smiling.

It wasn't a forced smile, the kind I had plastered on my face for weeks just to get through the day. This one felt different—genuine, almost like a piece of the old me was breaking through.

Sunny caught my eye and raised his glass. "See? I told you. This is what you needed."

I lifted my glass in response.

Sunny grinned at me, his eyes already glassy with the alcohol in his system. "Let's do some shots!" he said, practically bouncing with excitement. Before I could even think to protest, he was waving over the bartender.

We ordered Vodka Stinger shots. The first one burned like fire, searing a path down my throat as it made its way to my stomach. I could feel the heat spreading inside me, and I winced, but then laughed it off when Sunny gave me a knowing nod. We threw back two more shots, one after the other, the burn getting more familiar with each one, though it never really softened.

By the time we ordered a fourth, the room had started to blur at the edges. My thoughts felt fuzzy, the alcohol having struck my mind in a way that was both numbing and disorienting. I put my head down on the slab, closing my eyes for a moment to stop the spinning. The music was still thudding in the background, vibrating through my body, but my focus was slipping.

I don't know how much time passed before I lifted my head again. When I opened my eyes, Sunny was gone.

I sat up, squinting through the hazy lights, looking around for him. It didn't take long to spot him. There he was—sitting on the floor, staring at a group of girls, specifically at their legs.

"Oye, Sunny! Get up, you idiot." I nudged his arm with my foot, trying to jolt him back to his senses.

"She's sooo sexy!" he shouted, his voice slurred but loud enough to catch the attention of people nearby.

I cringed. "Sunny, for God's sake, keep it down." But Sunny, of course, was too far gone to care about being discreet.

"I want to dance!" he declared suddenly, staggering to his feet.

I reached out to grab his arm, trying to steady him, but he slipped out of my grasp, already making his way toward the dance floor. I groaned, debating whether or not to go after him. In the end, I let him go—what harm could a little dancing do?

Sunny was on the dance floor in seconds, his movements wild and erratic, and for a moment, I couldn't help but laugh. His dance moves were so ridiculous, so completely over-the-top, that it actually looked like he was doing it on purpose. His arms flailed, his feet shuffled out of rhythm, and I could see people around him watching in a mix of amusement and confusion.

"Come on, bro!" he shouted, waving me over. "Join me!"

I rolled my eyes, but a smile tugged at my lips. What the hell? Why not?

I made my way onto the floor, and before long, I was laughing harder than I had in months. The alcohol, the lights, the pounding music—it all blended together, taking the edge off my pain, at least for now. My body started moving to the beat, the trance music driving me to let go of everything, even if just for a few minutes.

Sunny, being Sunny, was all over the place. I saw him trying to talk to one girl, but she ignored him completely, stepping away with an awkward smile. Undeterred, he shuffled over to another, trying his luck again. She too gave him a cold shoulder, walking away without even a second glance. I couldn't help but laugh. Poor guy.

Still, it felt good to dance. The beats were heavy, pulsing through my body, and for the first time in what felt like forever, I didn't care how bad I looked. I wasn't thinking about Jojo, or the sleepless nights, or the unanswered texts. My body was moving, my mind was numb, and in that moment, I felt lighter. The music was pulling me out of the darkness, lifting me, bit by bit, from everything I'd been drowning in.

Eventually, we collapsed onto a nearby sofa, out of breath and sweating. My head was buzzing, my legs heavy from the dancing. I leaned back, placing my feet up on the table in front of me, letting out a deep, satisfied breath. The alcohol was still in my system, but I felt more in control—at least until I glanced over at the couple on the next sofa.

They were kissing, locked in an intimate moment, oblivious to everyone around them. Watching them, a sharp pang cut through me. It was like being hit by a wave I hadn't seen coming. I pressed my lips together, trying to shake off the feeling, but my thoughts drifted back to Jojo. Her absence suddenly felt suffocating, like no amount of music or alcohol could drown it out.

I sighed, turning my face away from the couple and closing my eyes, willing the feeling to pass.

Sunny had his eyes closed too, leaning back in a half-drunken stupor. I figured I'd use the moment to freshen up, hoping a splash of water might clear my head. Without telling him, I headed to the washroom.

As I stepped inside, the faint sound of voices reached my ears. Two guys were talking in low voices, and from the little I could hear, the conversation sounded off. I had a sinking suspicion they were talking about drugs, though I couldn't make out everything they said.

I hesitated near the sink, pretending to wash my hands, my ears straining to catch more of the conversation. But after a few moments, one of the guys stepped out of the stall and headed toward the sink. I glanced at him briefly, then decided it wasn't worth it. I didn't want to get involved in something I didn't understand.

As soon as the other guy appeared, I quietly slipped out of the washroom, letting the club's thudding music wash over me again.

After coming back from the washroom, I sat down on the sofa and told Sunny the whole story about the guys I had overheard. I pointed them out across the room, watching as they lingered near the bar.

Sunny squinted, leaning closer to get a better look. "Yeah, I know him personally. He's known to sell *maal*. I have met him couple of times." He shrugged it off casually, like it was just part of the scene.

"Let's just get out of here," I suggested. We both had work the next day, and the night was starting to wear on me.

We made our way toward the parking lot, weaving through the crowd of people still buzzing with energy. As we reached the car, I noticed something that made me pause. A few spaces over, there was a guy in a car, aggressively leaning toward the girl next to him. She looked drunk, her movements slow and uncoordinated as she tried to push him away.

For a second, I hesitated. My instinct told me to intervene, but Sunny nudged me toward the car. "Let it go, man. It's not our business."

I glanced back at them one last time before getting into the car, trying to shake the uncomfortable feeling settling in my gut. We drove in silence, both of us lost in our own thoughts.

When we reached my place, it was late—too late for Sunny to drive home. I offered him to crash at my room, and he agreed easily, too tired to argue. As we lay there in the quiet darkness, my thoughts kept drifting back to the night we had. I thought about the fun we'd had, the girls, the couple in the car, and especially the guys in the washroom talking about drugs.

The truth was, the idea of meeting those guys lingered longer than it should have. I wasn't thinking about confronting them or stopping them. No, my intention was different—darker. I wanted to buy drugs from them. But I didn't want to tell Sunny for now.

There was a part of me that just wanted the pain to stop. People always said, *Drugs are the end to pain.* I had no idea if that was true, but I was desperate enough to consider it. I wanted something—anything—that would numb the constant ache I was carrying inside. The partying had distracted me, yes, but it hadn't healed me. At the end of the night, the tears still came.

"Let's go back to the club tomorrow," I said to Sunny, half hoping he'd brush it off, but he grinned at me instead.

"Bhai, the girls there are awesome," he said, his eyes lighting up. It was the answer I'd expected from him, and I couldn't help but laugh, even with the ache lingering inside me.

We spent the rest of the night in silence, but even after all the fun, I could feel the sadness creeping back in. No matter how hard I tried to push it away, it lingered, pressing down on me like an invisible burden. As I lay there in bed, staring at the ceiling, the tears welled up again. My feelings for Jojo—the ones I had tried to drown in loud music and laughter—broke through everything. All the fun, all the distractions, none of it was enough to cover up the hurt.

Silent tears fell in the dark as thoughts of her overwhelmed me, each one making it harder to breathe. I was still hoping, in some small part of me, that she would come back, that maybe I could fix what had broken between us. Even though I knew the truth, even though she was gone, I couldn't let go of the hope that things might change. Sleep eventually came, but it wasn't peaceful. It was the kind of sleep that comes after you've worn yourself out from crying, a dull numbness taking over.

The next day, I went through the motions at work, barely present. By the time evening rolled around, I called Sunny again to make plans for the club. It was like I was chasing the high from the night before, hoping for another distraction, another temporary escape.

"Come to my place after work," I said. "Then we'll head to the club."

Later that night, he arrived, excited and ready for another night of fun. As soon as he walked in, he struck a pose and grinned. "How do I look? Think I can impress someone tonight?"

I couldn't help but smile. "Yeah, you look good, bro. Maybe tonight's the night you actually get a girl's number."

He laughed, but I could tell he was serious. "This time, for sure."

I didn't know where I was going, or what I was doing—maybe all of this was just supposed to give me some relief from the ache Jojo left behind.

We got to the club and, as expected, Sunny was immediately in his element. As soon as we ordered drinks, he made his way to the dance floor, already scanning the crowd for a girl to flirt with. But I wasn't paying attention to the girls. My mind was on something else entirely. I was looking for that guy—the one who had been selling drugs the night before.

I scanned the club over and over, my eyes darting from face to face, but I couldn't find him. The night wore on, and as much as I tried to enjoy myself, there was a growing frustration inside me. I wasn't here for fun—not really. I was here because I wanted something darker, something that would make me forget everything, if only for a little while.

But by the end of the night, I came up empty-handed. I hadn't found the guy. I hadn't gotten what I was looking for. Instead, I was left with the same emptiness I'd started with. The same pain. The same thoughts of Jojo.

We left the club, the buzz from the alcohol fading quickly, and I couldn't help but feel defeated. It didn't matter how many clubs we went to, how many nights we spent drinking and dancing—it wouldn't change anything. Nothing was going to take away the pain.

A few days later, I asked Sunny if we could make plans for the next week.

"Saale, I don't have that kind of money to waste all the time," he replied with a laugh, shaking his head. "You're starting to like this place, huh?"

I just shrugged, not ready to admit why I really wanted to go back. It wasn't about the fun, the drinks, or even the girls anymore. I was chasing something else. I had convinced myself that getting my hands on the drugs would somehow help, that it would be an escape from the pain that was suffocating me.

Sunny eventually gave in, and we made another plan. The night felt familiar—the loud music, the lights, the crowd. My eyes were scanning the room, searching for one face: the guy from the last time.

Hours passed, but as midnight approached, I finally spotted him near the bar. My heart started racing. This was the moment I'd been waiting for, but now that it was here, I couldn't move. My legs felt like they were rooted to the floor, my feet refusing to take even one step toward him. Fear and hesitation coursed through me, and I couldn't shake the worry of being caught, of something going wrong. Sunny was with me, so I tried to reassure myself that he'd have my back if anything happened. But still, my courage failed me.

I found myself mentally backing out of the plan, over and over. Every time I built up the nerve to approach the guy, I'd talk myself out of it at the last second. The weight of what I was about to do felt heavier than I had anticipated.

Then, I saw him heading toward the washroom.

I felt a surge of adrenaline. Maybe this was my chance. Alone, away from the crowd. I glanced at Sunny, told him to wait, and made my way to the washroom, my heart racing.

When I entered, there were a couple of guys already inside, and I lingered awkwardly by the sink, pretending to wash my hands while waiting for them to leave. My palms were sweating, and the mirror in front of me reflected my nervous expression. I barely recognized myself.

After what felt like an eternity, the others finally left. It was just me and him now.

I swallowed hard, trying to find the right words, but nothing came out. The silence stretched. I felt like my entire body was vibrating with fear. My throat went dry, and for a second, I considered walking away.

I went to Sunny. I took a deep breath, walked up to him, and said quietly, "Sunny, I need your help."

He looked at me, confused. "With what?"

I glanced over toward the bar, my eyes darting to the guy. "With him," I whispered.

Sunny's expression changed instantly. His usual carefree attitude dropped. He followed my gaze and realized what I was talking about. "Are you serious?" he asked, his voice sharp. "You want to mess with that?"

"I... I need it, man. I just... I need something," I said, my voice almost cracking. I hated how desperate I sounded, but I couldn't hide it anymore.

Sunny shook his head and took a step back. "No way. This is insane. You've never touched that stuff in your life, and now you want to start? Do you even know what you're getting into?"

I lowered my head, ashamed, but I pressed on. "Please, Sunny. I'm begging you. I don't know what else to do. I can't keep going like this. I need to shut my mind off, just for a little while."

Sunny sighed, running a hand through his hair. "This isn't the way, man. Trust me, it's not going to fix anything. This shit only messes you up more." He looked me over, his eyes narrowing. "You really want to go down this road?"

"I don't want to," I admitted, my voice low. "But I feel like I don't have a choice."

Sunny studied me for a long moment. I could tell he was torn—part of him wanted to pull me out of this, to tell me to forget about it. But another part of him could see how far gone I was. He knew I wasn't just asking—I was begging. The truth was, I wasn't going to stop until I found a way to numb the pain. And he could see it.

Finally, he let out a frustrated sigh. "Fine. But only a small quantity. Enough to get you through this night. And don't ever ask me for this shit again. Do you hear me?"

I nodded quickly, relief flooding through me. I knew Sunny wasn't happy about it, but he was doing it because he cared. He shook his head again, muttering something under his breath, then straightened up.

"Wait here," he said. "I'll talk to him."

I watched as Sunny walked toward the bar, feeling a knot tighten in my stomach. My legs felt weak, and my mind was racing with second thoughts. But now, it was too late. I had set this into motion.

I stayed by the table, nervously glancing around as Sunny approached the guy. They exchanged a few words, and I saw the guy look over at me briefly before nodding. A wave of nerves hit me as Sunny walked back, my pulse quickening.

"He'll meet you in the washroom in five minutes," Sunny said, his tone flat. "Go, and be quick about it."

I swallowed hard, feeling the fear and excitement swirl inside me. I nodded, grateful but still terrified.

I walked toward the washroom, my hands shaking as I pushed open the door. I stood near the sink, pretending to wash my hands, trying to steady my nerves. A few other people were in there, so I waited. When the last guy left, I was alone. I looked up at the mirror, trying to catch my breath. This was really happening.

Then the door opened, and the dealer walked in, his expression calm and collected, like he had done this a hundred times before.

I froze, unsure of what to say or how to start. He glanced at me and smirked, as if he could see my nerves written all over my face.

"You wanted something?" he said, his voice low and casual.

I nodded, my throat too dry to speak.

"Sunny said it's your first time," he continued, reaching into his pocket. "So I'll keep it light for you."

I watched as he pulled out a small pouch, holding it between two fingers like it was no big deal. I felt a wave of fear wash over me.

"How much?" I asked, my voice barely above a whisper.

He named the price, and I fumbled for my wallet, my hands shaking as I pulled out the money. I handed it to him with wobbly fingers, and he slipped the pouch into my hand in exchange.

Before I could turn to leave, he caught my eye. "Take it easy," he warned. "Small quantity. You're new to this, and if you take too much, it'll mess you up."

I nodded quickly, not trusting my voice. He gave me one last look before he left the washroom, disappearing as quietly as he had come.

For a moment, I just stood there, staring at the small pouch in my hand. My heart was still racing, and I felt a chill crawl up my spine. This was it. I had crossed a line I never thought I would.

I stuffed the packet into my pocket, washed my hands again—more out of nerves than anything—and stepped out of the washroom. But as soon as I was back in the club, I was hit by a wave of paranoia. It felt like everyone was watching me, like they knew what I had just done. My body was shaking, my legs wobbly beneath me as I hurried back to Sunny.

"Let's get out of here," I muttered to him, grabbing his arm.

He looked at me, his expression tense. "Alright, let's go."

We left the club quickly, stepping into the cool night air. I couldn't stop checking the rearview mirror as we drove back to my place, convinced that someone was following us, that something was going to go wrong.

We got back to my room, and Sunny gave me a quick look before he left for his place. I could tell he was worried, but he didn't say anything. I watched him drive away, then closed the door behind me, locking it tight. My hands moved automatically, pulling a towel off the rack and hanging it over the window. I didn't want anyone looking inside, didn't want anyone to see what I was about to do.

There was no doubt left in my mind. I was going to do it. My frustration had reached a breaking point, and I needed to silence it, even if just for a while. I pulled out the small pouch, hesitating as a flicker of anxiety ran through me. Following the dealer's instructions, I took a small amount, the tiniest dose, and braced myself.

At first, nothing happened. But then, slowly, my head began to ache—a dull throb that settled at the base of my skull and spread outward. I grimaced, but as the minutes passed, the pain started to fade. Instead, a strange calm washed over me. My body felt lighter, and the ever-present tension that had been twisting inside me for weeks finally loosened its grip.

It was the first time in what felt like forever that I wasn't being torn apart by my thoughts. No constant loop of pain, no images of her face flashing in my mind. Just quiet. For once, I felt... at peace. I staggered to my bed and collapsed onto it, the haze wrapping itself around me like a blanket. Within minutes, I was asleep—deep, dreamless sleep. The kind I hadn't had in weeks.

When I woke up the next morning, the sunlight was already filtering through the gaps in the window. I groggily glanced at the clock, then at my phone—*Shit, I'm late.* I scrambled out of bed, my head still aching, though not as badly as before. I shoved the packet into the desk drawer, hiding it from view, and locked the door behind me as I rushed out to work.

At the office, the usual weight settled back on my shoulders as soon as I saw her. My heart sank. The drugs had given me a brief escape, but now, faced with her presence again, everything came rushing back. My emotions, the hurt I had tried to push away, surged forward like a tidal wave. My eyes searched for hers throughout the day, hoping—*no, begging*—for a sign, for a smile. But there was nothing. Just the cold, indifferent way she ignored me, as if I didn't exist.

Her behavior haunted me all day. By the time I got back home, I was replaying every glance, every moment of her avoiding me.

It gnawed at me, made me angry, and then even more frustrated. I grabbed my phone, dialing her number almost without thinking, but at the last second, I hung up.

*No. Don't call her.*

But the urge to hear her voice, to feel connected, was overwhelming. I was desperate. I felt dead inside—like something essential had been stripped from me, and I didn't know how to get it back. I wasn't smiling, wasn't crying. I didn't even know who I was anymore. Everything felt empty, and I couldn't bear it.

I needed a distraction. Anything to pull me out of this void. I sat down at my computer, trying to lose myself in a game, but my eyes kept drifting toward the drawer. The drawer where the drugs were hidden. I fought the urge for a few minutes, telling myself it wasn't good for me. But as the minutes ticked by, the pull grew stronger.

Before I knew it, I had opened the drawer, staring at the small pouch inside. I wasn't sure if I should take it again, but my mind was already made up. Desperation had taken over. With shaking hands, I pulled the pouch out and took another small dose.

The effects hit quicker this time. My body felt weightless, like I was drifting above the ground. And then, suddenly, I started laughing. Not because something was funny, but because I could hear voices—whispers, like an echo in the air—telling me I was a fool.

I looked around the room, my vision blurring slightly, and I saw her. Jojo. Sitting in my computer chair, her eyes mischievous, staring at me the way she always did when she was teasing me, expecting a kiss. A sudden rush came over me, but deep down, I knew it wasn't real. It couldn't be. Yet, somehow, I didn't care. The drugs were keeping me from crying, from breaking down. They were blocking the pain, even if just for a little while.

I laughed again, this time at myself. I wasn't sure if it was a second version of me inside, mocking my misery, or if it was just my twisted way of coping. Either way, the laughter kept coming. It wasn't a happy laugh—it was the kind that bubbled up out of nowhere, masking the pain that was still hiding underneath.

But at least I wasn't crying.

For the first time in weeks, I felt like I had found a way to ignore the pain. A solution. Or so I thought.

A few days later, I went back to the club. This time, there was no hesitation, no second-guessing. I saw the dealer again, and he recognized me instantly, giving me a strange smile. I didn't even wait. I walked up to him when he was alone, feeling the familiar nervousness but ignoring it.

"Got any more?" I asked quietly, my voice steady, despite the adrenaline rushing through me.

He nodded and motioned for me to follow him. "Meet me in my car."

He gave me his car number, and I found it parked in the back of the lot. My hands were sweaty as I knocked on the window, feeling a flicker of paranoia that someone might see me. He rolled the window down and gestured for me to get in.

I climbed into the car, my heart hammering in my chest, and he pulled out a small bag from his jacket. "Same price as before," he said.

I quickly pulled out the money and handed it over with trembling hands. He took it without a word and gave me the pouch. I stuffed it into my pocket, feeling both relieved and uneasy at the same time.

As I got out of the car, I couldn't help but glance around, my paranoia returning. I half-expected someone to jump out of the shadows and grab me, but the lot was empty.

I started meeting him occasionally. But it was difficult to track.

One night, after we'd had a few drinks, he looked at me with a curious smile. "Man, why are you taking this stuff so much? What's your deal?"

I hesitated, but the alcohol had loosened my tongue, and before I knew it, I was telling him the whole story. About Jojo, the heartbreak, the constant pain, and how I just wanted to forget.

He listened, nodding occasionally, but when I finished, he laughed. Not a cruel laugh—more like someone who had heard this story a thousand times before. "Dude, it's just a girl," he said, shaking his head. "Why are you getting so worked up? Life's too short to waste on that kind of stuff. Just enjoy it, man. Let her go."

His words lingered in my mind. It seemed so simple when he said it—*just enjoy your life*. But how could I? I didn't say anything, just shrugged and took another drink, trying to drown the ache that never seemed to fully go away.

A few days later, Sunny called me out of the blue.

"Hey, bro," he said. "What are you up to this weekend? There's someone I want you to meet."

I frowned, slightly confused. "Who?"

"You'll see. Just meet me at the club on Saturday night," he replied cryptically.

I had no reason to say no, so that Saturday, I made my way to the club, curious about who Sunny was talking about. When I arrived, I spotted Sunny standing outside, talking to a girl. She was beautiful, with dark hair flowing over her shoulders and a confidence that was impossible to ignore. I hesitated for a moment, but Sunny saw me and waved me over.

As I approached, he grinned. "Finally! There you are. I've been waiting for you." He turned to the girl and introduced us. "This is Anjie," he said. "Anjie, meet my boy."

Anjie smiled warmly, her eyes sparkling under the neon lights. "Hey, nice to meet you." Her voice was soft, but there was something magnetic about her presence.

Sunny's phone rang, and after glancing at the screen, he excused himself. "I'll be back. You two enjoy," he said with a wink before walking off to take his call.

Suddenly, it was just the two of us, standing there in the middle of the crowded club. I felt awkward, not sure what to say. Anjie didn't seem to mind. "So, how are you?" she asked casually, as if we'd known each other for a while.

"I'm... good," I replied, though the word felt foreign in my mouth.

She gave me a small smile and then gestured toward the dance floor. "Come on, let's dance."

I hesitated for a moment, glancing around for Sunny, but then nodded. I followed her into the club, where the music was already pounding through the speakers. We moved onto the dance floor, and soon, I found myself lost in the rhythm. Anjie danced effortlessly, and as we moved, she crossed her arms over my shoulders, pulling me closer. Her hair brushed against my face with every turn, her movements perfectly in sync with the beat.

For the first time in weeks, a smile crept onto my face. It was real me, carefree. There was something freeing about it—being with her, the music, the energy of the club. Placing my hands on her waist and feeling her close to me was a strange but welcome distraction. The pain that had weighed me down so heavily seemed to fade, just for a moment.

After a while, her phone rang, and she excused herself to take the call. I stayed on the dance floor, swaying to the music alone. I didn't mind being by myself—it actually felt good, as if the loud music was pushing out all the thoughts that usually suffocated me. The pulse of the beat seemed to vibrate through my bones, and for a moment, it felt like my pain was dissolving into the noise.

Anjie came back a few minutes later, her hand brushing against mine. "Let's grab a drink," she said with a playful smile.

We headed to the bar, where we ordered two vodka shots. As we knocked them back, she grinned and leaned in close. "Back to the dance floor?"

Without hesitation, I nodded, and we returned to the center of the club. This time, our dance was slower, more intimate. Her hands were on my shoulders, mine resting lightly on her waist. We moved in sync, our eyes locked, the crowd around us fading into the background. At that moment, it was just the two of us.

Then, suddenly, she leaned in and kissed my cheek. My heart raced, but not with excitement. It was confusion, panic. The kiss felt wrong—like something I wasn't ready for. I pulled back slightly, lowering my gaze to the floor.

She smiled, sensing my hesitation, and didn't push any further. We kept dancing, but the moment lingered in the air between us, unspoken.

After a while, she took my hand again and led me outside. The shift from the loud, pulsating music to the calm, quiet street was jarring but soothing. We walked in silence for a while, her hand warm in mine. The cool night air was a welcome change from the heat of the club.

We walked for what felt like hours, though it was probably only a few minutes. There was something peaceful about it, about being out in the open, away from the noise, with someone who seemed to care. For the first time in a long while, I felt calm. Not healed, but calm.

Eventually, we reached her car. She unlocked it and we climbed inside, the quiet enveloping us. We talked, joked, and laughed—simple conversation that felt oddly comforting. She placed her hand on my chest, her eyes searching mine as she leaned closer.

She was beautiful. Wonderful, even. But as she moved toward me, I felt... nothing. No spark, no desire. It wasn't that I didn't like her, but something in me had shut down. I turned my head slightly, avoiding her kiss.

She noticed and smiled gently, as if she understood. There was no anger, no awkwardness—just a quiet acceptance. We sat there for a while, her hand still resting on my chest, both of us lost in our thoughts.

I couldn't explain it. She was everything I should have wanted, but I felt nothing. My heart was still somewhere else—still tangled up in memories of someone who wasn't coming back.

"I'm sorry. I should leave," I said to her quietly, avoiding her eyes.

Anjie smiled softly, her expression kind. She nodded and welcomed my request without question. There was no awkwardness, no disappointment—just a gentle acceptance, as if she could sense I wasn't ready for anything more.

I stepped out of her car, the cool night air hitting me as I walked away. My mind was spinning, and I couldn't shake the feeling of emptiness that had settled deep inside me. It was like I was a shell, walking through life without really feeling alive. Before leaving the place, I bought a few more packets. By now, the fear of getting caught or the hesitation I once had was gone. I had fully given in. Drugs were becoming my escape, my only way to numb the constant pain.

When I got back to my room, I also picked up a flask of whisky, something I could carry with me anytime, anywhere. The combination of the two—drugs and alcohol—had become my daily ritual. It was no longer about feeling better. It was about not feeling anything at all.

The doses I was taking grew larger by the day. It was a slow escalation, almost unnoticed at first, but I knew deep down that I was becoming addicted. There was a strange sense of apathy in that realization. I didn't care about the consequences. I just wanted the pain to stop, no matter the cost.

One night, in the haze of my intoxication, I did something impulsive. I took out my phone, snapped a few pictures of myself drinking, and uploaded them to social platform. I posted two pictures, along with a status: *I'm very sad and feeling alone.*

At first, I wasn't sure what I expected. Maybe I thought someone would reach out. Maybe I wanted attention, validation—something to prove that I wasn't as invisible as I felt. But the comments that flooded in were nothing like that.

Most of my so-called friends laughed at me. Some called me a fool, mocking me for constantly "crying like a baby girl." No one seemed to care about the real pain beneath the surface. I read the comments, feeling the familiar sting of rejection, and something inside me snapped.

I typed out a new status in anger: *Fuck off, all of you.* Then I logged out, slamming my phone onto the table.

That was when it hit me—truly hit me. I had no one. No real friends. No one who actually cared. All the people I thought might be there for me when I needed them had only laughed at my suffering. The loneliness I felt was so deep, so consuming, that I didn't know how to climb out of it. And worse, I didn't want to anymore.

Days passed, and the feeling only got worse. The drugs weren't working like they used to. The alcohol didn't numb the pain—it just drowned me in it. It was like I was sinking deeper into a black hole, and there was no way out. Depression had taken hold of me, and there was nothing left but the thought of ending it.

I sat alone in my room one evening, staring at the walls, feeling the weight of my decision pressing down on me. There was no relief. No hope. Just an endless ache that wouldn't stop. I was done.

I picked up the bottle of sleeping pills that had been sitting on my desk for weeks, and without thinking, I swallowed a handful. One by one, I felt them go down, each pill taking me closer to the edge. My body felt heavy, my eyes starting to droop, but there was no fear—only a strange sense of peace. Finally, it would all be over.

As the darkness closed in around me, I could hear an inner voice, faint but persistent. *I'm alive.*

When I opened my eyes, I was lying on a hospital bed.

Two guys from my building were standing nearby, both looking at me with concern. One of them, a neighbor who lived on the same floor, came and sat beside me. His face was pale, but his voice was steady.

"I saw you last night," he said quietly. "I was talking on the phone, and when I stepped outside, I noticed your door was slightly open. I found you on the floor, man. You... you weren't moving." His voice trembled for a moment, and he swallowed hard before continuing. "We got you here as fast as we could. My roommates helped carry you out."

I couldn't bring myself to meet his eyes. Shame washed over me in waves, and I felt so small, so utterly broken. I had wanted to end it, but here I was—still alive, still breathing. Saved by people who barely knew me.

"I'm sorry," I muttered, my throat dry. I didn't even know why I was apologizing, but the words felt like the only thing I could say.

He shook his head. "Don't be sorry. Just... don't do that again. You scared the hell out of us."

"Thank you," my voice barely above a whisper. I felt embarrassed.

The guy sitting beside me, my neighbor, gave me a gentle look. "What happened?" he asked, his voice soft but concerned.

"Nothing," I lied. I couldn't bring myself to explain the mess inside my head. I didn't even know where to begin.

"Don't worry about it," he said, as if sensing my discomfort. "It's okay."

He handed me my phone, explaining that I had been getting calls from the office. "I told them you're in the hospital and won't be coming in for a while. They know about the situation."

I blinked, my eyes widening. "What did you tell them?" I asked, my throat tightening with anxiety. A thousand questions raced through my mind.

"Relax," he said, noticing my sudden panic. "I didn't tell them too much. Just that you had a health issue. No police, no case. I handled it."

His calm reassurances soothed me a little, but there was still a knot in my stomach, twisting with shame. The doctor came in shortly after, checking my vitals before giving me a sympathetic smile. He recommended I stay in the hospital for at least three more days. The lack of food, combined with the drugs and sleeping pills, had taken a toll on my body, and I needed time to recover.

I thanked the guys for everything and told them they could head back to work. I didn't want to burden them any longer. "You've done enough already," I said. "Please, go to your jobs. I'll be fine."

One of them, the quiet one, spoke up. "We're not leaving you alone, man. Someone will stay with you." They had already taken the day off to stay with me, but I insisted, telling them I just needed some time to myself.

After they left, I was finally alone in the sterile quiet of the hospital room. For a while, I just stared at the ceiling, trying to make sense of everything. My body was weak, my mind foggy, and the weight of what I had done slowly settled over me.

*How did I let it get this bad?*

Two days passed in the hospital, and I couldn't stop my mind from wandering back to her—Jojo. The memory of her was like a ghost, haunting me when I least expected it. I thought back to that one time when I had called in sick to the office, and she had made *khichdi* for me. The warmth, the care—it felt so far away now.

But here I was, two days into a hospital stay, and she hadn't even called. Not a text, not a word. I was an idiot, still clinging to those memories, still hoping for something that wasn't going to come. Even after everything, I was thinking of her.

On the third day, the doctors finally discharged me. I went back to my empty room, feeling both relieved and terrified. The silence of the room pressed in on me, the loneliness suffocating. It didn't take long for me to realize that nothing had really changed. The hospital might have healed my body, but my mind was still trapped, still broken.

I took a few more days to gather myself before returning to the office. I was scared—petrified, actually—of facing my colleagues. What would they ask? How would I explain? The thought of their curious eyes, their whispers, it all gnawed at me. The shame felt unbearable.

Finally, I returned to work. I walked in, half-expecting whispers or sideways glances. But to my surprise, everything was normal. No one knew the full story. They had been told I hadn't been eating properly and that the stress had landed me in the hospital. Just a health scare—that's all they thought it was.

People greeted me with casual, "Glad you're feeling better," and "We missed you," but there were no probing questions, no concerned looks that went too deep. I realized that the truth had been neatly hidden away. They thought it was just physical exhaustion and stress. No one had any idea how close I'd come to disappearing entirely.

And for that, I was strangely grateful. It was easier this way. Easier to pretend that nothing had happened, that I was just recovering from a minor health issue.

I made my way to my desk, the routine of the office settling around me like a protective shield. There was a comfort in the normalcy of it all. I could just be another colleague who'd been out sick for a while, nothing more. For a few hours, I could forget about the weight I was carrying.

But even as they treated me like nothing had changed, something had shifted inside me. I was still trapped in my own world of despair, suffocating in the silence of my unresolved pain. I went through the motions at work, but there was a heaviness inside me I couldn't shake. I was quieter than usual, speaking only when necessary, not really engaging with anyone. My mind felt distant, consumed by thoughts of her—Jojo.

I missed her with an intensity that felt like an unbearable ache, as if something inside me was sinking under the heaviness of it. As the hours ticked by, the urge to hear her voice grew stronger. I picked up my phone and called her, my heart racing even though I knew how it would end. She didn't answer, like she usually didn't. I had become so accustomed to her ignoring me, but every time, it felt like a fresh wound. Her silence always hit harder than I expected.

But I couldn't stop myself. I kept calling her, over and over, desperate for any response. When she finally picked up, her voice was cold, distant—almost hostile.

"What do you want?" she snapped, her tone sharp enough to cut through the phone.

I sat there for a moment, stunned into silence. I had no words. I had been holding on to some small hope that she might be different this time, but her rudeness was like a slap in the face. For a second, I couldn't even remember why I had called.

"I..." I started, but the words died in my throat. There was nothing left to say. I hung up without another word.

My hands shook as I put the phone down. I had tried so hard to hold it together, but her coldness—it was too much. It was getting to me, more than ever. I thought about ignoring her, cutting her out of my life completely, hoping that maybe it would make her realize how much she was hurting me. But deep down, I knew it wouldn't matter. It was just a fantasy, a desperate hope that somehow, she'd care. But she wouldn't.

And yet, as I sat there, tears began to spill from my eyes. I couldn't help it. No matter how hard I tried, I was still tethered to her. I was still that fool, holding on to something that had long since died.

An hour later, my phone buzzed. I stared at the screen, hardly believing it—she was calling me.

I answered, bracing myself. "Hello?"

"Can you meet me?" she asked, her voice flat but not as harsh as before. "I've moved PGs. I'll send you the address."

For a moment, I hesitated. I wasn't sure what to think. Why now? What could she possibly want? But even as those questions ran through my mind, I found myself agreeing. I couldn't say no. Not to her.

She sent me the address, and before I knew it, I was driving towards her place. My heart raced the entire way, a familiar blend of hope and dread swirling inside me.

When I arrived, I saw her walking toward my car. She looked the same—familiar in a way that made my stomach twist. But there was no warmth in her eyes. No smile. I sat there, waiting, hoping against hope for even the smallest sign of affection, something that might remind me of the girl she used to be.

But as she reached the car, her expression was neutral, cold even. I had to face her as she was now, not as she had been in my memories. I couldn't help but recall the times she would come to me with a loving smile, eyes full of warmth. Back when everything felt right.

But now? Now, only God knew what had happened to her, to us. The girl I had once known was gone, replaced by someone I could barely recognize.

I opened the door for her with a courtesy that had always been there, and I knew, deep down, it would remain forever, no matter what happened between us. She stepped inside, not a trace of warmth or nostalgia on her face—just the same detachment she had shown the last few times we met.

She handed me the sketch she'd made of me, the one from when things were different, from when I thought there was something real between us. I took it from her, feeling like I was letting go of a piece of my own life. I placed it carefully on the back seat, but inside, it felt like I was setting down my heart, broken and bleeding.

I glanced at her, searching her face for something—*anything*—that would show me the girl I used to know. But there was nothing. She looked at me like a professional artist returning a commissioned work, as though I were just another task to be completed and forgotten. The contrast between her coldness and the memories that still haunted me shook me to the core. She was not the same. She wasn't Jojo.

A heavy silence settled between us, suffocating and thick. My mind raced with everything I wanted to say, a flood of words, emotions, and accusations rising inside me. I wanted to yell, to ask her why she was doing this—why she'd changed. But all that came out was the sound of my breathing, shallow and uneven.

Finally, I broke the silence. "Where do you want to go?" My voice sounded distant, like it belonged to someone else.

She shrugged, her voice flat. "I'm fine anywhere."

I started the car and pulled out, driving aimlessly, waiting—*hoping*—for her to say something that might crack through the ice between us. But the minutes ticked by, and neither of us spoke. The silence was unbearable, like we were both waiting for the other to make the first move.

Then her phone rang. She glanced at the screen, smiled slightly, and answered. It was her friend, I guessed. She started chatting casually, her voice warmer on the phone than it had been with me all evening. I kept driving, my hands clenching the steering wheel tighter with each minute, feeling a hollow sting inside—like I was just background noise while her real attention was elsewhere.

Twenty minutes passed, and she was still on the phone, laughing at whatever her friend was saying. Each second felt like a stab to my heart, the sound of her laughter mocking the pain swirling inside me.

I couldn't take it anymore. Without a word, I turned the car toward her PG.

She noticed the shift and asked, her voice finally acknowledging me again, "Where are we going?"

I kept my eyes on the road, my jaw clenched. "Back to your PG."

The tears started to well up, hot and relentless, but I blinked them away, refusing to let her see me cry. I didn't want her to know how much this was breaking me. I wiped my tears with the sleeve of my shirt, trying to stay composed, though it felt like my heart was shattering with each passing moment.

She hung up the call and broke the silence between us again, but this time with finality. "This is the last time we're meeting. I've given you the sketch, and now, please don't call me again. I never said I loved you, so don't blame me for anything. Don't say I cheated you."

Her words were cold, mechanical, like she'd rehearsed them before. She didn't even look at me while speaking, as though I wasn't worth her gaze anymore.

I sighed, a sound so deep and full of pain that I thought for a second she might feel it too. But she didn't react. She just stared out the window, waiting for this meeting to end.

I wiped away another tear and kept driving, saying nothing. There was nothing left to say. When I dropped her off at her PG, she waved goodbye with a half-hearted gesture, like this was just another part of her day. I watched her walk away, feeling a hollowness inside me that words couldn't fill.

After a few hours, my phone buzzed again. It was her. My heart leaped, betraying every promise I had made to myself. I picked up the phone, half hoping, half dreading what she might say.

"Can you come meet me again?" Her tone wasn't cold this time, but it wasn't warm either. "I need to go to the ATM. My landlord wants the money, and it's late. I don't feel safe going alone."

For a second, I just stared at the phone, trying to make sense of why she would call me for something so trivial after what had just happened. But I didn't ask any questions. I agreed, like a fool, and started my car again.

As I drove to her PG, a war raged inside me. My stupid heart was still clinging to hope, still wishing that maybe this time, things would be different, while my mind knew better. I knew she didn't feel the same. I knew that no matter how much I wanted it, we weren't going to work out. But hope is a dangerous thing—it keeps you tethered to the impossible.

I reached her PG and called her. She came out quickly, looking casual, almost indifferent. We didn't exchange many words as I drove her to the ATM.

Once we got there, she went inside while I followed, but the moment I stepped in, the weight of everything hit me again. Her indifference, her coldness—it was too much. I couldn't stand there and pretend I wasn't breaking inside. I left and returned to the car, closing the door behind me and burying my face in my hands. The tears flowed freely this time. I cried into my hands, gripping the steering wheel as though it could somehow hold me together.

When she came back, I quickly wiped my face and sat up, pretending nothing had happened. I didn't want her to see me like this—not again.

She got into the car, said a simple "thank you," and I drove her back to her PG in silence. There were no words left between us. I dropped her off, and without even a proper goodbye, she was gone again.

As I drove away, the empty space in the passenger seat seemed to echo the emptiness inside me.

That night, I was desperate. The kind of desperation that consumes you, makes your hands shake, makes your mind race in circles. I needed drugs. The addiction had wrapped itself around me so tightly that I couldn't think straight without it. I could feel it under my skin, in my bones—a gnawing hunger that wouldn't go away.

But I was running out of money. My earnings had already vanished into the void of drugs and booze, leaving me with barely anything. I didn't want to dip into my savings—not yet. But I knew I was already slipping. It scared me how quickly I had fallen, how clear it was now why addicts destroy themselves for that next hit. I was on the same path, and even knowing that, I still kept walking down it.

With my wallet nearly empty, I called up one of my friends. I hated myself for doing it, but I needed the money. "Can you lend me two thousand?" I asked, the shame heavy in my voice.

He didn't ask too many questions. It was a quick exchange, and soon I had the cash in hand. My next move was automatic—I headed straight to meet my dealer. But when I arrived at the usual spot, he was nowhere to be found. I tried calling Sunny, but his phone was switched off. Panic started to creep in. I needed this. I needed to find him.

Out of options, I called Anjie. "Do you know where he is?" I asked, trying to keep the desperation out of my voice.

"Where are you?" she asked, her voice soft but curious.

"I'm outside the club," I replied, pacing around anxiously.

"I'm close by. I'll be there soon." she said.

A few minutes later, I saw her pulling up. She stepped out of the car, looking stunning in a red dress that clung to her like she'd just walked off a magazine cover. As she walked up to me, she smiled warmly, and before I could react, she gave me a hug. Her warmth, her scent—it all caught me off guard. I wasn't expecting that kind of affection.

"You want to come inside?" she asked, nodding toward the club entrance.

I shook my head. "No, I'm... I'm not in the mood for it tonight."

She smiled again, not pressing the issue. "Let's take a walk then."

I hesitated but couldn't bring myself to say no. Something about her presence, the way she looked at me—it was comforting, and I didn't want to push her away. We started walking, the cool night air filling the silence between us.

After a while, she asked, "So why were you looking for Sunny? You didn't call him before coming. Was this unplanned?"

I sighed, not really wanting to answer, but there was no point in lying. "I needed to buy something. I came alone, but I couldn't get it. I thought Sunny could help me."

Her expression softened. She stopped walking and placed her hand gently on my cheek. The gesture was so tender, so unexpected, that I felt my heart twist. "Please stop this," she said quietly. "It's not for you. You're better than this."

Her words stung, but not in the way I expected. They weren't harsh. They were kind. She was showing me the care and concern I had longed for, but from someone else—someone who wasn't Jojo. It confused me. I wasn't used to kindness anymore. I was used to people mocking me, to being dismissed.

I looked into her eyes, and for a moment, I saw something I had been searching for. The care in her gaze was what I had always wanted, but not from her. It was supposed to be Jojo. *Why couldn't it have been Jojo?*

"I can't even sleep without it," I admitted, my voice breaking slightly. It felt good to confess it, even if it felt like admitting defeat.

Anjie reached into her purse and scribbled something down on a piece of paper. She handed it to me. "These are some meds that can help. They'll take the edge off, help you get through this." She paused and then looked at me with a seriousness I hadn't seen before. "But you have to promise me you'll stop. No more drugs."

I wanted to laugh at how simple she made it sound. Just promise, and it's over. But the way she looked at me, the softness in her voice—I couldn't say no. Not to her.

"I promise," I said, and I meant it in that moment. If only for her smile, I meant it.

"I don't trust you," she said, her voice firm, her eyes holding mine. "I'll stay with you until the moment you leave."

"It's really not necessary," I replied, forcing a casual smile. "I promised you, didn't I?"

She tilted her head, unblinking. "Let's spend some time in talking. Let's sit somewhere. Can we go to your place?" It wasn't flirtatious, or hesitant—it was a question that felt like it already had an answer.

I faltered, the words catching in my throat. For a few seconds, I just stared, trying to process. What was she really asking?

Sensing my hesitation, she laughed softly, brushing off the tension. "Don't worry. You're safe with me," she said, her tone light but sincere. "I'm not here to take advantage of you in alone or murder you in your sleep."

I couldn't help but laugh, shaking my head. Something about her made it impossible to refuse. "Fine. Let's go, then."

We took my car. She slipped in beside me, radiating a quiet confidence in that red short dress that turned every glance into a distraction. As I drove, she settled into the seat, occasionally resting her hand on my arm, a gesture that felt like both reassurance and something more. As we drove, we talked—about her work, her thoughts on the city, little stories from our pasts. When she mentioned Jojo, I felt that familiar ache, but she only squeezed my arm, as if to say, I see you, and I'm here.

When we reached my apartment, I opened the door, gesturing her inside. "Make yourself comfortable," I said, trying to shake off the sudden awareness of how messy I'd left things.

She looked around, taking in the clutter of empty bottles on the kitchen counter, the remnants of nights I barely remembered. I offered her a drink, a half-hearted gesture, already feeling the weight of memories pressing in.

It reminded me of Jojo, actually. I remembered a time when Jojo had wanted to drink with me, but back then, I didn't keep alcohol in my place. I wasn't that person yet. But now? Now I had enough bottles to last a month. I almost laughed at the irony of it, but it wasn't funny. Not really.

"You've got quite the collection here," she said, gesturing to the bottles with a raised eyebrow. "Enough to open your own bar."

I shrugged, giving a half-hearted chuckle. "Yeah. I guess..."

I offered her one, and she accepted. We ended up on my bed, side by side, with a playlist running quietly from my laptop. The conversation was soft, drifting from topic to topic. At some point, we leaned back, shoulder to shoulder, the silence between us surprisingly comfortable. She reached for my arm, guiding it over her, then rested her head on my chest.

I looked down at her, really seeing her for the first time. She was beautiful in a way that felt both powerful and unguarded.

She looked at me with a softness I hadn't seen before, her gaze warm and unguarded.

She started moving her fingers in my hairs, kissed my forehead. She cupped my cheeks and made a cute kiss gesture like she wanted to kiss me right then.

She lay down, loosened her waist belt for comfort, removed her heels. She was playing with her hairs. All of these were signs that she wanted me to understand that I should follow her lead.

I asked her why she was doing all of this—not just the kiss, but everything. Was she just trying to make me feel better, or had she actually started to like me? After all, we barely knew each other.

She reached up, gently touching my cheek. "You know... I noticed you months ago, at Sunny's birthday party," she said, her voice barely above a whisper. "You probably don't remember. But I do. You were there, glued to your phone the whole time." She smiled, a little sad. "I'm guessing that was Jojo? but I liked you. I wished to talk to you but it seemed you weren't single."

"I don't remember. Sorry." I feel ashamed that how could someone ignore such a hot girl.

She looked at me, her eyes soft but conflicted. "I don't know why I'm here, either. Maybe I just can't stand to see you like this. Or maybe... maybe I'm trying to finally win over my crush and want to be with the one I liked once.." She paused, her voice quiet. "But I do know one thing—I don't want to watch you destroy yourself."

She fell silent, then leaned in and gently pressed her lips to mine. I turned toward her, wrapped my arm around her waist, and let myself sink into the kiss.

But suddenly, I pulled back, avoiding her gaze. "I... I can't do this," I murmured, feeling a knot of guilt in my chest. "You're amazing, and I love being with you, but... I don't think I have it in me to give you what you want. Not right now."

"It's okay," she said softly, forcing a smile that didn't reach her eyes.

Then we decided to head back to the club, where her friends were waiting. When we arrived, she paused before getting out, touching my cheek gently. "Promise me... no more drugs, okay?"

I nodded, managing a small smile.

She broke into a big, genuine smile, her eyes warm, before stepping out of the car.

She smiled, the kind of smile that made me feel like maybe I could be better, like maybe there was still hope. And for the first time in a long time, I didn't crave the drugs. I just wanted to hold on to that smile for a little longer.

We parted ways, and I didn't even drink that night. I went back to my room, thinking about her words, about the way she had touched my cheek. It stayed with me, lingering in my thoughts like a warm memory I didn't want to let go of.

A few days later, I heard some news at work that I wasn't prepared for. The company was offering transfers to Mumbai office for a few employees. Jojo had applied. The results hadn't been officially declared yet, but I saw her status online—she had qualified.

I wasn't happy. Not at all.

I didn't want her to go. As much as I had tried to convince myself that I could let her go, that I could move on, the thought of her leaving the city for good felt like losing her all over again—like the final nail in the coffin. She was moving further away, not just emotionally, but physically. And I wasn't ready for that.

I tried to push it out of my mind. I wanted to keep her out of my heart, to bury her somewhere deep where she couldn't reach me. But it was impossible. She was still there, lingering in every quiet moment, in every thought that I couldn't control.

I picked up my phone and typed out a message, wanting to tell her she had qualified for the Mumbai transfer. My thumb hovered over the send button, but something inside me stopped. What was I doing? Was I trying to hold on to her, or was I just scared of being alone again?

I deleted the text.

But then, as the minutes passed, the familiar urge to connect, to hear from her, grew stronger. My resolve broke, and I typed out another message. This time, I sent it: *You've qualified for Mumbai.*

She didn't reply.

I had expected her not to, but it still hurt. It always hurt.

And so, I sat there, staring at my phone, waiting for something that wasn't going to come. Again.

The next day, I was on her shift. The air felt heavy, and not just because of the Mumbai transfer announcements. It was because of her. My heart raced, but I kept my face neutral, my tone professional.

It was time to declare the results. I stood in front of the group, a sea of familiar faces staring back at me, waiting for their names to be called. I had done this a thousand times before—called out names, handed over something—but today felt different.

When her name was about to come up, I couldn't help but remember that time when I was distributing cards for another occasion. I was about to call her by her nickname, *Jojo*, the name only I used for her in private. She had gotten nervous then, rushing up to me before I could say it, a playful panic in her eyes. We had laughed about it later. But now, those memories felt distant, like they belonged to someone else. This time, she wasn't my Jojo. Everything had changed. I called her name—*Jolene*—with no trace of emotion, as though I were calling a stranger. No tremor in my voice, no smile on my face. It felt cold, but maybe that's what it needed to be. Cold.

And strangely, I felt a small, unexpected satisfaction. At least I had that control over myself—to be cold when it mattered.

She came forward, just like everyone else, but I could see it in her eyes—there was no nervous energy, no spark, no history between us, just a name on a list. I gave the same instructions to the group about reporting to the Mumbai office on July 30th, and the leaves for relocation starting July 23rd. My voice was steady, rehearsed. I told them to collect their transfer letters before they left. It was just business, just another day at work.

Everyone filtered out of the room, one by one. But she didn't. She stayed, standing there, not moving toward the door. I could feel her presence behind me, that familiar tension hanging between us. I knew she wanted to talk, but I didn't want any drama—not here, not in the office. So I stayed quiet, hoping she'd just leave. But just as I was about to step toward the door, she finally spoke.

"I need extra leaves," she said, her voice softer than I expected. "I want to go to my hometown before heading to Mumbai. To see my family."

I nodded, keeping my gaze neutral. "You can go," I replied. "I'll approve your leaves."

She paused for a moment, then added, "Can I get my transfer letter now?"

I hesitated but kept my expression blank. "I'll give it to you after the shift ends."

She agreed and left the room. I exhaled. When the shift was over, I drafted her transfer letter, sealing it in an envelope. For a moment, I paused, staring at the envelope. I could have written *Jolene* on it, the name that had become so foreign to me, but instead, I wrote *Jojo*—her nickname, my last token of love, the only piece of her that still felt like mine.

I walked over to her desk and handed it to her. No words were exchanged. No smiles. Just silence.

Later that evening, I sent her an SMS: *"May I drop you at the bus stand for the last time?"*

She replied after a while: *"You can drop me."*

There was no warmth in her response, but it was enough. It was something. I couldn't let her leave without one final gesture, one last time to be close to her, even if it meant nothing to her now.

I decided to get her something before she left for good. She was going to her hometown the next day but would return to Panchkula briefly to collect her things before heading to Mumbai. That gave me a week. I logged into an online shopping site and ordered a pair of earrings and a bracelet for her. And for myself, I bought a brooch in the shape of a guitar—something to remind me of this chapter of my life, a chapter that was closing whether I was ready or not.

The next morning, I went to her PG as planned. She came out with two large suitcases, struggling under their weight. I didn't hesitate; I helped her load them into the car. She didn't say much, and neither did I. A thick silence hung between us as we both got in.

I started driving, the familiar route to ISBT Sector 17 stretching out ahead of us. The silence was unbearable, but I couldn't bring myself to fill it.

Halfway through the drive, she broke the silence.

"You promised you wouldn't send me any more messages or call me," she said, her tone laced with mild annoyance.

I kept my eyes on the road, my hands gripping the steering wheel tighter than necessary. "Now onwards, I won't," I said quietly, feeling the sting of her words.

She scoffed. "You say that every time, but you never follow through."

Her words hit me harder than I expected. I felt the sharp pang of regret and the familiar ache of loving someone who no longer wanted me. I could sense her frustration, but what she didn't know—what she couldn't possibly understand—was how hard it was to stay away, to pretend like I didn't care when every part of me still did.

"I will this time," I said, my voice almost a whisper, more for myself than for her.

The whole way to Sector 17, I held onto my silence with a kind of fierce determination. I didn't trust myself to speak; I had no words to say, nothing I wanted to share. My mind was a whirlwind, but I kept it all locked up, refusing to let anything slip out. Maybe it was pride, or maybe I just didn't want to open up any old wounds.

When we arrived at the bus stand, I parked in the lot, and we both stepped out, walking side by side in strained silence. A bus was already waiting. I glanced at her, remembering the last time she'd faced problems catching her bus. This time, I wouldn't let that happen.

I checked the details with the driver, making sure everything was in order. Then, without thinking, I went ahead and bought her ticket. It was automatic, a small gesture of care that I couldn't suppress, no matter how much I tried to detach myself from her.

I walked back to her and handed over the ticket. Instead of gratitude, her response was sharp. "Why did you buy me the ticket? I didn't ask you to."

Her words hit me like a slap. This time, it was unbearable. Something inside me snapped.

"Did I say anything to you?" I shot back, my teeth clenched. "Why do you always have to be so rude?"

I couldn't take it anymore. Without waiting for her response, I stormed onto the bus, leaving her standing there alone. My hands were trembling, a flood of anger, hurt, and frustration building inside me—an intense, uncontrollable surge that I could barely contain.

I went inside the bus and placed her bags in the overhead compartment, trying to push down the rage bubbling up inside me. She followed a moment later, wearing a smile that was so fake, so painfully forced, I could barely stand to look at her.

I didn't return the smile. I just gestured for her to sit.

"You can sit here too," she said, her voice soft, almost coaxing.

"No," I replied sharply, without looking at her. "It's fine."

She insisted again, "Please, sit here."

Reluctantly, I sat down in the front seat, keeping my body turned slightly away from her.

She tried to fill the silence between us. "Say something."

But I couldn't. I sat there, staring at nothing, refusing to meet her gaze. My lips stayed sealed, locked with all the things I wanted to say but couldn't bring myself to speak.

The minutes ticked by, each one dragging out the inevitable goodbye. The bus driver finally climbed into his seat, signaling the start of the journey. I stood up, waved her a quick, half-hearted goodbye, and got off the bus.

As I stepped back into the open air, my legs felt heavy, like the ground beneath me was dragging me down. I didn't turn around. I couldn't bear to see her leave, to know that this was it—this was the end of whatever we had, or thought we had.

But her memories refused to leave me. They clung to me, stubborn and unyielding, like the pain I couldn't escape. As I walked back to my car, my thoughts were a whirlpool of anger and sorrow, spinning out of control.

I wasn't just hurting. I was *angry*. Angry at her, angry at myself for still caring. Angry at the way things had fallen apart so completely. I wanted to unleash it, to scream, to hit something—*anything*—just to let the frustration out.

But there was nowhere for it to go. I was too much of a coward to take the anger out on anyone else, too afraid to confront the world that had turned on me. But I couldn't hold it in anymore. The stress, the rejection, the sheer weight of my brokenness was too much to bear.

When I got home, the anger was still burning under my skin, a heat that wouldn't cool. My mind was racing, wild and unmoored. I needed to release it, to do something—*anything*—to stop feeling like this.

I found a blade in my drawer. My hands were shaking as I held it, but I didn't hesitate. I dragged it across my palm once. Then again. And again.

The cuts multiplied, more than twenty by the time I stopped, but I barely felt the sting. The physical pain was nothing compared to the storm inside me. The soreness I felt in my heart drowned out everything else. This, at least, was something I could control—this was pain I could understand.

Blood dripped slowly from my hand, staining the floor, the bed, the sheets. I didn't care. I barely noticed. Exhausted from the rush of emotions, I fell asleep, the blade still lying beside me.

When I woke up the next morning, my head was throbbing, my eyes dry and sore. I looked around, disoriented for a moment, and then saw the bloodstained sheets. It hit me all at once—the mess, the shame, the disgust at myself.

I hated myself for what I had done.

My palm ached, but the deeper pain—the one buried in my chest—was still there, gnawing away at me. I stared at the cuts, the lines etched into my skin, and felt nothing but regret.

I got up, washed my hands carefully, trying to avoid the sting. Then I went out, bought some bandages, and wrapped my palm, covering the evidence of what I had done.

But the bandages couldn't cover the deeper truth: that I had become someone I didn't recognize. I had spent so much time in this city, hating every part of it—hating her, hating myself. I had lost myself in drugs, in memories, in the toxic cycle of longing and rejection.

The worst part? I wasn't just broken. I was *craving.* Craving for something real, for love, for anything that would make me feel whole again. But that desire had turned me into something unrecognizable—someone desperate and destroyed.

It was time to move on. I couldn't stay here anymore. The city, the drugs, the memories—it was all too much. Every street, every corner, reminded me of her, of the pain, of the person I had become. And I couldn't bear it any longer.

I hated this girl.

I hated my car, the one we had driven in so many times together. Every time I sat in it, I could still feel her presence, lingering like a ghost, haunting me with memories I couldn't erase. I hated the way the engine's hum reminded me of the long, silent drives we had shared when the distance between us had already started to grow.

I hated my phone, the way it buzzed with the occasional hope of her message. Every vibration was a cruel joke, making me expect a call or a text that would never come. And when it did, it was only to tear me apart further.

I hated that damn attendance sheet at work, the one I scanned every day, my eyes instinctively searching for her name, even though I knew I shouldn't care. But there it was, staring back at me, forcing me to confront the fact that she was still in my orbit, even if she didn't want to be.

I hated Facebook—the profile that once had her name linked to mine now only served as a painful reminder that I had been deleted, erased from her life as easily as a click of a button.

And this hate, this burning, relentless hate, had reached its peak. It was all-consuming, spreading through every aspect of my life. It wasn't just about her anymore. It was about everything—everything that reminded me of her, everything that tied me to her memory. My car, my phone, my office, my so-called friends, even the damn computer I stared at every day.

I wanted to quit it all. I wanted to disappear. To be isolated, away from everything that connected me to her. I wanted to vanish into a place where I didn't have to think about her, didn't have to feel this hate that was eating me alive. The desire to escape became overwhelming. My hatred made me desperate for an end, not just to my connection with her, but to everything. To life itself, because in some twisted way, it felt like my life belonged to her now, as though she had taken ownership of it the day she walked out of mine.

I looked at myself in the mirror, and what stared back at me wasn't someone I recognized. There was no trace of the person I used to be. The reflection was of a man broken, haunted, and consumed by something far darker than love. I looked at myself and felt... empty. The sensual, confident man I once knew was gone, replaced by someone I didn't want to be.

The next day, in the evening, my phone buzzed with an SMS. I almost ignored it, expecting another meaningless notification, but the sender's name stopped me cold: Jojo.

I opened the message, my heart constricting even though I wanted to feel nothing.

*"Hi all, please help me with a reservation as I'm unable to book a ticket to Mumbai."*

It wasn't personal. It wasn't even meant for me alone. She had sent it to all her friends, a group broadcast, but still... it was her.

I stared at the message, feeling a strange mix of emotions twisting inside me. The anger, the resentment, and yet... the urge to help her. Why was I still doing this? Why was I still chained to her? Maybe it was the hatred that drove me, the need to prove something to myself—or to her. Or maybe it was just the remnants of something deeper, something I couldn't admit to myself.

Without thinking too much, I grabbed my keys and headed out. I went to a booking office, determined to book her ticket. When I arrived, two girls were sitting behind the desk. I approached one and asked about railway reservations.

She asked me for the passenger details and the specifics of the journey. As she clicked away on the computer, checking availability, my mind raced. What the hell was I doing? Why was I still playing this role in her life, helping her when all I wanted was to forget her?

After some back-and-forth, the girl told me it was difficult to book a ticket on such short notice. For a moment, I thought about walking out, letting it go, but she made a phone call and after a brief discussion, confirmed that the ticket had been booked. The only issue was that she couldn't give me the physical ticket until the next day because of some problem with her Microsoft Outlook.

She reassured me, though. "She'll get an SMS confirmation soon," she said, her voice firm.

I stepped outside and called Jojo. My breath hitched as I waited for her to answer, the familiar dread creeping in. When she picked up, I asked if she had received the SMS about the reservation.

"No, I haven't," she replied, sounding distracted.

I confirmed that I had booked her a railway ticket from Delhi to Mumbai for July 28th. She thanked me, a short, hollow response that only added to the knot in my stomach. And then, like always, I disconnected the call, feeling a strange emptiness in its wake.

What was I doing? Why was I still doing this for her, this girl I supposedly hated? Maybe hatred wasn't the right word anymore. Maybe this was something else entirely—something darker and more twisted.

The next morning, I went back to the office to collect the physical ticket. It was ready. I stared at it for a moment before shoving it into my pocket. It felt like a strange symbol of my inability to let go, this simple piece of paper representing all the ways I was still tied to her.

I called her again, asking when she would be available to pick it up.

"I'll come tomorrow," she said, her tone indifferent.

I told her I'd give the tickets to Preeti at the office, and she could collect them from her. It would be easier, less personal—another step toward detaching myself. But she said she'd rather take them directly from me. "I'll meet you before I leave for Mumbai," she added, her tone matter-of-fact.

Something in her words twisted inside me, as if she still had some invisible thread tied to me, tugging just enough to keep me close, but never enough to pull me back in fully. That day in the office, while all the staff members were filling their TDS returns, I asked her casually if she had received her Form 16 on her email. She nodded, confirming she had it.

"Forward it to me," I offered, trying to sound detached. "I can file the return on your behalf."

She sent the emails without a second thought. It was an automatic gesture, just like it had always been—like she trusted me to take care of the small things, even if she didn't want to deal with the bigger ones anymore.

I asked her for her bank details so I could finish the filing. She said she'd give them to me later. I realized after I'd asked that I already had access to her information through the database, but somehow, asking her directly felt different. Maybe I just wanted her to share something with me willingly, even if it was as simple as her account number.

The next day, she called me. My heart did that ridiculous leap it always did when her name flashed on my screen, even though I knew better by now.

She told me she was preparing to leave for Delhi, that she would be going by bus. "Who are you going with?" I asked, hoping she wasn't entirely on her own.

"I'm going alone," she said, her voice steady, though I could sense a hint of unease. "I'll take a bus to the Delhi Railway Station."

Without thinking, I found myself offering, "I can drive you to Delhi. I'm free, and it'd be easier than going by bus."

She paused, considering the offer. Then, to my surprise, she agreed. It wasn't much, but it was something. Maybe it was just practical for her, but for me, it was another chance to be with her—another chance I shouldn't have wanted but still did.

We agreed that we'd leave for Delhi on the 28th. There was no emotion in the arrangement, just a plan, but it was enough to keep me tethered.

On the evening of July 27th, I called her again. I couldn't help myself. "Did you finish packing?" I asked, trying to sound casual.

She had, but there was something in her voice that made me uneasy. She sounded... unhinged, like she was barely keeping it together.

"What's wrong?" I pressed, unable to ignore the tone in her voice.

"I'm so worried about going to Mumbai," she admitted, her words coming out in a rush. "I'm going alone because the other girls got reservations on a different train. I don't know what to do when I get there. I haven't even arranged for a PG yet. I don't know where I'm going to stay."

Her anxiety washed over me. I could hear the worry, the fear she was trying to hide. She'd always been good at that—keeping her fears under the surface, showing only calm to the outside world. But now, in this moment, she sounded vulnerable in a way she hadn't before. And something in me stirred again, that old need to protect her, to fix things.

"Don't worry about that," I said quickly, trying to calm her down. "My sister lives in Mumbai. You can stay with her until you find a PG."

She didn't answer right away, and I could tell she was weighing the option, trying to decide if she could accept my help.

"I haven't slept for the last two nights," she confessed. "I keep thinking about the journey. I don't want to go alone."

Her words cut through me. The idea of her, the girl I had once loved so deeply, alone and afraid in a city she didn't know, gnawed at me. I wanted to be the one to make things easier for her, to take away her fears, just like I had tried to do all those times before.

I took my leave for the next day, planning to drive her to Delhi, and then I hung up, feeling both hopeful and heartbroken. I wanted to fix her problems, to be the person she turned to when things got hard. But I knew, deep down, that she didn't want that from me anymore. She didn't want me to be her protector. She just needed someone, anyone, to fill a temporary void.

That evening, my online order for her arrived. The earrings and bracelet I had bought for her were finally here. I stared at them for a long moment, wondering if she'd even care. Would she smile? Would she appreciate the gesture, or would it be another thing she discarded, like the memories we once shared?

I called her again in the evening. "Are your bags ready for tomorrow?" I asked.

She was still tense, still worried about going alone. The same fears she'd expressed before lingered in her voice. The other girls weren't arriving until later in the evening, and the idea of her being in a strange city by herself seemed to be eating away at her.

Without thinking, I offered again, this time going further. "What if I come with you to Mumbai?" The words were out before I could stop them.

There was a pause, and then, her voice firm, she said, "No. Don't do that."

Her refusal was sharp, like a cold splash of water. She didn't want me there. Not in Mumbai. Not in her life. Not in the way I still wanted to be.

And just like that, the illusion of being her safety net shattered. I realized, painfully, that while I was still trying to be her anchor, she didn't need or want one anymore. Not from me, at least.

I kept turning over alternatives in my head. Jojo's anxiety about the journey to Mumbai weighed heavily on me, and though she had refused my offer to accompany her, I couldn't just leave her to fend for herself. I wanted to make the process easier for her. I couldn't let go, not yet.

The next morning, before heading to the office, I went to Mohali Airport. With what was left of my savings, I booked her a flight to Mumbai. I chose the timing carefully, making sure her flight would arrive after the other girls. That way, they'd already have some arrangements in place, and she wouldn't have to navigate a strange city alone. It felt like the best solution, a way to protect her even from a distance.

Once everything was set, I sent her a message: *"I've booked a flight for tomorrow. We're not going to Delhi anymore."*

Her response was almost immediate. She called me while I was driving. I pulled over to the side of the road, turning off the engine, and answered.

She was angry, her voice tight with frustration. "Why did you book a flight without asking me?" she demanded, though there was something softer beneath her anger, a kind of reluctant gratitude.

I sighed, keeping my voice steady. "I just thought it'd be easier for you. You won't have to worry about the train or getting there alone."

She fell silent for a moment, and I could sense her emotions shifting, the anger retreating. But she wasn't ready to fully admit that I had done something kind. Instead, she just said, "We'll talk later."

"I'm heading to the office now," I replied, cutting the conversation short before she could dig deeper into her mixed feelings.

When I arrived at the office, everyone looked surprised to see me. I was supposed to be on leave that day. "Plan changed," I told them, forcing a smile. "I'll take my leave tomorrow instead." It felt strange, pretending everything was normal, when inside, I felt the weight of the previous night's conversation and the uncertainty of what was coming next.

Later that morning, we were finalizing the transfer details for the employees heading to the Mumbai office. It was a routine task—going over names, checking their paid leave balances, ensuring everything was in order. When her name appeared on the list, my heartbeat increased. I tried to focus, to treat it like any other name, but it wasn't.

Her leave balance showed zero. No paid days left. For a moment, I stared at the screen, fingers hovering over the keyboard. I knew what I was about to do was unethical. But when has love ever been logical?

Without thinking twice, I added two extra days to her balance. It was a small, almost meaningless gesture in the grand scheme of things, but somehow, it felt like something I had to do—one last act of love, hidden in the numbers. A silent goodbye.

It didn't change anything. It wouldn't bring her back. But I did it anyway—because I loved her. Because, despite everything, she was the one who taught me what love could feel like. Even if it was over, even if she was gone, a part of me still held on, refusing to let go of the pieces she left behind.

In the afternoon, I called her. I kept it brief, telling her I'd leave the flight ticket with Preeti, and she could collect it from her at the office. I thought it would be a cleaner break, not seeing her again. But she insisted on meeting me.

"Let's meet in the evening," she said, her voice calm, but I could sense the expectation behind it. She wanted to see me, not because she needed to, but because she felt obligated after I bought the ticket. I didn't want to meet her. I didn't want the awkwardness, the mix of emotions that always followed. But, as always, I couldn't refuse.

"Okay," I replied quietly. "I'll see you in the evening."

When evening came, I drove to her PG and parked outside, feeling the familiar tension creep into my chest. She came out and got into the car, her expression a mix of irritation and something else I couldn't quite place. She immediately started expressing her anger about the flight booking again, her words sharp and full of frustration.

I stayed silent, gripping the steering wheel and staring at the road ahead. Her words washed over me like a wave, but I didn't react. I just let her talk, let her anger spill out without engaging with it. I was too tired for this. Too tired of trying to explain myself, too tired of trying to justify my feelings or actions to someone who didn't want to hear them.

After a while, she ran out of steam. The car was quiet. She glanced at me, waiting for me to say something, but I remained silent. The tension in the car was thick, heavy with everything left unsaid.

I reached into the console and pulled out a chocolate I had bought for her. It was a small gesture, one I had done countless times before, back when things were different. She took it, a faint smile playing on her lips, the kind that wasn't real. She even made a small joke, saying at least this time it wasn't melted.

But there was no warmth behind the words.

Her eyes fell on my bandaged hand, and her smile faded. "What happened to your hand?" she asked, her voice softening. There was concern there, but it was distant, like she was checking on an acquaintance, not someone she once loved.

I shrugged, giving her a lie I had rehearsed. "Just hurt it on a table. It's nothing."

She looked at me, her gaze lingering longer than usual. "I know what happened," she said quietly, but I didn't respond. I kept my eyes fixed on the road, refusing to meet her gaze. I didn't want her to see the truth. I didn't want her to see how much I was still hurting, how much I was still holding on. Silence stretched between us, and I felt the weight of her words pressing down on me.

We drove to the CCD in Sector 11. It was a familiar place, one we had been to before, but now it felt different. The memories of our past seemed to linger in the air, heavy and suffocating. When we sat down, she seemed to sense my distance, my unwillingness to engage.

At first, she tried to pretend everything was fine, talking casually about her travel plans and Mumbai. But when she realized I wasn't paying attention, she grew quiet.

I sipped my coffee and flipped through a magazine, doing everything I could to avoid looking at her. I could feel her eyes on me, watching me with that same intensity she used to have when we were in love. But this time, I didn't respond. I kept my attention on the pages in front of me, even though I wasn't reading a single word.

She finally broke the silence between us, her voice softer now. "Put the magazine down and talk to me," she said, her eyes pleading for connection.

I sighed, reluctant but resigned, and set the magazine on the table. I turned to face her, meeting her gaze. Her eyes, once so full of warmth, now seemed burdened with uncertainty. I could see the weight of her thoughts, her fears etched in the way her lips quivered slightly.

I gestured for her to sit closer. "Come here," I said softly.

She hesitated for a moment, then got up from her seat and came to sit beside me. The closeness was familiar, yet different now, charged with an unspoken tension neither of us could quite navigate.

"What's really bothering you?" I asked, my voice low and steady.

She sighed, her shoulders slumping a little as the defences she had been holding onto began to crumble. "I'm just... I'm tense about everything. About going to Mumbai. About being alone there. I don't even know where I'm going to stay yet," she admitted, her voice cracking slightly. "And I'm worried about my career. What if things don't work out? I'll miss my friends... I haven't slept in three nights thinking about all of this."

I looked at her more closely, noticing for the first time how exhausted she looked. Her lips were trembling, and her eyes glistened with unshed tears. She was on the verge of breaking down, and for a moment, it was as if all her bravado had faded away, leaving her raw and exposed.

She was about to cry.

I reached over and gently rubbed her shoulder, offering what little comfort I could. "Hey, you're stronger than you think," I said softly. "You've made the brave decision to go to Mumbai alone, and that takes a lot of courage. Most people wouldn't even dare to take that step. You're going to figure it out once you get there. And yes, it'll be hard at first, but it's a big step for your career, and I know you'll thrive."

Her wet eyes met mine, and I could see the gratitude flickering there, even if she didn't say it out loud. I continued, trying to lift her spirits. "You've already made a decision that I'm not even sure I would have had the guts to make. That shows how capable you are. You've faced challenges before, and this is just another one. I believe in you."

Her expression softened, and I could see the tension slowly easing from her face. She took a deep breath, as though my words had given her some relief, even if it was just temporary.

"Thank you," she whispered, her voice barely audible.

I nodded, sensing that the moment needed no further words. Then, after a pause, I asked, "Do you want to go to the lake with me? Just one last time before you leave."

I wanted to hold onto those memories, to live those moments with her again, even if only for a little while—one last chance to feel what we once had, before it all became just another memory.

She nodded, a small smile tugging at the corners of her mouth. It wasn't much, but it was enough.

As we walked to the car, she broke the silence again, her voice more composed. "Why did you book the flight for me?" she asked, her tone less accusatory now, more curious.

I glanced at her and then back at the road. "I didn't want you going alone on the train, especially at night. You don't know who's going to be sitting near you, and I didn't want you feeling uncomfortable. I was also worried about your stuff, all your belongings. The flight seemed like the safest option. Plus, this way, the other girls will already be in Mumbai when you arrive, and they'll have figured out some arrangements by then."

She murmured a soft, "Hmm," as if she was processing what I had said, but didn't push further. Her mind seemed to drift back to her worries, still weighed down by the thought of the journey ahead.

When we sat back in the car, her sadness lingered, like a shadow that refused to leave. I glanced at her, sensing her unease, and asked quietly, "Do you need a hug?"

She shook her head, trying to force a smile. "No, I'm fine."

I didn't press her further. Instead, I reached into the back seat and pulled out the gifts I had bought for her. "Here," I said, handing them over without much fanfare.

She looked at the neatly wrapped boxes in surprise, her fingers running over the edges of the paper. "Why did you buy me gifts?" she asked, almost accusingly, but her voice was soft.

I didn't answer. I didn't know how to explain it, or maybe I just didn't want to. I watched her unwrap the bracelet and earrings, waiting for her reaction.

Her eyes lit up slightly when she saw the pair of earrings, but she let out a small laugh as she held up the bracelet. "Preeti has this exact same bracelet," she said, smiling faintly.

I smiled back, shaking my head. "Figures. I've got a talent for picking disaster gifts."

But she liked the earrings, and that small victory made me feel a little better. At least it wasn't a complete failure.

As we drove to the lake, the silence between us felt heavy but oddly familiar, like so many other silences we'd shared recently. Then, breaking the quiet, she asked, "Do you ever think about going to Mumbai?"

Her question caught me off guard. For a brief moment, my mind flashed back to a conversation I had with my dad months ago, when everything between Jojo and I was still good, when the future seemed full of possibilities. I had asked him casually, almost excitedly, *"What if I don't join the family business and move to Mumbai instead?"*

I remember the thoughtful pause on the other end. My dad had agreed, surprisingly open to the idea. *"If that's what you want, go for it."*

Back then, the idea of moving to Mumbai had felt exciting, like a new adventure, and I'd imagined evenings with Jojo, exploring the city together. It had seemed so simple, so full of promise.

But now, the thought of Mumbai only brought a deep, sinking pain. That future wasn't mine anymore. I didn't tell her about the conversation with my dad—I couldn't. It felt like revealing a dream that had already slipped through my fingers, like holding on to something that had long since crumbled.

So instead, I kept my voice steady and said, "There's nothing in Mumbai for me."

She didn't push further. Maybe she sensed the weight behind my words, or maybe she was too lost in her own thoughts to notice the shift in mine.

We reached the lake as the sun was beginning to set. We found a quiet spot and sat down, looking out at the water as the soft breeze played with the surface. It was peaceful, serene, but the silence between us was still charged with unspoken things.

She turned to me after a while and confessed, "I haven't told my parents I'm flying to Mumbai. They think I'm going by train." Her voice was low, almost guilty. "And I couldn't tell them that you booked the flight for me. They've been calling to check where I am, and I haven't answered their calls."

I glanced at her, a mixture of concern and amusement tugging at me. "Why didn't you just tell them?"

She sighed, glancing at her phone. "I don't know. I just... I didn't want to deal with their questions. And now they're probably worried."

At that moment, her phone buzzed, and her sister's name flashed on the screen. Jojo looked at me with a tired, apologetic expression. "It's because of you," she said, half-joking but with an edge of truth. "I'm having to avoid all these calls because of you."

I smiled gently, not taking the bait. "Just send her a message. Tell her you're fine, but the network's bad or something."

"You always have a tricky solution for everything, don't you?" she said, smiling at me.

I forced a small smile in return, but my thoughts were elsewhere. She had no idea how lost I felt, how helpless I had become. Solutions? I wasn't finding any—not for the mess my love life had turned into. Not for the tangled web of emotions I was caught in, spinning in circles with no way out.

Her phone started ringing. The familiar chime cut through the air, interrupting our moment. It was her friend calling. I gestured for her to pick it up. "Go ahead, take it," I said.

I stood up, giving her space, and moved a few steps away. She answered the call, and I could hear her voice relaxed and carefree. The conversation lasted for twenty minutes, and all the while, I waited, standing off to the side, lost in my thoughts.

When she finally hung up, she came back over to where I was standing, as if nothing had happened. We tried to restart our conversation, but something inside me had shifted. I knew we had little time left, and there was still so much left unsaid. I wanted to clear the air before she left for good, but just as I opened my mouth, her phone rang again.

"Who's calling?" I asked, though I already had a sinking feeling.

"Nikhil," she said, almost casually.

A familiar hollow feeling crept over me. Of course. Him again.

I sighed, trying to suppress the bitterness rising in my throat. I stood up once more, moving further away to give her privacy. I didn't want to hear any of it—didn't want to listen to her talking to him, knowing full well that no matter how much I tried to be here for her, he was always lingering in the background.

She motioned for me to stay, to sit with her while she talked, but I shook my head. I couldn't do it. I couldn't sit there and pretend that listening to her speak with her ex-boyfriend didn't tear me apart. So, I walked a little further, distancing myself from the conversation that was already pulling me down.

The minutes stretched into more than half an hour. I sat down on the stones, trying to distract myself with the peacefulness of the lake, the breeze rustling through the trees, the faint sounds of the world moving on around me. The quiet serenity of the environment was a stark contrast to the turmoil inside me.

*It doesn't matter*, I told myself. *This is why she wanted to meet me today—just to keep me on the sidelines while she talked to him.* I lay back, feeling the coolness of the stones against my skin, trying to numb myself to the hurt.

Eventually, she came back, her call with Nikhil finished. She sat down beside me, as if nothing had changed, and asked me to stand up. I did, but the weight of everything was too much. The disappointment, the frustration, the sense of rejection that had become all too familiar.

"I think it's time to go," I said, my voice quieter than I intended. "Let's head back." I didn't want to stay anymore. I didn't want to sit here, pretending like everything was fine, like we could still have a normal conversation after she'd spent more time on the phone with her ex than with me.

As we walked back to the parking area, she broke the silence. "Nikhil asked if he could come with me to the airport tomorrow," she said, looking at me carefully. "But I told him no. I want you to come with me."

Her words didn't bring the comfort they should have. Instead, they felt hollow. I knew the only reason she was coming with me was because I had booked the flight. If it hadn't been for that, she would have had no reason to meet me at all. I felt like a second choice—like an obligation rather than someone she wanted to be with. She was only coming along to pay her gratitude, a polite gesture rather than a genuine desire to be by my side.

"You should go with him," I said, trying to keep my voice neutral, even though the words felt like they were burning in my throat. "He clearly wants to be with you, and you two have so much history. Why not let him take you?"

But she shook her head, brushing off my suggestion. "I'm going with you," she insisted.

Her words made no sense to me, and neither did this entire situation. I was so tired of trying to figure out where I stood with her. Everything felt like a painful loop of contradictions, with her giving me just enough to keep me close but never enough to make me feel secure. Our conversation was going nowhere, and the more I tried to understand, the more confused I became.

As we neared the car, I turned to her, the heaviness in my heart impossible to ignore. "Can I hold your hand one last time?" I asked, my voice barely above a whisper.

She looked at me, her expression unreadable. "You don't need to ask," she said. "You can hold my hand whenever you want."

But her words didn't comfort me. If anything, they made everything feel more distant, more confusing. I reached out and took her hand, feeling its familiar warmth, but the connection we once had was gone. I was holding on to someone who was no longer truly there with me, and the realization was crushing.

*Why is she behaving like this?* I thought, my heart aching with the weight of all the unspoken feelings between us. If she didn't care, why did she ask me to meet her? Why did she hold my hand? Why was she here at all?

I wanted her to love me the way I loved her. I wanted to believe that there was still something between us, that somehow, all of this would matter. But deep down, I knew it wasn't working anymore. Trying to make her love me was like trying to hold on to water—it slipped through my fingers, no matter how tightly I tried to grasp it.

Perhaps, for her, all of this love—everything I was feeling—meant nothing. But for me, it was everything. It was all I had left.

We got into the car, the familiar tension hanging between us like a weight that neither of us could shake off. I tried to break the silence. "Do you want to grab some dinner?" I asked, though part of me already knew the answer.

She shook her head. "I'll eat at my PG," she said flatly.

So we drove in silence. The streets seemed darker than usual, or maybe it was just my mood. As we neared her PG, I glanced at her, hoping for some kind of smile, a gesture, anything to soften the goodbye. But as usual, there was nothing. She stared out of the window, distant, as though she had already left.

I pulled up outside her building and parked. It should have ended there, but something inside me wasn't ready to let the day close on such a cold note. I needed to leave her with something—something that wasn't just emptiness. I reached into my pocket, feeling the small brooch I had bought for myself. It had been a symbol, a little piece of something just for me, but now it felt like it had to be hers.

"I have one more gift for you," I said, trying to sound casual.

She sighed, her tone tired and impatient. "Now what?" she asked, like she was getting sick of me. Her words stung, but I tried not to let it show. I knew her irritation wasn't really about the gifts or even me—it was about something deeper, something unspoken that neither of us could name.

I pulled out the brooch and held it out to her. "Here," I said, my voice softer than I intended. "Give this to the person you fall in love with in the future."

Maybe it was a way to release her, or maybe I just wanted her to feel a fraction of the hurt she'd left me with. A bitter satisfaction crept in as I said it—a final act of letting go, even if it stung.

She frowned, her face hardening. At first, she didn't want to take it, her expression making it clear she didn't understand why I was doing this. But after a moment of hesitation, she took it from me, her fingers closing around it with reluctance. Her face was set in a kind of angry frustration, as though this last gesture was a burden she didn't want to carry.

She opened the door to step out, but something inside me held on. There was a finality to this that I wasn't ready for, even though I had been preparing myself for weeks.

Before she could say anything, I reached into the dashboard and pulled out the printed flight tickets. The papers had been sitting there all day, waiting for this moment.

"Take this," I said, handing them over to her. She looked down at the papers, her expression unreadable.

"You can go with him tomorrow," I continued, keeping my voice steady, even though a lump was building inside me. "I've already spent this day with you. I don't need to come to the airport. I have work anyway." I delivered the words casually, not giving her a hint of the ache buried beneath them, refusing to let her see how much it hurt.

She didn't move to take the papers. She just stared at them, the silence stretching between us like a chasm. I could feel her hesitation, but I pushed forward, trying to make it easier for her. "It's fine, really. He wants to take you, and... I have things I need to do tomorrow."

She shook her head slowly, her lips pressed into a thin line. "No," she said, her voice firm but quiet. "You're coming with me."

I sighed, feeling both relief and frustration welling up inside me. "Jojo, it's okay. I don't need to—"

But she cut me off, her eyes hardening. "I want you to come. He's not coming. You are."

There was no room for argument in her tone, but I could still feel the wall between us, the same wall that had been there for so long now. She wasn't choosing me out of love or care—it was obligation. I could feel it in the way she refused to meet my gaze, in the way she grabbed her bag and stepped out of the car without looking back.

I watched as she walked into the building, still holding the tickets in my hand

Back at home, I thought about how I had wanted to leave her with something simple—something sweet. So I grabbed a packet of small chocolates, wanting, for once, to give her something that wasn't melted or broken. A final gesture of care.

Later that night, I called her, reminding her about the ID proof she'd need at the airport.

"Make sure you carry your ID tomorrow," I said. "You'll need it at the gate."

She sighed on the other end, sounding tired and slightly exasperated. "What should I take?" she asked. "I don't have my driving license or anything else."

"Just bring your office ID," I suggested.

"But my photo on that isn't clear," she replied, her voice softening. "Even the security guard at the airport is going to laugh at my photo. I don't want to carry this."

I couldn't help but laugh. There was something so familiar about the way she said it—like the Jojo I had known before everything got so complicated. "Don't worry," I reassured her. "It'll work. And besides, we don't really have another option."

She hesitated, then spoke in a playful, almost childish voice, "But... I don't know..." She sounded like a child on the verge of tears, and it made me smile.

It was in moments like these—small, fleeting moments—when my heart melted for her all over again. Her vulnerability, even if brief, reminded me of why I had fallen for her in the first place. "My baby," I said softly, my voice full of affection. "You look beautiful. It doesn't matter if your picture on the ID isn't perfect."

"Hmmm," she murmured, like she didn't fully believe me but appreciated the words anyway.

"Now go to sleep," I said, trying to sound firm but gentle. "I'll pick you up at 9:30 in the morning."

As I hung up the phone, a hollow emptiness washed over me—a longing to kiss her goodnight like I used to. But all I had now were words over the phone and the echo of memories that weren't coming back.

The next morning, her flight was at 11:30 AM. I woke up early, not because of Jojo but because I had to drop my brother off at the train station—he was headed to Gurgaon.

The drive to the station was uneventful, but on the way back, something jolted me out of my thoughts. A dog darted in front of the car, too quickly for me to swerve. I felt the sickening thud as the car struck it.

I slammed on the brakes and looked in the rearview mirror. The dog was limping, its leg clearly broken. Guilt surged through me, heavy and immediate. I whispered a quick "sorry" to God, feeling the weight of yet another thing gone wrong, another thing I couldn't fix.

There was nothing I could do. So I drove on, the image of the injured dog lingering in my mind like a bad omen.

When I got home, I collapsed back into bed, exhausted in every way. Sleep came quickly, but it was a restless kind of sleep, filled with dreams I couldn't quite hold on to.

I went to move the car to the parking area, taking my time, as if delaying the inevitable would somehow make it easier. Once I returned, I bought a visitor ticket for myself. I wasn't quite sure why I was still doing this—why I was still so determined to see her off. Part of me wanted to run away, but another part couldn't let go.

As I stood near the entrance, a man approached, extending his hand toward me. I blinked, caught off guard. Before I could react, Jojo said, "That's Nikhil." Her voice was soft, but I could hear the undercurrent of something warmer.

*Of course,* I thought, my stomach sinking. I reached out and shook his hand, trying to mask the bitter thoughts rising inside me. I looked him over quickly, wondering what it was about him that had captured her heart. He didn't seem like anything special to me. But then again, maybe that's what love is—beyond logic, beyond reason. It's just a choice. Her choice.

I let them talk, stepping aside to give them privacy, but my eyes betrayed me. No matter how much I told myself to look away, they kept focusing on the two of them. I couldn't help it. She was so animated with him, her smile wider and brighter than I'd seen in ages.

*That smile,* I thought, *the one I had been waiting for all this time... she gives it so freely to him.*

They were touching each other, their hands naturally intertwining as they spoke. She laughed with him, playfully hitting him the way she used to do with me—once upon a time when that laughter was mine to share. A deep, burning jealousy welled up inside me, followed by a searing pang of anger. I wanted to look away, but my body refused to cooperate.

I stood frozen, watching as she moved closer to him, wrapping her arms around his neck in a long, tight hug. I felt my heart twist violently in my chest, the slow ache becoming a stabbing pain. My breath quickened, and I knew that if I didn't pull myself together, I might fall apart right there. But I couldn't look away. I couldn't stop watching as her head rested on his shoulder, as if it belonged there, as if that was her true place of comfort.

A single tear slipped down my cheek before I could stop it. I bit into my lip hard, hoping the sharp pain would distract me from the emotional storm raging inside. But it didn't. Another tear followed, tracing the same path down to my lips. I bit harder, tasting salt and metal, forcing myself not to scream, not to break.

She looked so at peace in his arms, as if the world outside them didn't exist. And in that moment, I wished I didn't exist either. I wiped my tears quickly, hoping she wouldn't notice. But the truth was suffocating me—*her happiness was killing me inside.*

*Why is she showing me this?* I thought bitterly. *What did I do to deserve this?*

I knew from the start that he would come. She had always wanted him to be here. The only reason I was here at all was because I had booked her flight ticket. That realization stung more than anything.

As they finally pulled apart, still exchanging soft smiles and whispers, she walked back toward me. I was struggling to hold myself together, my hands clenched in fists. I didn't know how much longer I could stand there.

"You should call him back," I said, my voice flat. "Ask him to buy a visitor ticket so he can take you inside. I'm sure you'd be happier with him."

She shook her head, her face unreadable. "No," she said firmly. "You're coming with me."

I stared at her, confused and hurt. *Why?* Why was she doing this? Why was she dragging me through this if she didn't care? But I didn't ask. I couldn't find the words.

I followed her, but the emotions inside me were spiraling out of control. I tried to hide them, but it was impossible. As I pushed her luggage trolley toward the entrance, it got stuck on a small pillar outside the gate. Frustration welled up in me. I yanked the trolley hard, but it wouldn't budge. My anger surged, and I kicked the trolley with a sudden burst of fury, sending it jolting forward.

She watched me, her face blank, offering no reaction. The silence between us only fueled the fire in my chest, the weight of everything I'd held in for so long threatening to explode.

Finally, I sighed, forcing myself to calm down. I pulled the trolley back and moved it in a different direction, pushing ahead toward the security gate. She followed quietly beside me, as if the incident hadn't even registered.

When we reached the guard, she showed her office ID. The guard chuckled, clearly amused by the grainy, awkward photo. He looked at her, then at me, still smiling. "This is your ID?" he joked, shaking his head.

She turned to me, a playful smirk on her lips. "You're the one who told me to use this," she said, her voice light, almost teasing.

I forced a smile in return, but it didn't reach my eyes. It was a small moment of levity, something that should've been lighthearted, but all I could feel was the unbearable weight of what was about to happen.

Once we entered the terminal, I asked the security guard again about the process, not really because I needed to, but because I was stalling. I wasn't ready for this to end. He explained everything clearly, but my mind was elsewhere, focused on the fact that I couldn't follow her any further. I repeated the instructions to her, my voice softer now, as though I was telling myself just as much as her.

This was it.

I stood there, waiting, hoping—*expecting*—something before she left. A hug, at least. Something small to hold on to. But instead, with a quick toss of her head, she turned away without a word, pushing the trolley ahead of her. No look back, no pause, just gone.

I stood rooted to the spot, watching her disappear into the crowd, her figure getting smaller and smaller until she was swallowed by the airport bustle. Only then did I let the tears fall, wiping them away quickly, though no one was around to see.

*What did I expect?* I thought bitterly. *Hope's a shameful thing sometimes.*

I had taken leave from work that day, so I had no obligations, nothing to distract me. On a whim, I decided to drive to Kurukshetra, needing something—anything—to fill the hours. The road was long, but my thoughts were longer. Everything felt suspended in that moment, like the drive was just a way to keep myself from drowning in all the emotions I hadn't let out.

Then, as I was heading back home, my phone buzzed. A message.

*"Sorry I couldn't hug you."*

I stared at the screen for a moment, the words twisting in my head. She couldn't? Or she just didn't want to? The difference seemed huge now, though I wasn't sure why.

I typed my response quickly, my fingers moving before my mind caught up.

*"It was not needed,"* I wrote, pressing send. The lie settled heavily in my chest.

A few minutes later, another message.

*"Sorry for everything."*

I could feel my throat tighten, the words clinging to me like they had more weight than they should. What was she sorry for?

Everything? Or just the part of everything that still hurt me?

I sighed and sent back something simple, something I hoped would end the conversation without more disappointment.

*"When you reach there, please inform me."*

*"I'll call you upon reaching,"* she replied quickly.

I tried not to put too much stock into her promise. Part of me wanted to believe it, wanted to cling to the idea that she still cared enough to call. But the other part of me—the part that had watched her walk away without looking back—was already bracing for the silence.

That evening, though, my phone rang. Her name flashed on the screen. For a second, I just stared at it, feeling that familiar flutter of hope that had become too ingrained to shake. I answered quickly, before I could overthink it.

"I've reached here and I'm fine," she said. Her voice was soft, almost distant, like she was distracted.

We didn't talk much. She was with her friend, and the conversation felt like something she had to do, a formality. I knew there wouldn't be much more than that.

The next day, I tried to call her again. No response. I wasn't sure about her office timings or what her day looked like, so I tried not to overthink it. But as the hours passed without any reply, that familiar anger and anxiety began to creep in.

I sent her a message. *"How are you? Where are you living?"* The questions felt hollow, like they were just ways to fill the space between us, but I was genuinely worried about her.

Still, no response.

By the evening, my frustration had reached its peak. I called her again, this time with more urgency. I hated feeling this way—like I was chasing after her, like I couldn't let go even though everything pointed to the fact that I needed to.

Finally, she answered.

She shouted at me, her voice cutting through the silence like a blade. "Why are you making me annoyed? I'm so frustrated here. I haven't even found a PG yet. Please, just stop contacting me right now!"

For a second, there was silence on the line.

"Bye." I said.

I didn't wait for her to say goodbye. I slammed my phone shut, my hand trembling with a mix of anger and pain. I had wanted a goodbye, something final, but not like this. Not with this bitterness.

It was the last time we spoke. And in that moment, I hated her for it.

With trembling fingers, I picked up my phone and sent Jojo one final message. *"I promise I'll never contact you again. But if you ever need help, don't hesitate. My sister and a good friend are in Mumbai. Love you. Take care."*

A few minutes passed, and then the phone buzzed again—her name flashing on the screen.

I hesitated before answering, already bracing myself for the worst. "Why didn't you talk to me earlier?" I asked, my voice cracking under the weight of all the unanswered questions.

And then she told me.

All my faults. Everything I had done wrong. And as she spoke, I realized, painfully, that this was exactly why I loved her. She was a mirror, reflecting back my mistakes with brutal honesty.

"I loved you truly," she began, her voice steady but full of hurt. "But when I asked you to give me some time to sort through my problems and confusion, you thought I was avoiding you. Rather than being patient, you pushed me away. I was trying to make myself stronger, to take a decision in favor of our relationship. But you had no patience."

Her words pierced me, each one cutting deeper than the last.

"My impatience was my biggest mistake," I admitted, though I knew it was too late.

She didn't stop. "You talked to me so rudely," she continued, her voice colder now. "The words you used in anger... no one would tolerate that kind of disrespect. I'll never forgive you for that."

There it was. The unforgivable.

After the call ended, her words echoed in my mind, each one cutting deeper than the last. *"I told you that I can't tolerate avoidance at all. But you did it anyway,* I thought bitterly. *You pushed me into a corner, made me do things, say things I never wanted to say."* I wanted to shout this at her, to let her know how her silence had driven me mad, how her absence had shifted my life upside down. I didn't know how to pick up the pieces, didn't know which direction to take, or even what my life was supposed to look like anymore. Everything felt scattered, chaotic—a mess of half-finished thoughts and dead ends, with no clear path forward. But I held back. It didn't matter now.

And maybe, deep down, she was right. I had let my fears take control, let my own insecurities ruin what we had. I should have trusted her, trusted what we'd built together. But instead, I'd let doubt and impatience consume me, leaving nothing but wreckage in their wake.

In the end, it was easier to blame her silence than to face the truth of my own actions. But the truth was unavoidable: I had destroyed everything we had, with my own hands.

I sat in silence, the reality of it all sinking in. There was no hope of her coming back. No more chances. I was filled with a sadness I couldn't shake, knowing I had been the one to tear us apart.

I needed to distract myself. To numb the pain. Facebook seemed like a good place to lose myself for a while, so I logged in, scrolling mindlessly through posts. But it didn't help. I felt empty.

Without thinking, I posted a status: *"I can't live without her. I should have trusted my love. I lost her because of my stupidity."*

The moment it went up, the comments started flooding in. But instead of offering comfort, my so-called friends turned it into a joke. Some called me a fool, others laughed at my constant crying over her. The cruelty of it hit me hard.

I didn't need friends like this.

"Fuck off, all of you," I typed out in anger, before permanently deleting my account. I was done with them. If these were the people I had been calling friends, I didn't want any part of it anymore.

Her birthday was coming up on August 13$^{th}$. It would be her first birthday in Mumbai. I had promised myself I wouldn't contact her again, but something inside me couldn't let go. I wanted her to forgive me, to come back—even though I knew she wouldn't.

I decided to send her a final gift. One last gesture.

This time, I wasn't going to trust an online shopping website. I wanted to pick something myself, something meaningful. A real gift that would show her how much I cared. A way to make things right, even if only in a small way.

I reached out to a friend, who also moved to Mumbai. They were living together now, and I asked her if he could give me her address so I could send the gift. She agreed and sent me the full address in the evening.

I got my salary on August 7$^{th}$. With the money finally in hand.

I didn't know exactly what I was looking for, but I hoped that when I found it, I would know. Something that might say all the things I hadn't been able to say. Something that might make up for everything I had done wrong.

But deep down, I knew—no gift could ever fix what had already been broken. I called off a friend to come shopping with me.

We reached the mall, and I couldn't help but feel a bit out of place. Two guys browsing the women's section, searching for the perfect—it was awkward, to say the least. But there I was, determined to find something beautiful for her, something that would make her pause and maybe, just maybe, remind her of the love we once shared.

After some time, we found ourselves at Patiala House, surrounded by elegant suits in every color and fabric imaginable. I gravitated toward a stunning white suit, intricately embroidered, soft to the touch. It was beautiful—just like her. It was also way beyond what I could comfortably afford, but I didn't care. This was supposed to be my last gift to her, the last piece of me I would give. If that meant dipping into my savings, so be it.

I handed over my debit card, wincing slightly at the total, but reassuring myself that it was worth it. *This was for her,* I kept thinking. The weight of the suit in my hands felt like the weight of my emotions—too heavy, yet something I couldn't let go of.

Afterward, we stopped by the DTDC office to ship it to Mumbai. The shipping alone cost 400 rupees—just another small price to pay for the love I was still trying to hold on to. As I watched the courier seal the package, I couldn't help but wonder what her reaction would be. Would she be excited? Would it soften her heart, even just a little?

A couple of days passed, and I checked the consignment number on the DTDC website. To my dismay, the status was still pending, and worse, the address displayed on the site was wrong. Panic crept in as I quickly sent an email to DTDC, hoping they hadn't botched the delivery. I explained the error and asked them to confirm the package was headed to the right place.

The following day, they responded, promising to notify me once it was delivered. I waited anxiously, checking my phone constantly, hoping for some kind of resolution. I wasn't just waiting for the package to be delivered—I was waiting for some sign from her, some acknowledgment that she hadn't forgotten me entirely.

Then, on August 12th, a day before her birthday, I got a call from an unknown number. It was the DTDC delivery boy.

"Sir, she refused to accept the courier," he said bluntly, his words hitting me like a punch to the gut.

My heart sank. *She refused it?* I struggled to process the rejection. After all the thought and care I'd put into choosing the suit, she wouldn't even accept it.

I quickly told the delivery boy to leave it with the security guard. "Just hand it over to him," I muttered, trying to keep my voice steady. He agreed and hung up.

August 13th. It was her birthday.

I couldn't help myself—I sent her a simple text: "Happy Birthday." No long message, no extra words—just that. I didn't expect a reply, and deep down, I knew I wouldn't get one.

In the office, we had this tradition of listing the names of employees who had birthdays on the notice board. It was a small gesture, something simple to acknowledge the day. She wasn't part of the office anymore, but I found myself adding her name anyway, right at the bottom of the list. I didn't use her full name. No, I wrote "Jojo."

She didn't work here anymore, and no one would expect me to write her name. But there it was, standing out quietly among the others.

A part of me knew it was foolish. Another mistake to add to my collection of senseless acts. But what did it matter? As if one more act of stupidity would make a difference now

About the courier, I waited, still holding on to the faint hope that maybe, once she saw the gift waiting for her, she would change her mind. Maybe she would pick it up, take a moment to look at the beautiful suit inside, and reach out to me. But the hours passed, and no call came. Not that evening, not the next day.

Ten days. Ten long days, and the gift remained with the security guard, untouched.

I felt hollow. I had bought it with so much love, but she didn't even want it.

In the evenings, I found myself talking to Preeti, hoping she could shed some light on the situation, give me some kind of insight into what was happening. I tried to keep it casual at first, but eventually, I couldn't hold back. I asked her if she could ask Jojo to take the suit, just so it wouldn't go to waste.

Preeti hesitated. She didn't want to get involved, afraid that it would only make things worse. "Every time I mention you, she starts a fight with me," Preeti admitted. Still, she promised to try, for my sake.

But later, I found out that it had only made things worse. Jojo had scolded her, accusing her of taking my side. Their conversation had spiraled into a fight, and Jojo stopped speaking to Preeti altogether after that.

I felt sick with guilt. Not only had Jojo refused my gift, but now I had caused a rift between her and one of her oldest friends. Preeti had only been trying to help me, and I had repaid her by straining their friendship. I had never wanted that.

"Don't be sad. Be happy," I whispered to myself, but the words rang hollow. I tried to push it out of my mind, to stop thinking about that suit and what it symbolized.

But deep down, I couldn't escape the truth.

I had wanted to make things right. I had wanted her to remember me, even just for a moment. But the gift, the gesture, everything—it was all in vain.

It was time to let go. I made a firm decision.

But then, after a few days, I heard from Preeti that Jojo had finally taken the courier from the security guard. For a brief moment, hope flared up inside me, a small, foolish flicker. *Maybe she had forgiven me,* I thought, *maybe this was a sign.* But just as quickly as the hope came, I stamped it out. I knew better than to believe in something that wasn't there anymore. She hadn't accepted the gift because of love, but probably out of respect, or maybe out of some lingering sense of obligation.

I wasn't happy. I wasn't sad either. I felt... nothing. I was neutral, a hollow shell of what I once was. It didn't matter if she took the gift or not. My emotions had been drained dry long ago. I was already broken inside, beyond the point where any external gesture could affect me.

Even though I missed her badly, the ache gnawing at me every single day, I had made a promise to her. I had sworn I wouldn't contact her again, and this time, I meant to keep my word. But that didn't stop me from asking Preeti about her. I couldn't resist.

"How is she?" I'd ask.

Preeti would tell me that they had started talking again, though not as much as before. Jojo, she said, was struggling to make ends meet. Her salary was only 8000 rupees in-hand, a pittance for surviving in a city like Mumbai. She was worried about how she'd manage until her promised raise in December. I knew how hard it must've been for her, how she was probably scraping by, every day a grind.

I wanted to help. Without telling anyone, I decided to start depositing money into her account. I found her bank details in our office database—something I probably shouldn't have done, but I didn't care. I needed to do something for her, even if she didn't know it was me.

I went to the bank and quietly deposited 3,000 rupees into her account. It wasn't much, but it was what I could afford. My own salary wasn't great, but I figured I could manage this until December. It wasn't about the money—it was about doing something, anything, to ease her burden.

I continued depositing money into Jojo's account until she received her long-awaited increment. I applied for jobs on her behalf, quietly working behind the scenes to make sure she was okay, even though she had no idea I was doing any of it.

But even after that, nothing changed inside me. I still felt abandoned, like I had been used and discarded. My life had become a routine of pretending I wasn't missing her, but deep down, I knew the truth. Every breath I took, every sleepless night, was filled with thoughts of her. I was living in a cycle of pain, telling myself I was moving on when all I was doing was sinking deeper into my own sorrow.

My nights were hell. Sleepless. Endless. Every day started with a bad morning, the kind where you don't even want to get out of bed because you know the day is going to be as empty as the one before. And every night ended in tears. No matter what I told myself, no matter how much I tried to bury it, I couldn't escape her memory.

And the drugs... I had promised Anjie I'd quit. But I broke that promise too, just like I had broken so many others. I couldn't help it. The drugs were the only thing that dulled the pain, that made the nights bearable.

One night, I was with Anjie and Sunny, the only people who still brought some kind of joy into my life. We had a good time—probably the only real fun I ever had anymore. They had become my escape, my new everything. I relied on them more than I realized.

We were having a wild night at the bar—dancing, drinking, shouting along to the music. For a moment, everything felt light, almost easy. Anjie kept looking at me with a mix of love and concern, her eyes lighting up every time I laughed. My smile seemed to make her genuinely happy.

After a while, we stepped out to the parking lot, still laughing and catching our breath. Anjie went off to use the restroom, and as soon as she was gone, I saw my chance. I turned to Sunny.

"Call the dealer," I said, keeping my voice low but firm.

He shook his head with a laugh. "Pagal hai kya?"

"I'm serious," I replied, my tone flat. I wasn't asking; I was demanding.

Sunny's face hardened as he studied me. "You keep this up, and it's going to kill you. You know you can't handle this stuff."

The craving gnawed at me, a restless, insistent need. I felt the urgency rise as I glanced toward the restroom, worried Anjie might come back any second. My voice turned sharp. "Just call him you asshole. Stop acting like this is a big deal."

He denied again.

The craving pulsed in me, urgent and heavy, like an itch I couldn't scratch. Anjie could be back any second, and I didn't have time for his lectures. I scoffed, frustration rising. "Saale, You take this stuff too, Sunny. So why deny it to me? Don't start this fake 'caring' drama now. Just call him and stop making a mess of things."

"Yes, we do, but we do this for fun and we know our limits. You are becoming addicted and yes I care for you because you are my friend. You just can't see now because you are desperate." He replied to me in higher volume.

Anger flared, hot and uncontrollable. "Oh, you care?" I scoffed, voice dripping with sarcasm. I was abusing continuously. Without thinking, I lunged for his pocket, trying to grab his phone. He pushed me back, and in the scuffle, the phone clattered to the ground. I scrambled to pick it up, but he shoved me away.

Something snapped inside me. I grabbed his collar, pulling him close, my voice a low, furious growl. "Just fucking call the damn dealer, Sunny."

He pushed me off, trying to get me to calm down. "You're out of control," he said, but his words only fueled my rage. I shoved him harder, and he stumbled back, eyes wide with shock.

At that moment, Anjie returned. She saw the chaos unfolding and rushed over, grabbing my arm. "Stop it!" she yelled, her voice pleading.

I barely registered her touch, my mind clouded by anger and need. I shook her off roughly, sending her stumbling back. She steadied herself and came closer, but I shoved her again, harder this time. She fell to the ground, her face a mixture of shock and hurt.

The world froze. I stared at her, realization crashing down like a weight on my chest. Sunny broke free of my grip and ran to her, helping her up, picking up her purse that had fallen to the ground. People around us were watching, their whispers cutting through the silence. Anjie didn't say a word, but tears glistened in her eyes.

Sunny led her toward his car, one arm around her shoulders as he whispered something to comfort her. Before he opened the car door, he turned back to me, his face twisted with anger and disappointment. "You only care about one thing," he said bitterly. "Not us. Not her. Just your damn drugs."

He pulled out his phone and dialed the dealer. "He's coming. Talk to him yourself. And don't call me or Anjie again."

He helped Anjie into his car, gave me one last look of disgust, then drove off, leaving me alone in the empty parking lot.

And yet, even as I stood there, ashamed and alone, I still felt the pull. The dealer arrived shortly after. I paid him, took the packet, and walked back to my bike, unchanged, clutching my fix like it was the only thing that mattered.

Usually, I saved the drugs for when I was alone at home. But that day, I couldn't wait—I took it right there.

I was riding my bike home, my head spinning from the drugs. I don't even remember how it happened. One minute I was riding, the next I was lying on the footpath, my body sprawled out on the ground. I tried to stand, but the world was spinning too fast, and my head felt like it was splitting in two. I couldn't move. I broke my knee and elbow. I just lay there for what felt like hours, my body numb, my mind lost in a fog.

Eventually, I made it back to my room, barely conscious, and collapsed onto the bed. The drugs hadn't numbed the pain this time. Instead, they just made me feel more lost. I fell asleep as soon as my head hit the pillow, not caring what would happen when I woke up.

Nothing had changed in me. I was still the same—crying, broken, searching for the smallest glimpse of hope, needing *Jojo* just to smile. My mind kept spinning around the same thought: *I need to see her. I need to meet her, even if it's just once.*

On a whim, I decided to go. I packed a small bag. In morning, I headed to the airport, and booked the first flight I could find. The whole thing felt impulsive, almost surreal, but I couldn't turn back now.

I didn't know why I booked the flight. I had no idea what I was expecting or what I hoped to accomplish. But deep down, I couldn't deny the flicker of hope still burning inside me, the absurd belief that maybe—just maybe—if she knew I was in Mumbai, she'd want to see me too.

When I reached Mumbai, the city buzzed around me, completely indifferent to my arrival. I booked a small room in a hotel, barely bigger than a box, and collapsed onto the bed, staring up at the ceiling, my mind consumed by thoughts of her. She was all I could think about. *What would I say to her? What would she say to me? Would she even agree to meet?*

I needed to know. So, before doing anything else, I confirmed her shift timings from a friend—she was working the evening shift now. I waited, restless, until the next day came. As the afternoon bled into evening, I found myself near her office, just wandering, waiting for a glimpse of her.

Hours passed. I felt like a ghost, drifting through the streets with no real purpose. And then, finally, I saw her.

She appeared with another girl, walking casually as if the world was hers, wearing a purple top and blue jeans. My heart jumped, pounding in my chest. Instinctively, I ducked behind a corner, hiding myself because I wasn't ready for her to see me. Not yet.

But I couldn't take my eyes off her. She was beautiful—God, she was beautiful. She had changed her hairstyle since the last time I saw her, and her red lips, painted like they had been in the old days, brought every kiss rushing back into my memory. The way she walked, her posture, her confidence—it reminded me of every step we had taken together, every journey we shared. And her smile... it was like a dagger in my heart. That smile used to be for me.

I stood there, tears stinging my eyes, unable to move. I wanted to run to her, to tell her everything that had been building inside me since the day we fell apart. But I couldn't. I was frozen, stuck between the past and the present, too afraid to take that final step.

People walked by, brushing past me without a second glance, but I stayed hidden. I noticed a few familiar faces, people who worked in the same office as her, and that only made me shrink further into the shadows. I couldn't risk being recognized, not like this.

Eventually, she and her friend disappeared down the street, laughing and chatting as they went. She looked happy. It killed me inside, but I was glad she hadn't seen me. Not like this.

I decided to go back without talking to her or even letting her know I'd come. A wave of regret washed over me. What would I even say to her? Being here felt pointless—like my presence held no meaning for her anymore. The things I'd wanted to say all this time suddenly seemed trivial, foolish even. Maybe she had moved on, maybe I was just a memory she'd already filed away. I couldn't bear the thought of finding out.

I decided to leave immediately. As I waited for a taxi, my mind was racing, the image of her walking away playing on repeat. I stood there, lost in thought, until a man approached me.

"Kaali-Peeli?" he asked.

I blinked, confused for a moment.

He raised an eyebrow. "Taxi?"

"Ah," I nodded, offering a small smile. *Mumbai's style,* I thought, amused for a second.

The taxi arrived, and I climbed in, the weight of the day sinking in around me. I stared out the window as the driver navigated through the crowded streets, but all I could see was her face, her smile, her walk. My chest ached. Tears slipped down my cheeks, but I didn't bother wiping them away.

I thought about calling her—about telling her I was in the same city, so close to her, hoping, just hoping, she'd want to meet me. But I stopped myself. What if she didn't want to see me? What if she didn't care?

No, it was better this way. I could leave with a shred of hope. I could convince myself that maybe, if I had called, she *would* have come. It was easier to live with that possibility than to face the reality of rejection.

I reached the hotel, went straight to the washroom, and splashed cold water on my face.

The man staring back at me in the mirror wasn't me. At least, not the version of me I used to know. The reflection felt foreign, almost mocking. I had never been a fool, but now, all I saw was a fool in that mirror. I had never been a coward, but the person looking back at me was exactly that—a coward, too afraid to move on, too stuck in the past to face the present.

My eyes bore into my own reflection, burning with frustration. I could feel the anger building in me, rising like a wave that was too big to control. My hands began to shake, not from fear or cold, but from pure, unfiltered rage.

Without thinking, I raised my hand and slapped myself across the face. The sting on my cheek wasn't enough. It didn't match the fury boiling inside me. Again, I lifted my hand, slapping my cheek with all the strength I could muster.

*This is for being weak,* I thought.

Another slap.

*This is for not moving on.*

Again and again, until my cheek burned and my hand ached. Until the anger subsided, replaced by a deep, hollow sadness. I stared back at myself in the mirror, red marks now visible on my face, but the same empty eyes staring back at me. *What have I become?*

The next day, I boarded back to Chandigarh. My time in Mumbai was over, and yet nothing had changed. I hadn't seen her, hadn't spoken to her, but the weight of her absence still hung over me like a shadow.

Back in Chandigarh, I made a decision. I stopped taking drugs. They had been my escape, my crutch, but I knew if I wanted to rebuild my life, I had to face my pain head-on—no more hiding.

Something inside me had shifted. I had gone there hoping for some kind of closure, but the truth was, there wasn't any closure to be found. Nothing had changed. I was still the same—haunted by her absence, unable to let go. But I knew I couldn't keep living like this, trapped in a cycle of pain. I had to move on.

Or at least, I had to try.

Before this, I had to fix something. I wanted to reach out to Sunny and Anjie, to make things right.

Unsure of who to call first, I dialed Sunny. He picked up, and though his voice lacked the usual warmth, he answered—as if he'd been expecting me. I felt a wave of guilt and mumbled an apology. He hit me with a few sarcastic remarks, but I could tell he wasn't abandoning me. He was still my friend.

I asked about Anjie. He sighed, "She was hurt, but she's not going anywhere. She's been waiting for you to call. Reach out to her and fix this."

So I did. To my surprise, Anjie didn't even complain. I apologized more than ten times, but each time, she cut me off, saying there was no need. She only thought of my welfare; all she wanted was for me to keep the promise I'd made to her that I won't take drugs again.

I promised her I wouldn't break it again.

We agreed to meet up soon. The dance floor was waiting for us, and this time, I intended to show up as someone she could trust.

The next day, I went back to the office, walked straight to my manager's desk, and handed in my resignation. It wasn't a spur-of-the-moment decision—I had been thinking about it for a while. The truth was, everything in this city reminded me of her. Every street, every café, every corner of the office held a memory. Her presence lingered in the air, and I wasn't strong enough to face it every single day.

I couldn't move on while staying here. I wasn't built that way.

Leaving was the only option left.

As I packed up my things from my desk, I felt a strange mixture of sadness and relief. Sadness because this place, this life, had once meant something to me—*she* had once meant everything to me. And relief, because now I could finally start the process of letting go, even if it was slow and painful.

That night, I sat in my room, staring at the sketch she had drawn for me. I had framed it and hung it on the wall, like a piece of her that I could hold on to. It had become my daily reminder of what I had lost—and, in a way, what I had once loved so deeply.

I knew that *Up* would always remind me of her. That one scene—the couple growing old together, building a life filled with love—it was everything I had imagined for us. But it wasn't my reality. It wasn't our story.

I packed my bags and moved, carrying the memories with me but leaving everything else behind. In morning, I left the city.

I thought about the mistakes I had made, about the times she had asked for space, and I didn't give it to her. I was too impatient. Too afraid of losing her. I didn't see that she was struggling in her own way, and instead of supporting her, I let my fear turn into anger. I had been so focused on my own pain that I couldn't see hers.

Looking back now, I know that she truly loved me. But love doesn't always survive under pressure. If I had been more patient, if I had trusted her more, things might have been different. I was the one who broke us. Not because I didn't love her enough, but because I didn't know how to give her what she needed when she needed it most.

Two years passed.

The world had moved on, and so had I—or at least, I had convinced myself of that. But her memory, like a shadow, never fully left me. It lingered, subtle yet constant, in the quiet moments of the day and the restless hours of the night. Then, one afternoon, out of nowhere, her name lit up my phone screen. In that instant, my heartbeat spiked, racing in a way it hadn't in years. Everything—every moment, every smile, every heartbreak—came rushing back with such force that my hands trembled as I stared at the screen.

I couldn't bring myself to answer. I just watched the phone ring, paralyzed by the flood of emotions that gripped me. The call ended after a few moments, leaving me in a silence that felt heavier than before.

For a long while, I just sat there, trying to make sense of it all. Why now? What could she possibly want? I wondered if she was in trouble, if she needed something. My mind raced, and before I knew it, I had dialed her number back.

"Hello," her voice—soft, familiar, and heartbreakingly gentle—came through the phone.

I swallowed the knot in my throat and, with my voice barely steady, asked, "How are you?"

She said she was fine. She told me she was visiting Bahadurgarh for a short holiday and would be heading back to Mumbai in a couple of days. For now, though, she was in Delhi. "If you want to meet," she added casually, "you can."

Without hesitation, I agreed. It was as if no time had passed, as if all my attempts to distance myself, to forget, crumbled in that moment. We planned to meet the next day. That night, I told Gaurav, my friend who was staying with me, about my trip to Delhi. He just smiled knowingly and said, "We're all fools when it comes to matters of the heart. But sometimes, being a fool is all we know how to be."

The next morning, I left early, setting off on a journey that felt both exciting and painful. The four-hour drive to Delhi passed in a blur, my mind consumed by the thought of seeing her again.

By 10 AM, I arrived at the place she had directed me to. I called her to let her know I was there. "Give me a little time," she said. Strangely, I didn't mind waiting. Maybe I had learned patience over the years—patience that I wished I had had back then.

A while later, she called again, sounding a bit confused. "I've been looking for your car, but I can't seem to find it. Where are you parked?"

I smiled to myself and replied, "Oh, I changed my car. It's not the old one anymore. Look for a white Skoda Rapid with 303 on the plate."

"I see it," she said, and moments later, I saw her approaching in the rearview mirror. I stepped out, opened the door for her, and there she was—just as beautiful as I remembered.

It was as though time had preserved her in my mind. My heart ached, but I kept my emotions in check, refusing to let myself fall again. I reached into the dashboard and pulled out a chocolate—something I had gotten into the habit of keeping, a piece of the past that never quite faded. I handed it to her. She glanced at the familiar melted chocolate, and laughed.

"Still melted?" she teased, her smile lighting up her face, "Some things never change, do they?"

I chuckled, feeling a warmth I hadn't felt in a long time. "Yeah, I guess not." Her words stirred something inside me—a flicker of the past, of late nights and easy laughter, back when things were simpler.

It was a small moment, but it felt like a glimpse of the past—a memory that made us both smile.

Trying to move past the wave of nostalgia, I asked, "Where do you want to go?" She shrugged, saying she didn't mind. I suggested the Lotus Temple, and she agreed.

As we drove, we fell into conversation. She told me about her life in Mumbai —how she had grown to love the city, how it gave her a sense of freedom, even at night. She asked how I was, and I simply said, "Life is normal." When she asked about the family business, I admitted that I still had no plans to join it.

Parking at the Lotus Temple was, as expected, a challenge, but eventually, we found a spot. As we walked toward the entrance, she asked what the temple was like inside. I laughed, recalling a long-forgotten school trip. "Honestly, all I remember is that we had to stay quiet inside."

Inside the temple, the silence was palpable. She began to pray, and I watched her, unsure of what to say myself. I thought to pray. A simple prayer to God: "Whatever she's asking for, let it come true."

Afterward, we decided to visit a nearby mall. Parking, again, was a hassle, but it didn't bother me as much this time. We wandered through the mall, talking, catching up, and reminiscing. We grabbed lunch at the crowded food court, and she started talking about her career, her dreams of becoming a cinematographer. Her eyes sparkled as she described how she would film the very moment we were living—where she'd place the cameras, how she'd capture the light. She was so passionate, so alive when she spoke about her dreams, and it reminded me why I had fallen in love with her in the first place.

After lunch, we asked a passerby to take a photo of us. The first picture was awkward—he suggested we stand closer. She moved toward me, and without thinking, I placed my hand on her waist. She smiled, and for a moment, it felt like we were exactly where we had once been—together. She looked at the picture afterward and smiled. "Your dressing sense has really improved," she joked.

I nodded, but inside, the moment was bittersweet. There was a time when I would've been overjoyed by that compliment. Now, it felt like a small consolation for all that had been lost.

The day wound down, and we drove back toward her area. I asked if I could get a hug before she left. She hesitated and then said, "No." It stung more than I expected. She stepped out of the car, and we waved goodbye.

That was it. I had hoped for a closure, maybe even a hug to make up for the one I never got at the airport, but I should have known better. The hurt lingered, but I told myself not to expect anything more.

After that, we never spoke again. She was gone, and this time, I didn't chase after her. I had learned my lesson. I needed to keep my distance, to protect myself from the loneliness and sorrow that always came flooding back whenever I thought of her.

"Move on," I kept telling myself. And yet, even after seven years, I couldn't.

I hadn't fallen in love again. A few women showed interest, but I was impossible to handle. My heart was still trapped in the past, and I knew I could never give anyone else what they deserved. No matter how hard I tried, I couldn't move on.

So I chose to live with the memories. To keep loving her in my own way. And maybe, just maybe, that was enough.

..

I kept telling myself to let it go,
To close that door, leave the past alone.
But some love stays, no matter the time,
Like the taste of melted chocolate, sweet and fine.

..

And I tried to move on, but the heart knows best,
Some things stay, while the rest fades to rest.

..

So I'll live with the memories, carry them free,
Hold onto the warmth of what you gave to me.
I'll love you in silence, in peace, and in dreams,
And maybe, just maybe, that's enough for me.

..

Years have gone by, but I still feel the grace,
Of the laughter we shared, of time we embraced.
When I see nail art, bright colors and style,
I think of your hands, how they'd move, how they'd smile.

..

I may walk alone, but I don't feel alone,
With the love that remains, I've made it my home.

..

So I'll live with the memories, carry them free,

Hold onto the warmth of what you gave to me.
I'll love you in silence, in peace, and in dreams,
And maybe, just maybe, that's enough for me.

..

I still have the sketch you once made for me,
Lines and shadows of who we used to be.
It's faded and worn, but it's there in the light,
A reminder of love that felt endless, felt right.

..

So I'll live with the memories, carry them free,
Hold onto the warmth of what you gave to me.
I'll love you in silence, in peace, and in dreams,
I too had a break-up story, or so it seems.

..

Yeah, maybe, just maybe...
That's enough for me.

# Thank You

This journey was never easy, and I wouldn't have made it through without the people who stood by me when I couldn't stand on my own.

**To Anjie**

You are a rare kind of beautiful—inside and out, full of empathy and understandings. You walked into my life when I was at my lowest and refused to let me stay there. I can't thank you enough for your love, for your unwavering support, and for always seeing the best in me, even when I couldn't see it myself. Though I may not be able to give you everything you desired for, I am honored to call you my bestfriend. I'll hold tight to the promise I made to you, and I'll never forget what you've done for me.

**To Sunny**

You are my best friend and my lifeline. Thank you for being real with me, for never sugarcoating the truth, and for keeping me grounded when I was ready to drift. You didn't let me get away with my worst moments—you held me accountable, even when I pushed back. Your loyalty has been my anchor, and your sarcasm, my saving grace. I'm incredibly grateful to have you in my life.